ITEMS FOR A MYSTERY
LOVER'S WISH LIST . . .

"The Season of Giving"
by Richard T. Chizmar and Norman Partridge
A little girl's desperate request moves a store detective in a Santa suit to grant her wish . . . even if it means committing murder.

"Mad Dog" *by Dick Lochte*
Author/sleuth Leo Bloodworth accepts a radio talk show host's invitation to solve a thirty-year-old crime of passion involving a dead Santa and "The Woman Who Killed Christmas."

"Ho Ho Ho" *by Barbara Paul*
Who strangled the trainer of Biedermann's Department Store's Santas with a string of Christmas lights? The thirteen suspects all wear red suits and fake beards.

"The Man in the Red Flannel Suit" *by Jan Grape*
An Austin policewoman goes after the hit-and-run killer of a homeless woman, and her only clue is the victim's little girl, who thinks Santa Claus is the scariest man in town.

. . . AND 17 MORE TALES OF
KRIS KRINGLE AT HIS KRIMINAL BEST

CLUES

SANTA CLUES

EDITED BY

Martin H. Greenberg
and
Carol-Lynn Rossel Waugh

A SIGNET BOOK

SIGNET
Published by the Penguin Group
Penguin Books USA Inc., 375 Hudson Street, New York, New York 10014, U.S.A.
Penguin Books Ltd, 27 Wrights Lane, London W8 5TZ, England
Penguin Books Australia Ltd, Ringwood, Victoria, Australia
Penguin Books Canada Ltd, 10 Alcorn Avenue, Toronto, Ontario, Canada M4V 3B2
Penguin Books (N.Z.) Ltd, 182–190 Wairau Road, Auckland 10, New Zealand

Penguin Books Ltd, Registered Offices: Harmondsworth, Middlesex, England

First published by Onyx, an imprint of Dutton Signet,
a division of Penguin Books USA Inc.

First Printing, November, 1993
10 9 8 7 6 5 4 3 2 1

REGISTERED TRADEMARK—MARCA REGISTRADA

Printed in the United States of America

PUBLISHER'S NOTE
These stories are works of fiction. Names, characters, places, and incidents either are the product of the author's imagination or are used fictitiously, and any resemblance to actual persons, living or dead, events, or locales is entirely coincidental.

CONTENTS

SANTA CLUES

Back in the 1950s, Norman Rockwell did a series of magazine covers that captured perfectly the joyous aspect of the holidays.

There was Dad, dress hat tilted back, pipe slanting out of his mouth, walking awkwardly down a snowy street beneath the burden of all those gift-wrapped boxes Mom kept piling on his arms.

And then there was the snowman, two large boys holding up a much smaller boy so he could put the stovepipe hat on the snowy head.

And then there was the skating rink, the very cute young girl being followed on the ice by three very intent young men with Rockwellian pug noses and freckles.

You know: the holiday spirit.

But then there's the other side of the holidays. Inordinately high suicide rate. Increased arrests for drunken driving. Soaring domestic violence statistics.

While millions prefer the song "White Christmas." a formidable number would rather hear "Blue Christmas" (especially the mournful version by Elvis).

Which brings us to the book at hand.

Ask a group of good writers to reflect on Santa Claus and you're bound to get innumerable different responses. That's why you'll find holiday moods of every kind in this collection.

The common trait shared by all these stories is their sense of fun. Some of it just happening to be a little darker than others.

Whatever your feelings about Yuletide, you'll like these tales of good times gone astray . . . beneath the baleful gaze of Santa Claus as he decides who has been naughty, and who has been nice.

—Martin H. Greenberg

HO, HO, HO

by Barbara Paul

"He used to be Santa Claus," the store manager said.

"Used to be," Sergeant Murphy repeated.

"Until he was promoted. Now he trains all our Santas. Or did train them, I should say."

The two stood looking down at the fat man lying spread-eagle on the floor. "How many Santas do you have?" the police sergeant asked.

"Two for the main store and two for each of the four branches, plus three on standby. That's thirteen altogether."

"So any one of the thirteen could have killed him."

The store manager sighed. "So it would appear."

The dead man was named Harvey Nye. He was about fifty, weighed over two hundred pounds, and was dressed in sweats and Reeboks. A burly man, thick-necked and big-shouldered. But that thick neck hadn't protected him; he'd been strangled with a string of Christmas tree lights, which, grotesquely, had then been plugged into a nearby socket. Nye's seasonal garrote blinked off and on, off and on. The ex-Santa had died clutching a fake white beard in his right hand, a scrap of red cloth in his left. "Who found the body?" Sergeant Murphy asked.

"Santa Number Five. They were just coming back from their morning break, you see, and Number Five was first into the room."

The room was located on the ninth floor of Biedermann's Department Store and had been set up as a classroom. Christmas decorations ornamented the windowless walls, and in the corner sat a small tree—

without its lights. "You number your Santas?" Sergeant Murphy asked.

"Harvey did. He said it made it easier to call on them during the three-day training session."

Sergeant Murphy told the store manager he could go. The Crime Scene Unit came in and took pictures of Harvey Nye and his necklace of twinkling lights. When the body was finally removed, Murphy sent for the Santa Clauses. They came bouncing in, thirteen jolly old elves who jingled as they walked, ushered along by two police officers who then stationed themselves on both sides of the door. The Santas were a mixture of retired older men, college students looking to make a few bucks for Christmas, unemployed men taking anything they could get, and one or two who just liked playing Santa. They were all corpulent, either naturally or with the aid of padding, and they were all in costume and wearing numbered placards pinned to the fronts of their suits. "Hee, hee, hee!" Santa Number Ten was snickering. "Somebody decorated old Harvey."

Number Five growled. "Show some respect for the dead!"

"Why?" Number Ten asked reasonably. "Nobody respected him alive."

"Ain't that the truth," Number Four chimed in. There were murmurs of agreement as the Santas took their seats.

"Why didn't anyone like Harvey Nye?" Murphy asked.

"Ah, he was too full of himself." Number Five.

"He was a bully." Three.

"He made you feel like shit." Nine.

"Aw, Harvey wasn't that bad. A little bigheaded is all." Six.

"Bigheaded? The man was a mini-fascist!" Ten.

"Just because he gave you a hard time—"

"I'm not the only one he gave a hard time! What are you, teacher's pet?"

Then everybody was shouting at once and Murphy had to yell for silence. *The Case of the Squabbling*

Santas, he thought. "Okay, so Harvey was not a popular guy. But is that a reason to kill him? The training session is only three days long, for Pete's sake. There has to be some other motive."

"Not necessarily," said Santa Number Seven. "Harvey had the most aggravating personality of anyone I've ever met. I consider myself a mild-mannered, peace-loving man, but there were times when I would gladly have strangled the man myself. But I didn't," he added hastily.

"Truth is," Number Twelve added, "most of us felt that way, Lieutenant. Captain?"

"Sergeant," Murphy said. "I'm Sergeant Murphy, and for now I think we'll just stick with numbers for you." He let a silence develop as he looked over these living icons of goodwill toward all men and found what he was hunting for. "Number Eight!" Murphy barked. "Where's your beard?"

"I don't know," Number Eight said in a frightened young voice. "I got here late, while the others were on their break, and when I got changed I couldn't find the beard."

"How about that, Number Three?" Murphy asked, picking a number at random. "Was Number Eight late getting here?"

"Er, I didn't notice," Number Three said, startled at being singled out.

"I did," said Number Eleven, nodding vigorously and making the bell on his cap jingle. "He missed the first part of the session."

"Yeah, I saw him come in," Number Four confirmed. "He was late. He couldna done old Harv."

"I dunno," Santa Number One said with a surprisingly squeaky voice. "Harvey was always picking on Number Eight."

"Because Number Eight was always late!" snapped Number Thirteen.

"Now wait a minute!" Number Eight wailed.

"Let's all wait a minute," Murphy said. He wanted to know how long their break lasted. Fifteen minutes, they told him, from ten to ten-fifteen. Not really long enough for the killer to get out of his costume, put on Number Eight's, kill Harvey Nye, and change back into his own Santa suit before Number Eight showed up. "Number Eight, is your costume torn anywhere?"

The young Santa looked down at himself. "I don't think so."

"Then whose is? *Somebody's* suit is torn."

Silence for a moment. Then: "Mine is," Number Two said reluctantly. He lifted his beard to show a piece of red missing from the top of his suit. "It was all right when I took it off yesterday. And I might as well tell you—I couldn't find my beard either, so I took Number Eight's. But I didn't kill Harvey. I was with Number Seven and Number Thirteen all during the break."

"That's right," two voices spoke up.

"You took my beard?" Number Eight asked indignantly.

Murphy waved him to silence. "Did you all go to the same place for your break?"

They didn't. Santas Number Two, Seven, and Thirteen were in the employees' cafeteria drinking coffee. Santas Number Five and Eleven went to the men's room. Numbers Three, Four, Ten, and Twelve spent their break in the Smoking Lounge. And Number Eight was late. That left Number One, Number Six, and Number Nine unaccounted for.

"I had to make a phone call," said Number One.

"I had to drop off a form at the Personnel Office," said Number Six.

"I got a Coke from the machine down the hall and stood there drinking it," said Number Nine.

Did anyone see them making the phone call, dropping off the form, drinking the Coke? No, three times. Murphy paused to think a moment. Harvey Nye had been alive and well before the break, busily instructing his students in the art of Santa-ing; the only difference from the day before was that today his class numbered twelve instead of the usual thirteen. Sometime during the break one of the Santas had slipped back into the classroom and strangled Harvey with the Christmas tree lights. And the killer had to be Number One, Number Six, or Number Nine—since the remaining ten alibied one another.

But before the session began, the killer had stolen Number Two's beard and ripped a piece from his costume in a clumsy attempt to incriminate the other Santa. Premeditation, no doubt about it. Sergeant Murphy asked, "Did any of you know Harvey Nye before this training session began?"

Haltingly, four hands went up into the air. The three suspects' . . . and Number Two's. "We've worked this gig before," Number Six explained. "The store makes us repeat the training session, though."

"That's okay," Number Nine said. "You forget the drill from one Christmas to the next. And we want to be the best Santa Clauses we can be, don't we?"

"Ha ha ha," said Number One mirthlessly.

Murphy told the two police officers to get the names and addresses of the other nine Santas and let them go.

"Hey, what about me?" Number Two protested. "I got two witnesses that say—"

"You were with them all during the break, I know," the police sergeant said as the other Santas got up and started filing out. "But the killer took your beard to plant as false evidence. I want to find out if he picked you at random or whether you were a deliberate choice."

The words "the killer" got through to them. Number Two stared at the other three Santas. "One of you guys is a-a *murderer*!" he blurted. It was just sinking in on the others as well. Numbers One, Six, and Nine eyed one another warily. They'd been so caught up in the not altogether unpleasurable notion that Harvey Nye was dead that they hadn't yet given much thought to how he got that way.

"Which one of you dropped off the form in the Personnel Office?" Murphy asked.

"Me," said Number Six.

"What's your name?"

"Jack Billings."

Murphy went to the door and motioned to one of the police officers. "Go to the Personnel Office," he said. "Find out if a form was left there this morning by Jack Billings. If it was, see if you can pin down the time."

"Jack Billings," the officer repeated and left on his errand.

Murphy went back to Number Two and the three suspects. "So. You've all had this training session from Harvey before."

"Naw," squeaked Number One. "This was Harvey's first year as the instructor. Last year he was just a Santa like the rest of us."

Number Two nodded. "Me and Harvey and Will here—Number One—we been doin' this for six, seven years now."

"What about you two?" Murphy asked the others.

"This is my second year," Number Six said.

"My third," Number Nine added.

"Take off your beards," Murphy said abruptly. "Your hats, too . . . and wigs? Let me see what you look like."

The four near-identical Santa Clauses gradually metamorphosed into four individual men. Numbers One and Two were much older than the others, obviously retirees with time on their hands. Physically, they were of a type with Harvey Nye, evidently the build the store preferred in its Santas: burly, barrel-chested, big-shouldered, making Number One's squeaky voice all the more surprising. Number Two appeared to be the older of the two, with a full head of thick, wavy white hair. He was the only Santa who didn't have to wear a wig.

Number Six was in his forties, with a down-on-his-luck look about him. An enigma: Murphy couldn't get a fix on him. But it was Number Nine who surprised him. Like the tardy Number Eight, Number Nine was clearly a student. He was very young, and skinny to the point of emaciation. Murphy looked at the boy's thin wrists, thought of Harvey Nye's thick neck, and mentally dismissed Number Nine as a suspect.

He said, "What happened to the previous instructor?"

"Moved to Florida," Number One answered.

"And so Harvey was promoted. Why Harvey instead of one of you two?" Murphy meant the two older Santas.

"Because Harvey sabotaged us," Number Two said bluntly. "He went into Personnel and convinced them neither of us could do the job."

"He said nobody would listen to me," Number One squeaked. "Because of my voice. He said people laughed at me."

Number Two sighed. "He told them I was too old. Not enough stamina."

Professional jealousy among Santa Clauses? "And they believed him?"

"Personnel don't know squat," Number One said viciously. "Harvey wasn't even a good Santa Claus. He made the kids uncomfortable. He loved to lecture them—he was such a bully, he even bullied the little kids. Kids don't come to Santa Claus to be lectured. They want to talk about their wish lists, about what *they* are going to get out of Christmas this year. Some of the kids are unbelievable, and you want to squash 'em like the bedbugs they are. But even the good kids went away from Harvey on the verge of tears. But Harvey loved kids. Oh, yeah. He loved them because they couldn't fight back." Number One's squeak got higher. "You think Personnel noticed? You think they even had an *inkling* of what a sadist Harvey Nye was? Ha! No, he smiled and turned on the charm and filled their ears with poison about me and George here, Number Two, I mean. He stole that job from me. From us. One of us shoulda got that promotion."

The other three Santas were listening to his tirade with fascination. "Who *is* Number One?" Six whispered to Two.

"You are Number Six," Number Two replied cryptically.

Just then a knock sounded at the door; it was the

officer Sergeant Murphy had sent to the Personnel
Office. "Learn anything?" Murphy asked.

"Yeah. Woman in Personnel says Jack Billings
dropped off his GSK-440D form this morning. She
says she stepped out of her office at ten o'clock, and
when she got back ten minutes later the form was on
her desk."

Number Six whooped and threw his arms into the
air. "Then I'm cleared?"

"You're cleared," Murphy agreed. "You can go.
Leave your address and phone number with the
officer."

Number Six, aka Jack Billings, jingled his way out
of the room, not even glancing back at the three remaining suspects. Not his problem. The officer raised
an eyebrow and closed the door.

Murphy turned to Number Nine. "Strip."

"What?"

"I want you to strip down to your underwear. Go
on. Do it."

Uncertainly, the boy started taking off his Santa
costume, unwrapping what seemed like a ton of padding to reveal the full extent of his natural skinniness.
When he was finished, he looked like a skeleton
standing there in Jockey shorts and a T-shirt that said:
I think, therefore I is.

Murphy stared straight into Number One's eye.
"You know as well as I do that that kid could never
have taken Harvey Nye in a struggle. Look at him,
Number One! Harvey could have broken him in two
like a stick. But you, on the other hand—you could
have pulled that string of lights around Harvey's neck
tight enough to get the job done. And, Number One
. . . you're the only one left."

Number Two stared at his companion aghast.
"Will?"

"You killed him," Murphy said flatly. "Nobody else
had means, motive, and opportunity. Number Nine
there had opportunity but not the rest of it. You're
it, Number One. Cooperate and things'll go easier for
you."

The other man's eyes were watering as he turned away from Murphy to face Number Two. "That promotion shoulda gone to *me*, George!"

"Aw, Will!" George put his hand on Number One's shoulder.

Murphy noticed the gesture and said, "In case you've forgotten, Number Two, it was your beard and a piece of your costume that he left at the scene of the crime. You were his only remaining competition."

Slowly Number Two withdrew his hand.

"Wow," said Number Nine.

Murphy had almost forgotten him. "Get dressed, kid. Go on home. And don't forget to leave—"

"My name, et cetera, with the officer. Gotcha." Number Nine gathered up his Santa clothing and left.

The two old Santas sat staring at each other. "I'm sorry, George," Number One said. "I was just feeling so . . . so *cheated*, ya know?"

"So you decided to put the blame on me?" Number Two stood up and shook his head. "I'm sorry too, Will. I'm sorry you thought you had to do this. You deserve whatever you get." Still shaking his head, he trudged heavily out of the room, not a happy Santa.

Number One didn't even seem to hear his rights being read to him. "That promotion shoulda gone to me!" he insisted stubbornly. "I was a better Santa Claus!"

"Ho, ho, ho," said Sergeant Murphy.

COLD COMFORTS

A Koko Tate Tale

by *Peter Crowther*

Christmas Eve in the city.

Detective Charlie Bieglemann telephoned me out of the blue a little after 2 P.M. just when I was about to get festive and start celebrating the Saviour's birthday the way I celebrated everybody's birthday—even people I didn't know. No tree, no lights, no presents, just an awful lot of bourbon in a few bars well off the main drags, where I can sit around with the other misfits and listen to Frank and Julie and Peggy and kill time till Christmas is just another bleary memory of someplace I might have been, but couldn't be sure.

So, you might say Charlie's call was timely. You *might*.

He reminded me about my college days, checked that I'd majored in English, and asked if I was too busy to help him with something. If I'd felt any more festive I might've laughed but the bottle was still only half-empty. All I'd managed in the weeks leading up to the first snows was a couple of seedy photo sessions to pass on to expensive-looking wives who didn't look at you when you spoke to them and who were concerned more at the audacity of their husbands than at their infidelities; a little repo work that netted me $500 and a busted cheekbone; and two days' protection, me and Eddie Gonzalez, for a Miami bag man who'd come to "visit" Eddie's boss, Phil Maumstein.

"Oh, I figure I could spare the time," I told him.

It turned out Charlie was up to his fat neck in bodies. He had kept the details out of the papers which explained why I hadn't read about it. The truth was I didn't read the papers, but I hated to appear illiterate.

18

"Bodies?" I said.

His voice was characteristically gruff on the other end of the line. "Three old women wrapped up like early presents and then smothered," he said. "Or maybe the other way around. And now there's been a fourth one. Grocery boy found her, down in the Village."

"Grocery boy? I thought they went out with 'Cal's My Pal' election buttons and bearskin coats."

"You wait long enough, everything comes back around."

"How's the kid?"

"Thinner. Five days is a long time, Koke."

I nodded to the empty room. "At least it's not summer."

"Summer, we'd have found her earlier," he said. "Heat *we* get, could've smelled her up in Harlem."

I smiled in spite of myself.

"There's something else."

"That why you wanted to check my grades?"

"You're not bad, you know that?"

"I try."

"Yeah," he agreed. Then, "Poetry."

"Poetry?"

"I'll tell you about it. Three o'clock, outside Macy's, corner of 34th."

"I'll be there," I told the dial tone.

It was the coldest afternoon in the coldest snap of the coldest winter for twenty-seven years. That meant it hadn't been this cold since before the night all the lights went out when, to keep warm, people made babies in stranded elevators and small back rooms on the higher stories of the monoliths that keep the streets in constant shroud.

Statistics, I love 'em.

And I love the people that give them out, too. All the fresh-faced collegiates and the greasy-haired, wall-eyed boffins who schlep onto the tacky cable shows—between reformed ax murderers and people who've had sex with dolphins—to amaze with a torrent of

figures second only in size to a few miles of used, Wall
Street ticker tape the assembled horde of pasty-faced
troglodytes who live in the shadow of the windowed
towers. Then, while glancing side to side to see if
maybe a camera is picking them up and returning their
drool-mouthed image to the folks back home (who
never even watch the show anyway), the cardboard
studio audience nods its collective approval and belts
out a tumultuous applause that is, itself, merely a response to a Walkman-clad technician who leaps
around with a board that tells them what to do.

Face it: cold weather makes me cranky.

I was standing alongside an emaciated Santa outside
Macy's, basking in the rheumy warmth of exhaled
bourbon that had gathered by the doors on the corner
of 34th and Broadway, and beginning to feel forgotten.
In a moment of reckless abandon, I figured Charlie
maybe wasn't coming after all and I waved a snow-
encrusted arm at a passing Yellow. The driver, a long-
haired guy lost in a morass of seventy-decibel rap
music and wearing a head scarf like Douglas Fair-
banks, leaned over and mouthed "Merry Christmas"
at me through the window. Then he gave me the bird
and drove up 34th, his shoulders going up and down
like he was holding a road drill. If you ever want to
get me a seasonal present, forget the egg nog and the
nuts—a pint of Huckleberry and a big tub of New
York cabbies' balls'll do it for me every time.

The December wind blew around the fast-disappearing
cab and continued down toward me to search out the
thin areas of my old thermal drawers, there to bestow
an early Christmas gift of frostbite to my pecker. In
so doing, it wafted thick flurries of exhaust-darkened
snow up into the gathering gloom of an early Christmas Eve. Meanwhile, the faint sound of recorded
Christmas carols drifted constantly out of Macy's re-
volving doors to meet the milling throng of last-minute
shoppers, bag ladies, drunken nine-to-five Casanovas
feeling guilty about slapping typists' fannies at the office party, and slant-eyed dips in zoot suits that looked

like they'd blown in straight from a Damon Runyon short-short.

All human life was there, and then some.

Hell, there was even Charlie Bieglemann.

I saw his blue-and-white pulling in to the curb just as Santa's beard slipped. The car kept moving as I opened the door and stepped in. Inside, it was Florida.

Charlie held out a can of Sprite. "Here, hold my drink for me willya . . . cool it down a little," he said with a big smile, smokey chuckles shaking thick, unshaven jowls.

"Who're you," I asked him, "Woody Allen?"

"Naw, he's taller and has more luck with women."

"The second bit applies to anybody with a pecker," I replied while attempting to sink myself into the relative warmth of the seat.

"That lets you out," he said. Another chuckle.

"You're late," I said as we pulled away into the traffic. I stomped my feet like I was at a Springsteen concert and we headed up Broadway toward Times Square. "Where we going?"

"Tenth and 46th," he said around the can. "Number five's come in and it's recent."

The house was one of those twenty-step walk-ups where, in the summer, every step provides an occasional home to the city's luckless. Two uniforms were already there, shuffling side to side on the sidewalk, banging their arms against their coats and breathing out thick plumes of fog into the white-speckled air. We got out and Charlie flashed his badge. The first cop nodded and ushered him by, then put an arm in front of me. "He's with me," Charlie said over his shoulder as he jogged up the steps.

"I'm with him," I confirmed with a mock swagger. "Poirot's the name." The cop said nothing but made a mental note to watch out for me parking next to a fire hydrant. The cold weather plays hell with humor.

The inside of the house hadn't realized it was Christmas. No holly, no ivy, no wise men. Just graffiti

in a language I couldn't read, a couple of dog turds
with a layer of frost that made them look like the
cakes they serve with afternoon tea at Rosoff's, and
an old man wearing a fur jacket. The old guy asked
me if I'd seen his son, coming to take him home for
Christmas. I said I hadn't but then traffic was bad and
maybe he'd been held up. His face lit up. He hadn't
thought of that. It would keep him going until he gave
up and just went back to his room to make another
excuse.

On the second floor was another uniform standing
by a half-open door. He knew Charlie and moved
aside. Charlie let me in first so I wouldn't make my
Poirot crack again, and there she was. A guy from
Forensics was placing her in the bag, folding her arms
over her chest and generally making her as comfortable as dead people can be. Her face was light blue,
lips bloated and turning black. Looking around the
room—it was as much an apartment as a back alley
was a rest room—I figured it was probably a lot more
comfortable than she'd been when she was alive.

The room was decorated in late dust bowl. An open
door to the right showed a toilet bowl and a sink
hanging from the wall with what looked like sticky
tape and rope. One of the panels in the door was
missing so it wouldn't have made much sense her closing the door when she was on the john. But just thinking that, with her lying out on the floor, made me
feel like a heel. In the other corner was a thrift-store
cupboard with one of the doors out of the slats and
leaning up against it. On top was a small gas ring and
a lot of open cans. I knew without looking that there
would be bits in each of them.

Charlie stood by the guy from Forensics. "Same?"

The guy nodded. "Wrapped up like she was in the
Arctic and then smothered." He zipped up the bag
and I watched her face disappear from her home for
the last time. "No signs of a struggle, Charlie, before
you ask."

"Mmmm." Charlie drained the remains of his Sprite

and crushed the can, put it in his coat pocket. "And the note?"

The guy stood up and handed Charlie a note in a police-issue plastic wallet and Charlie handed it to me. "Read it, Koke."

I read. " 'All is a blank before us; all waits undream'd of in that region, that inaccessible land.' "

He shrugged. "Poetry," Charlie said. It wasn't a question.

"Who can tell," the Forensics guy answered anyway. "Sounds old."

I handed the note back to Charlie and looked down at the zipped-up bag. "Like her," I said. "Old and tired."

"And fucking cold," Forensics added. "Jesus Christ it must be getting on for ten below in here."

Charlie pocketed the note and looked around the room. "What did she do for heat?"

"She didn't," he said. "No radiator, no stove."

"Some life," I ventured.

Back in the car, heading downtown, Charlie didn't speak. I decided to break the silence.

"It getting to you, this one?"

He nodded slightly. "I guess," he sighed. "They don't make any sense. Five old ladies, suffocated, and wrapped like they was going on an expedition to the Pole."

As we drove through Times Square, we passed a bunch of carol singers standing outside the Flame Steaks restaurant. It was like passing a scene in an old Hollywood movie and, just for a second, I half dreamed I saw Pat O'Brien dressed like a priest laughing good-naturedly and tossing a handful of dimes into an upturned hat. "Ho, ho, ho!" I said.

Charlie let it pass.

"You got the other notes?"

He stook his head and cursed an old Impala that mounted a curb to beat the lights. "I got it written down, though . . . what they said."

"On you?"

He reached into his inside pocket and took out a sheet of paper. On it were four small verses. I read them out loud. " 'All at once a fresher wind sweeps by, and breaks my dream, and I am in the wilderness alone.' Don't any of these mean anything to you?"

"Listen: the only poetry I've ever remembered is 'Hard Rock Goes to Prison' . . . or something like that." He smiled as he remembered. "The opening line goes 'Hard Rock was known not to take no shit from nobody.' "

"That's a *poem*?"

Charlie nodded proudly. "Ethel Ridge Knight, I think her name was."

I thought a minute. "I know that." Somewhere amidst all the beatings and all the drinks, in a musty cupboard I'd not looked in since—well, just "since," there it was. " 'And he had the scars to prove it: split purple lips, lumped ears . . .' Hell, I don't remember the rest."

"That's the one though."

"Yeah . . . it's Etheridge Knight."

"Huh?"

"Etheridge Knight, not *Ethel Ridge* Knight."

"Yeah? Hey, you're the guy for the job, okay! Secret of being a good cop is knowing who to call on."

I shrugged. "You say."

"Right, I say," he said, speeding to make a light. "You know the one you just read?"

"Nope."

"How about the others?"

I looked back at the sheet. " 'As cool as the pale wet leaves of lily-of-the-valley, she lay beside me in the dawn.' That one's familiar. I think I know that one."

"How'd you remember those things, Koke?"

"I used to like reading poetry. I read a lot of it." I hoped he wouldn't ask why, and changed the subject. "So, what are we looking for here?"

Charlie grunted while I settled back in my seat and stared into the gloom. Snowflakes swirled in front of us and you could hear the steady *thrlush* and occasional chain-rattle of tires cutting through the thickening black slush. "You tell me."

"Okay: one," I checked them off on my fingers, hoping to God I'd have a *two,* "a poetic serial killer."

"Every town should have one."

"Two . . ." I struggled on the second finger. "Two is, well, why do murderers leave notes?"

"Clues," Charlie said.

"So why give clues?"

"So we can catch 'em."

"So, two: our man wants us to catch him."

"Or *her.*"

"Or her."

"What's three?"

He had to ask, just when we were getting somewhere. "Three . . . three is the victims. Who are— hey, shouldn't you be doing this?"

"You're on a roll, go with it."

I went back to the finger. "Who's he killing?"

"Little old grannies who don't have heating, don't have much food, and don't have no relatives."

"That was a double negative."

"What was a *what*?"

"A double negative. 'Don't have no relatives' is a double negative. The 'don't' is canceled out by the 'no.' It becomes '*Do* have relatives.' "

Charlie whistled. "Thanks."

I stared out the window some more.

"I said 'Thanks.' "

"No, I'm thinking." I thought. Charlie drove. "What if the killer was trying to avenge his own—no, that doesn't work out."

"It don't?"

"We need to get a line on the motivation," I said. "Then maybe we'll get a picture of the type of guy we're looking for." I thought some more.

"Maybe it's one of the bohos, the poetry freaks, hang around the coffee bars in the Village . . . all black sweaters and sandals, Kerouac and Ginsberg—"

"Charlie, it's 1993," I pointed out. "The Village is porno houses, metal joints, and brothels, little men with big egos and long knives. Dylan and Baez moved on about thirty years back . . . those places don't exist anymore."

"Shame," Charlie said, and he started humming *Eve Of Destruction*.

I looked across at him. "You're starting to feel better now, huh?"

"Some," he said, nodding in the darkness. "But only cause you're on the case, Sherlock."

I held back the smile and tutted for him, loudly. He didn't fool me for a minute. "How about access to the victims?"

"You mean how's he get into them?"

"Well, not just '*in* to them'—how does he know where they *are*?"

He kept silent. We drove.

"Welfare." He said it softly.

"Right! These *cannot* be random killings. The guy must know where the victims are beforehand."

"And that means—"

"He works for the Welfare department!"

Charlie made a U-turn and I made a mental note to empty my pants at the first opportunity. A Dodge Rambler, a guy on a bike, a rusting Thunderbird, and two Yellows probably made similar mental notes. As we drove back uptown I checked to see if I recognized either of the cab drivers.

"Where we going?"

"West Village . . . there's a Welfare office over on Ninth."

"Oh." I thought for maybe a full minute and then said, "Where *were* we going?"

"Just driving," Charlie said, "waiting for you to get inspired."

Every cloud has a silver lining, or so they say.

The cloud in question was that the Welfare office was closed for the night. In fact, it was closed for the next day. The silver lining was that we didn't have to figure out what we were going to ask, and of whom we were going to ask it. Some days, good luck just falls from the skies.

Back in the car, Charlie said to me, "Now what?"

"Back to the inspiration, I guess."

He shifted the blue-and-white into Drive and drove.

After a while, I said, "He can't only work for Welfare."

"Go on."

"I mean, if he's so *au fait* with poetry, then maybe he's a student. Maybe he studies by day and—"

"And smothers little old ladies by night."

I slapped my knee in exasperation. "Look, Charlie, Welfare runs with a lot of voluntary help. Maybe our guy's got a beef against somebody."

"Hmmm," Charlie said thoughtfully. "A student with a chip on his shoulder."

I nodded.

"Kind of narrows it down a little."

"And anyway, we already decided that he doesn't have a beef . . . there's nobody to hurt. No relatives, no friends, and the women themselves aren't molested or beaten in any way?" I phrased the last part as a question.

"Nope, he just smothers them. Bill Tanakowa says it's a very humane way to go, particularly if you're old and weak." He lifted his right hand from the wheel and snapped his fingers. "Like that, Bill says."

I shook my head. "Doesn't sound like a student. I don't know why. It just doesn't."

"Maybe he's not a student, maybe he's a teacher."

I felt my face light up and then, just as quickly, the light went out. "Uh-uh, he wouldn't have the time."

"An academic?"

This time, the light stayed on. "Yeah, maybe he's not a teacher, maybe he's a professor."

"A professor who does voluntary work for Welfare."

"Who *does* have a relative," I added, remembering Charlie's double negative.

"Right," he said enthusiastically.

"Right," I agreed. The enthusiasm was infectious.

We drove.

"So where to, Inspector?"

"I wish I knew."

"Maybe the guy is an expert on poetry? Like the head of a university department or a dean or something."

Ninth became Columbus and we hit the corner of Broadway and 65th at the same time as about two million others. "We need to look at some kind of academic register . . . look for . . ." I shook my head. "It's impossible."

We drove in one place for ten minutes, silent.

"We're looking for a link, right?"

I didn't speak.

Charlie went on. "You ever played bridge, Koke?"

I remembered the games I had with Mary, playing her brother and his wife. "Some," I said. "Not much."

"Well, I played a little . . . not much either, but I remember the guy that taught me saying that, sometimes, when you need a card to be in a certain place so you can make the contract, then you play the cards assuming it's going to be where you hoped it was." He looked around at me. "That make any sense?"

"You're saying you play the hunch."

"Yeah," he nodded and looked back in front of him. "Yeah, you play the hunch."

"And the hunch is?"

"The hunch is . . . *shit,* how the fuck do I know!"

"No, you're saying that if the logical play isn't safe, then you play for the drop."

"I don't know, Koke."

"So the hunch is—"

"The hunch is that the link isn't just in the fact that it's poetry, maybe it's in the poet or the different poems."

I looked back at the lines Charlie had written out. As I looked, Charlie said, "The point I was making is that it's only impossible if the only link is that it's poetry. We don't want it to be impossible, so we have to go for something else."

"Drive," I said.

"You're the boss," he said. "What's the idea?"

"The library."

When we finally got moving again, Charlie made a left and worked his way onto Amsterdam. To his credit, he didn't ask me which library. I read some more. " 'My friends are estranged, or far distant, I bow my head and stand still.' " I turned around to Charlie. "I think I've heard that one before, too."

"So much culture," he said, "in such a small brain."

I ignored him and read the final verse. " 'I do not think Life provides for all and for Time and Space, but I believe Heavenly Death provides for all.' This the five-day one?"

He nodded. "We're here."

"Where's 'here?' "

"West 53rd," he said. "Donnell Library Center."

"Why here?"

"It's the nearest. We got to start somewhere."

I looked at my watch. It was ten after five. "Jesus Christ, Charlie, it's after five on Christmas Eve . . . they're not going to want to talk to us about poetry." I looked out through the snow at the plaque on the wall. "And, anyway, it says 'Central Children's Room, Nathan Strauss Young Adult . . . Foreign Languages . . .' this is no good, Charlie. We need somewhere that'll specialize in poetry."

He leaned over and looked at the plaque and pointed. "So, that must be the Public."

I followed his finger. The top of the plaque said BRANCH OF THE NEW YORK PUBLIC LIBRARY.

"On 42nd Street?"

"That's the one," Charlie said.

And we drove some more.

It was five-forty by the time we tried to get across Times Square. It seemed like coming home, we'd been through it so many times.

When we pulled onto the sidewalk beneath the Latting Observatory, it was nearly six o'clock and I was beginning to think we were wasting our time. But at least I had made a small discovery.

"Ezra Pound," I told him as we got out of the car.

He stood looking at me over the roof, eyebrows raised.

"Ezra Pound, the poet. That's the two I know. 'As cool as the pale wet leaves of lily-of-the-valley, she lay beside me in the dawn.' That's all of it. 'Alba,' it's called." I muttered through the five-day-old poem again. It was one of the ones I *had* known and I had known it well . . . but now it was gone.

A thin layer of snow was building up on Charlie's head but he didn't seem to notice.

I looked back at the sheet, squinting back through the years while trying not to think of Mary's face. It was hard. " 'My friends are—' Yeah, that's Pound, too. Don't remember what it's called, though."

"Could they *all* be Ezra Pound?" Charlie's mouth picked its way around the alien name with difficulty, like he was speaking a new language.

"I don't think so." I looked up at Patience and Fortitude, sitting statuesque in the gentle, twinkling whiteness, and thought of Bryant Park just behind the building. Mary's face suddenly smiled at me and then disappeared. "Let's go in," I said and, without waiting for him, I ran past Charlie and up the steps between the old marble lions into the library.

The guy on the reception desk did a couple of double takes on his watch and then tried not to raise his eyebrows when Charlie flashed his card. He almost made it. He told us we wanted John Coucher up on the third floor, CLASSICS SECTION—you could hear the capital letters—and wave-pointed up-and-across directions.

John Coucher wasn't there but a nimble little lady wearing an obligatory hair bun, pince-nez glasses, and forearms like Popeye the Sailor *was*. She looked to be in her early forties, but dressed older and as we walked toward her, she appeared flustered. When

Charlie pulled out his ID, I thought she was going to faint.

Coucher was the Classics Controller, she said, and he knew all there was to know about poetry. *She*— "My name is Miss Carlisle"—usually only worked in the research area. Mister Coucher would be back soon, she told us defensively. I said it didn't matter, that she would do just as well if not better.

She said the name almost before she'd started reading. "Walt Whitman. 'I know it not O soul, nor dost thou, all is blank before us, all waits undream'd of in that region, that inaccessible land.' " She looked up at me and, just for a second, I thought I saw her eyes moisten. "It's called 'Darest Thou Now O Soul,' written in the 1860s, '67 or '68, I think."

Charlie nodded. "And the others, Miss Carlisle?"

"I know the two Pound poems," I told her, "but what about this one?" I leaned over and pointed at the verse. She read it with a slight shaking of her head.

"No?"

She looked up and straight at me. "No, sir." She looked across at Charlie and shrugged with a half smile. "Sorry."

I pointed to the last one. "This one?"

"No." She shook her head. "No, I'm sorry. I can't help you any more."

I smiled at her and watched her look away. Over beside me, Charlie nodded.

"If that's it, I have to go now," she said, glancing at her watch. "My mother . . ." She let her voice trail off and I smiled winningly, wondering how she looked without the bun and whether John Coucher knew. I guessed not.

She disappeared along a row of shelves and by the time we'd taken down the few details she'd provided, reappeared pulling on her coat and hat. She nodded as she went past us.

"That tell you anything?" Charlie said.

I was watching Miss Carlisle sashaying along the room to the swing doors. "No, nothing at all."

He slipped the note and paper back into his coat and we started out. That was it. We'd tried and failed. It was 6:30, and Santa was coming. I could hear a bottle I'd written and asked him for sloshing around in his sleigh.

As we got to the elevator, the doors opened and a tall man with a college-style crewcut and more pens in his wool jacket pocket than you'd find in an average office block stepped out onto the floor. He looked at me and then looked away, adjusting his glasses. On a hunch, I said, "Mister Coucher?"

The guy stopped dead, looked at me and then over at Charlie.

"Mister *John* Coucher?"

"Yes, I'm John Coucher," he said at last.

Charlie flashed the trusty ID card and said, "We're investigating a crime, Mr. Coucher and looking for some help."

Coucher looked amazed, adjusted his glasses, and blinked twice in quick succession. "From *me*? You're looking for help from *me*? I haven't done anything."

It was a fact that would probably be chiseled onto his headstone. "Here lies John Coucher: he didn't do anything."

"Show him the poems, Charlie," I said.

Charlie fished them out of his pocket and handed them to Coucher, who accepted them with a slightly shaky hand.

"I wonder if you might be able to tell us the names of the poets who wrote these lines," I said. "I know that—"

"*Me?*" He laughed and held out the two pieces of paper without even looking at them. "I'm afraid you have the wrong guy, here, gentlemen. I know absolutely nothing about poetry. It was never an interest of mine."

Charlie accepted the papers with his mouth slightly open.

"But Miss Carlisle said—"

"You've spoken to Vanda?" He shook his head and shrugged. "Listen, if Vanda couldn't help you, then nobody can. I mean, she is just *the* expert on poetry. Me? Ask me about the classics—Melville, Shakespeare, Poe—but poetry? No, sir."

"She said *you* were the expert."

John Coucher shook his head. "You must have misheard her."

"No," I told him. "She did say you would be able to help us. She had to rush off . . . something about her mother."

"Her *mother*?" He looked at my eyes and then at Charlie's. "Look, if is this some kind of—" He stopped and took a deep breath. "Vanda's mother died a few weeks ago. She's only just started to get over it."

"Her mother's dead?"

"How did she die?" I asked him.

"Hypothermia. Tragic case. They were very close." He settled his shoulders down and seemed to get more comfortable. "For a while, she just went to pieces. Then she started doing voluntary work for the Welfare office over near Gramercy Park . . . corner of 23rd and Lexington."

"Voluntary work?" Charlie was buttoning up his coat.

Coucher nodded and adjusted his glasses again. They hadn't moved, but it seemed to make him feel better. "Yes, visiting old folks who live alone. You know, getting groceries, making them something to eat, that kind of thing."

"Do you have Miss Carlisle's address?" I said.

He frowned. "It's down by Port Authority, I think . . . they'll have it downstairs. Ask the man on the desk."

I hit the elevator button. "Thanks."

"For what?" he said.

"Yeah," said Charlie, "you've been a big help."

Coucher shook his head so hard as to make it fall right off his shoulders. "But I didn't *do* anything!"

Back inside the car, now cunningly disguised as an igloo, I said to Charlie, "Remind me never to play you at bridge."

He started the engine and crunched through the gears. "I was never any good," he said. "It's only right that I win one hand after all these years."

The address was 85½ Lunan Court, a small street off Ninth Avenue. Not a good area. We parked the blue-and-white outside a store on 34th in the hope that would-be automobile dismantlers might think we were inside and could see them schlepping away with fenders and wheels and other assorted goodies. A vain hope, perhaps.

The sign on the mailbox said V. CARLISLE: APT 12. There was no intercom and the inside door stood wide open, a thin layer of snow on the first few feet of worn linoleum.

We went in, checking door numbers. Apartment 12 was on the second floor. I made to knock but Charlie shook his head and motioned me to stand to the side of the door, like they do in the movies. Standing against the wall, he stretched out his arm and rapped on the door. "Miss Carlisle? It's Detective Bieglemann . . . from the library. Could we speak with you again?"

The door opened straightaway and Vanda Carlisle stood in front of us, coat still on, a small smile tugging at the corners of her mouth. "Come in," she said. "Please." She turned around and we followed her inside.

The room smelled of air freshener or potpourri, the strong kind that you get from the cheap supermarkets to cover up the aroma of busted drains.

"I was expecting you," Vanda Carlisle said.

Charlie said, "John Coucher told us that *you* were the poetry expert, not him."

She nodded. "Yes, that is correct."

"He also told us that your mother . . ." He let his voice trail off the way that she had done earlier.

She nodded again. "She's in the bedroom."

Somebody dropped a slab of ice down the back of my shirt. "She's *here*? In the apartment?"

"Oh, yes, I couldn't bury her."

Charlie just looked at her.

"Too cold," she told him, matter-of-factly. She turned to me and said, "The ground. It's as cold down there as it is up here," she said. "That's why I've been helping the others."

"The other women?"

"Yes," she said softly. Then, to me, "It was Whitman, the other poem. 'I do not think Life provides for all and for Time and Space, but I believe Heavenly Death provides for all.' It's from 'Assurances.' I had to look after them, didn't I?"

Neither of us said anything.

"Nobody else could."

Charlie read her her rights and told her she would have to come down to the precinct with us.

"Will you look after my mother?"

"Yeah," he said, "we'll take care of your mother."

As he led her out of the apartment I walked across to a door that bore a small plate containing a picture of a bed. I turned the handle and pushed it gently. Inside, in the darkness, the *warm* darkness, I could see a figure in a chair beside the bed. The room smelled like a busted drain. I closed the door again and left.

I told Charlie I'd walk home. He asked me if I was sure and I nodded. "Sure."

In the back of the car, Vanda Carlisle sat quietly, her wrists handcuffed on her lap, looking out of the window . . . not at us but at the steadily falling white coldness. I wondered how many other women—and men—were sitting in cold rooms, in cold houses, looking out of dirty windows and searching the heavens for a solitary star.

"We blew it," I told him, watching my breath gather in a fog and then disperse.

"*Blew* it? Hell, we made it, didn't we?"

"It was luck, Charlie. Okay, she worked for Welfare, and, okay, she's a she . . . like you said. And she *did* have a relative, which was a link. Just. But the rest of it was chance. Remember your hunch?"

"My hunch?"

"The link. It didn't exist. We were just lucky. If we'd not been lucky—*damned* lucky—she could still be out there . . . writing poems."

"It was a break, Koke. We had it coming." I watched his eyes searching mine. "That's what card games are all about, Koke. We played for the drop, and we got it."

"We didn't play for the drop, Charlie. She as good as showed us her cards." I was starting to feel cold and in bad need of a drink. "It fell in our lap. You and me, the intrepid investigators. Denny Colt and Commissioner Dolan."

Charlie screwed up his face and shook his head. "Koke," he said, shrugging his shoulders and holding out his hands, palms up, "it's Christmas. We got a present. And like you said, she wanted to be caught."

"Yeah, she wanted to be caught."

"You know what, Koke?"

I shook my head.

"You're a bad winner."

"Merry Christmas, Charlie."

As I turned my back and walked toward the first of many bars and of many bottles, I heard a car door slam and an engine start up. It sounded as tired as I was. It was seven-fifteen. Santa must have made his delivery for me by now. Hell, I hadn't asked him for much.

But then, so many people don't ask for much.

I wondered if we'd done the right thing.

I still say we blew it.

THAT BELLS MAY RING AND WHISTLES SAFELY BLOW

by Margaret Maron

"Deck the halls?" snarled Jane as she untied a rope of tinsel from a file cabinet and added it to the pile growing beside her reception desk. "I know one Hall I'd love to deck."

"And I know where I'd like to stick a few boughs of holly," Sheila agreed. She stood atop a step stool and unhooked the cluster of shiny stars that dangled from an overhead light.

I didn't speak. I believe actions speak louder than words and I was using all my breath to stuff our four-foot artificial fir tree into a huge plastic bag—lights, ornaments, icicles, and all.

'Twas two nights before Christmas, and we were three angry middle-aged mice as we stripped the office of every decoration. Santa Claus was a bully, Scrooge had triumphed, why continue the peace-on-earth-goodwill-to-men charade?

The annual Christmas party downstairs had put us in such a bleak mood that when we came back up for our coats, the jingle-bell festivity of our office repelled us. As one woman, we decided to bundle everything up and give it to someone deserving. The way our boss's bosses had reacted to Bridget's whistle-blowing, a shelter for battered women seemed the most appropriate.

Not that Sheila wasn't put out with Bridget herself.

"If she hadn't gone off half-cocked—" She tossed the stars atop Jane's pile of tinsel and paused to help me close the top of the tree bag.

"She's young," I said. "Things are more black and white when you're nineteen."

In truth, Bridget reminded me of myself at that age, which was more years ago than I like to contemplate: naive, idealistic, and full of youthful misconceptions.

Here in the Budget Department of the City Planning Commission, she'd soon learned that very few public officials actually serve the public. Clerical staff does most of the work while department heads hide incompetence, gross negligence, and outright dishonesty by playing the bureaucratic shell game: You cover my rear, I'll cover yours, and Santa will fill both our stockings with sugarplums.

Our boss was one of Santa's best little helpers. Nicholas T. Hall exuded an air of confident ability. He spoke the jargon. He had an endless fund of risque stories that were clean enough to be told in mixed company, and he knew to the millisecond when to cut through the laughter with a "But seriously, guys, this problem we have here means we're gonna need to . . ."

As a result, he'd been promoted two notches above his level of competency. Nothing terribly unusual about that. We "girls" were used to covering our bosses' worst blunders. But then he began to muddle ineptitude with greed. Before his arrival, most contracts were still awarded to the lowest or most efficient bidder. Now reports had their figures padded or deflated depending on what was needed and what could be glossed over, and kickbacks ranged from bottles of scotch to God knew what.

Business as usual, right? It was only taxpayer dollars. Who gave a happy damn?

Well, as it turned out, Bridget did.

She'd seemed as militant as dandelion fluff when she first floated into our department right out of high school back in May. We soon learned that she'd fudged her application form and that she had no burning desire to work her way up from file clerk to senior administrative aide in the city's civil service system. She merely wanted to earn more than a student's usual summer job paid and she planned to quit at the end of August and go off to college.

Jane was a bit ticked because it would mean training someone else in the fall, but Bridget proved a quick learner and, though clearly not a dedicated worker, was at least willing to follow directions, so Jane kept her mouth shut to Mr. Hall.

Which was lucky because in mid-June, Bridget's parents and three perfect strangers were killed in a car crash that was clearly her father's fault. Funeral expenses and settling two messy civil lawsuits out of court took the house and most of her parents' modest estate. There were no relatives and Bridget's college plans had to be put on hold. She did manage to salvage some of her mother's furniture and a few family keepsakes from the sale of the house, and Jane and Sheila helped her find a cozy little apartment near enough so she didn't need a car to get to work.

Bridget changed overnight. She'd been an adored only child and was very close to her parents. After their death, the lightness went out of her steps; and all through the fall, she threw herself into the job with a passion that gave a whole new meaning to the term workaholic. We knew her reaction wasn't completely healthy, but compulsive dedication was certainly easier to deal with than the crying jags that had gone before. Jane was pleased with her new thoroughness, Sheila was skeptical as to how long it could last, while I, keeping to the real agenda, was indifferent.

There were other, younger women in the department, but for some reason Bridget attached herself to the three of us even though we did little to encourage her. At coffee breaks she brought her hot chocolate to my cubicle, or she tagged along at lunch. Occasionally, she and I were even mistaken for mother and daughter. I'd seen pictures of Bridget's mother and knew there was a vague resemblance, but it wasn't something I wanted to promote. I had two perfectly satisfactory Siamese cats, thank you, and I certainly didn't want an emotional involvement with anyone's orphaned child. Nevertheless, there were times when something I said would remind her of happier times and tears would spill down her smooth cheeks. That's when it got hard to stay completely aloof.

Early in December, when Mr. Hall's Christmas booty began pouring in, Bridget started to notice. Soon she had matched the names on the gift cards with names on certain city contracts, and she came to us in outright indignation.

"Look at this!" she cried. "Davis Corporation's original bid. Here are their first figures and this is how Mr. Hall let them change it. And now they've sent him two bottles of scotch? They're going to get an extra four thousand a month from the city for two bottles of scotch?"

Sheila and Jane and I exchanged glances. We knew the scotch was but a socially acceptable token of Davis Corp's real appreciation, which was delivered every month in an unmarked envelope.

"And see what Mainline's done! They—"

"And just where did you get those contracts?" Jane asked sternly, snatching them out of her hands. "You have no business rummaging in those particular files."

Bridget's big blue eyes had opened even wider. "Don't you care that they're robbing the city blind?"

"Small potatoes," Sheila said heartlessly, "compared to what some others are doing."

I gave Sheila a cold glare and she shut up as I pulled on my boots against the snow falling outside. "I'm going to spend my lunch hour Christmas shopping," I announced. "Anyone interested?"

"I'll come," said Jane. She quickly refiled the contracts and closed those drawers with a crisp finality. "Rowan's has a sale on men's flannel shirts."

"Maybe I'll get one for Bill," said Sheila.

"How can you shop when—" Bridget's outraged protest broke off as the inner door swung open and our boss breezed through in his overcoat, heading out for his usual two-hour lunch.

He smiled at us in genial bonhomie. "Going Christmas shopping, girls?"

"Yes, Mr. Hall," I said.

If he ever remembered how long it took me to teach him his job here, and if he ever realized he still couldn't handle it without me, he never showed it. I could appreciate the irony, and unlike Sheila and Jane, I didn't resent the institutional unfairness of the situation. Might as well resent December for not being June. Make as much sense. So what, if I still knew more about how the department functioned than he ever would? Clerical experience wasn't worth a reindeer's damn to the hierarchy. The job description for department head specified a college degree.

I didn't have one.

Nicholas T. Hall did.

That's why we called him Mr. Hall and he called us "girls."

"You got some Christmas presents," Bridget said, thrusting the beribboned boxes toward him. Unexpected acid etched her voice.

Mr. Hall held one up to his ear and beamed happily as he heard the expected liquid slosh from the bottle inside. "Good old Davis!" he chuckled. "Why don't you help me put these in my office, little lady?"

Davis Corp knew their man. He would probably take a quick nip before leaving and two or three more nips when he came back from his three-scotch lunch. Then he'd shove a few papers around his desk, sign the ones I'd left there, and about midafternoon ask us to hold his calls. At times like that, the rest of the staff thought he was concentrating on a project. Only Jane and Sheila and I knew that he sneaked long naps on the couch in his office, and he trusted us to cover for him. Four years of such indulgence had added an extra chin and puffed the bags beneath his eyes.

Indignation still burned in Bridget's eyes as Mr. Hall held the door for the three of us; and when we returned an hour later with our shopping bags crammed with gaily wrapped bundles, she spoke not a word but went straight on with her work on the far side of the office.

We let her sulk. December was hurtling past, the

year was coming to an end, and we were so pressed for time on our own special project that we had none to spare for her. In fact, we used her sulks to rational-ize our neglect. That was the guilt that gnawed at us and had sent us back up to the office to rip down the Christmas decorations that afternoon.

"If only we'd paid attention!" said Jane. "We could have headed her off."

"Who'd expect someone that young to get so up-tight about morality?" asked Sheila.

"It's the young who do," I said slowly. "Once they get our age, most of them are too cynical to care anymore."

"They didn't have to fire her though," Sheila muttered.

Jane snorted and I gave Sheila a jaundiced look.

"Okay, okay," Sheila said. "You're right. But . . . I mean— Well, darn it all, it *is* Christmas."

"That's what *they* said," I reminded her.

As senior administrative aide in this department, I'd had to stand and listen that morning while Nicholas T. Hall and G.W. Parry, Hall's superior, fired Bridget.

When the flow of Christmas bottles reached its crest, that naive little bit of dandelion fluff had care-fully listed all the donors and keyed their names to various contracts Hall had awarded. This morning, bright and early, she'd marched down to Parry's of-fice, handed him the list, and stood there expecting to be told what a good little girl she was for blowing the whistle on crooked contractors.

Instead, she'd gotten a rude blast of reality and or-ders to clean out her desk before five o'clock.

"What else did you expect?" I'd asked her as we climbed the stairs back to our office. She was shaking in nervous reaction and trembling on the verge of tears, and I'd chosen stairs over the elevator so she'd have time to collect herself. "Okay, so city employees aren't supposed to take gifts. Nobody considers a few bottles of hooch a bribe. You're lucky they're satisfied just to fire you. You could have been sued for slander."

"Sued?" she whimpered. "Again?"

She'd endured agonies when everything her parents amassed had gone to settle the lawsuits over her father's car wreck. I hated to touch a hurt that had almost healed, but she needed to understand the consequences of going off half-cocked.

"Do you know what this is going to do for morale in our department?"

Tears did stream from her eyes then. "Oh, Glenna. I'm so sorry. I wasn't thinking."

I sighed and put my arms around her and let her cry. Inside, I burned with white-hot rage and impotence, but I kept my voice soothing as I patted her back and told her everything was going to be fine, just fine. She was such an emotionally fragile kid and here she was, being cut adrift at Christmas with no immediate job prospects and no shoulder to go home and cry on. Not even a cat.

When we reached our landing, the humiliation of having to clean out her desk while the whole department watched was more than she could take at the moment and she clutched at my hand.

"Don't make me go in there. Please, Glenna?"

I offered to do it for her, but she shook her head and began to edge down the stairs. "No, I'll come back this afternoon while everyone's at the Christmas party, okay?"

Reluctantly, I agreed but made her promise to wait while I got her coat. She seemed ready to bolt off into the snowy day with nothing on her arms but a thin pink sweater, and I didn't want her pneumonia on my conscience, too.

My return to the office coincided with Mr. Hall's. It was his year to play Santa Claus, to hand out the gag gifts and Christmas bonuses, and he had his red suit and wig in one hand and white beard in the other.

"Damn shame," he said, fluffing out the beard. He'd decided to be noble and magnanimous, more sinned against than sinning, this hurts me more than it hurts her. "Such a pretty little thing. I thought Parry was a bit hard on her, but he seemed to think we had no choice."

What G.W. Parry had said, with more force than originality, was that when an apple (i.e., Bridget) turned rotten, it had to be plucked out before it spoiled the whole barrel (the Budget Department).

"And I agree," I told him with more sincerity than he realized.

"You do? Ah, Glenna, you girls always surprise me. Will you tell the others?"

"I thought I'd wait till just before the party, if that's all right with you?"

"Good thinking. The party will take their minds off it, and then with the whole Christmas weekend— You're right. By Tuesday morning they'll have forgotten this whole unpleasant situation."

On the whole, he probably hadn't underestimated his staff's compassion. In an announcement shortly before the party was due to start at two-thirty, I explained that Bridget had made certain unfounded accusations against Mr. Hall and that she'd been asked to resign in light of her poor team spirit. Rumors would fly, but except for Sheila, Jane, and me, Bridget had made no close friends among the other ten women in the department. Unless we discussed her actions in public, there'd be nothing to keep the rumors going.

Of course I'd told Jane and Sheila everything over lunch and by the time we'd had a few cups of the spiked punch down in Central Planning, the three of us had gone from rage to despair to a melancholy pity for poor Bridget. As the others drifted off early to their varied merry Christmases, we went back upstairs and found that Bridget had been and gone.

Her desktop was bare, the empty drawers stood ajar, but everything that had made the desk hers— nameplate, coffee mug, even a cloisonné brass pot full of pencils, pens, and scissors—had been dumped in the nearest trash can as if she'd suddenly changed her mind about taking anything with her.

That's when we got angry all over again and attacked the Christmas decorations. We were almost finished when Nicholas T. Hall staggered in, beard awry, reeking of scotch, and slurring his words. He made a half-hearted joke about mistletoe and pretty girls as he shucked off his red jacket, hat, and attached wig, and slung them toward the nearest coat rack.

We ignored him.

Wounded, he retreated to his office and a moment later we heard the tinkle of glass, then the whooshing sound that his leather couch always makes when he sprawls upon it full length. By the time we'd bagged all the decorations to take over to the women's shelter, muted snores were drifting through our boss's half-open door.

It was only a little past four, but the sky had darkened and a fifty-percent probability of fresh snow was predicted. The telephone rang just as we were putting on our coats.

"Glenna? Oh good. This is Louise Hall. Is my husband still there? He promised he'd be home early."

Automatically I spoke the sort of lies Mr. Hall had instructed me to speak in such circumstances. "I'm sorry, Mrs. Hall. He left about a half hour ago. I think he planned to do some Christmas shopping on the way home. I was just leaving myself."

As I opened my desk drawer for my purse, I found a small gaily wrapped package with my name on it.

"I thought we agreed no presents," I said. Then, across the room, I saw that Sheila and Jane had discovered similar boxes.

I looked again at the name tag and recognized the handwriting.

"From Bridget," I said.

"Oh, gee," said Jane, ripping the paper from hers. "With all her troubles, she went and did this for us?"

She lifted the lid from the box and gasped with delight. Inside was a beautiful snow dome, one of those glass balls filled with water and white flecks that create a swirling snowstorm when shaken. This one was old, almost an antique. I knew because I was there the day Bridget showed it to Jane, who collects snow domes. It held a miniature elf who trudged across the snowy field carrying a decorated tree on his shoulders. It had belonged to Bridget's grandmother.

My gift was a sterling silver bracelet I'd once admired. Her mother's.

Even Sheila was touched. "I can't take this," she said though she tenderly cradled the old-fashioned gold pocket watch in her hand and traced the intricate initials with the tip of her finger. "It was her great-grandfather's. Almost a hundred years old. She loves this watch."

Jane inverted the snow dome and watched the white flecks dance inside its polished glass. "This is one of her favorite things."

The thin silver bracelet suddenly felt like a sliver of ice on my wrist. "These *are* her favorite things. Why has she given them away?"

I looked into their faces and saw my own startled apprehension reflected.

My reserved parking space was nearest the back entrance and Sheila and Jane piled into the car with me. Bridget's apartment was only a few short blocks away and though we made it in minutes, we were at least a half hour too late.

She'd left the door unlocked.

She was still wearing the pink sweater, but now the front was drenched in blood. She must have come home and sat down in her mother's wingback chair, then pressed a needlepoint cushion against her chest before pulling the trigger, as if the cushion would somehow soften the shot.

Nicholas T. Hall's gun.

Every once in a while he had to go out and inspect deserted job sites in the rougher sections of the city. Legally registered. We recognized the fancy bone handle. He kept it in his desk drawer and whenever he cleaned the damn thing, he'd leave his office door open so that we *girls* could catch a glimpse of the he-man in action, ready and willing to face all dangers, the city's very own rootin', tootin' gunslinger.

And now his gun had finally notched its first kill.

Bridget's blue eyes stared into eternity. With infinite tenderness, Jane leaned over and closed them; then, almost wordlessly, we did what had to be done.

Christmas arrived two days later and that morning, the police apologetically summoned the three of us back to the office. They had a search warrant.

Mr. Hall was there, too. He looked as if he'd discovered rats and spiders in his Christmas stocking.

"Tell them, girls," he said hoarsely. "Tell them how I fell asleep on the couch night before last and didn't wake up till after eight. Jane? Sheila? You were here when I came back from the party and—Glenna! You were still working when I woke up. Remember?

We looked at him blankly.

"I'm sorry, Mr. Hall," I said. "You left the office immediately after the party. If you came back again, it must have been after we'd gone."

"Besides," added Jane, "why would Glenna work late that night? It was the beginning of our Christmas holiday."

"Fits with what Mrs. Hall said," one of the detectives muttered to another. "Let's get on with it."

They soon found the gun behind the couch where it'd dropped from Mr. Hall's comatose fingers. (Jane's idea, and a nice touch, I thought.)

They were equally pleased with the red jacket and white beard still dangling from the back of Mr. Hall's door. "The old lady across the hall said she saw a Santa ringing the girl's bell."

So many people had worn the company's Santa costume over the years, it wouldn't matter whose hairs they found on the cap and wig as long as one or two of them belonged to Mr. Hall.

The detectives were very good at their job. Within hours after the anonymous call late Christmas Eve, they'd also found the computer disks I'd hidden in Bridget's lingerie drawer as well as the papers I'd stashed in her flour canister.

Taken together, the papers and floppies documented four years of corruption that stretched from the Budget Department right up to the City Council itself. There were names and dates and bank account numbers and Xerox copies of dated deposit slips. Every allegation wasn't backed with solid proof, of course. Not as much as Sheila and Jane and I'd hoped to provide before Bridget so abruptly forced our hand, but more than enough to fuel the public investigation we'd been planning for almost a year—especially when linked to the shooting of a pretty young city clerk.

Bridget's death, an apparently cold-blooded murder so she wouldn't go public with her tale of bureaucratic corruption, wasn't the sort of thing that could be glossed over like a few bottles of complimentary Christmas booze. Not if that television van parked downstairs meant what I hoped it did.

Scotch had fogged Mr. Hall's perceptions more than he realized. It was closer to nine than eight when he woke up and found me still stripping the electronic data of all links to the three of us and transferring it to the sort of floppies that Bridget's computer used. Sheila and Jane had families; so they had washed the sulfites from Bridget's hands, taken away the cushion, and gone straight home. The rest was up to me; and if it'd taken longer than any of us expected, if Bridget's delicate young face kept coming between my tear-blurred eyes and the numbers on my computer screen, who would know? Siamese cats can't tell time. Can't testify.

Open and shut, said the detectives. "The kid let slip what she had on you; you got her fired. Then she threatened to blow an even bigger whistle and you got drunk and shot her."

"No!" whimpered Nicholas T. Hall.

"Drunkenness is no longer a defense against murder," warned the younger detective.

"Why won't you girls tell them?" Mr. Hall asked plaintively as they hauled him away like a defective Christmas present.

I pulled on my gloves and my own Christmas present gleamed against the soft leather, a slender shining hoop too delicate for everyday wear. Too easily crushed.

If Sheila and Jane and I had been younger, less cynical, perhaps we could have trusted her.

As soon as Cameron Jewelry begins its January clearance sale next week, I shall buy a tiny gold whistle to hang on Bridget's silver bracelet.

I shall blow it every Christmas.

NO GAOL FOR THE BUDGIE

by Jon L. Breen

Hummingbirds made good solicitors, Mr. Justice Owl reflected, watching one from the bench that overlooked the crowded courtroom. So much energy, and so adept at backing out of tight situations. True, they seldom made the grade as barristers. They talked so fast and found the wigs heavy. Coots were the ones most frequently called to the bar. Indeed, they looked like barristers even without their wigs, and they seemed to enjoy a good fight.

The prisoner perched in the dock, charged with an accumulation of breaches of the peace, was a budgerigar whom the Crown was endeavouring to have caged. If these chaps could get on with it, court might be recessed at a decent hour this Christmas Eve. Judge Owl hadn't wanted to sit today—indeed Lady Owl had done some pointed hooting about it—but, after all, some of the highest quality justice was dispensed in the waning days before Christmas.

This was a large tree, the judge thought, but still the Law Courts were outgrowing it. The jury box was perfect for twelve sparrows, but when larger birds perched there, they seemed crowded and uncomfortable. Everyone in court was surely anxious to leave for that last-minute Christmas shopping, but Judge Owl was determined there be no undue haste in the pursuit of justice.

Sir Graham Goose, Q.C., rose to lead for the Crown. "M'Lord and members of the jury, I shall be honored to prosecute in the case of *R.* v. *Bo Budgie.* Representing the prisoner is my learned brother at the bar Sir Cuthbert Coot, Q.C. Knowing the pressures of the season of the year, and also cognizant of the rare intelligence of this fine jury, I shall not make any extended remarks in my opening address to you this afternoon, trusting in your discernment to recognize from the evidence here adduced that the caging of Bo Budgie, for his own protection as well as for the good of society, is the inevitable course that must be taken. You shall hear . . ."

Sir Graham was a thorough advocate if seldom an exciting one. It was not an easy time for him, Judge Owl knew, bearing the brunt of tasteless japes that all geese and turkeys must face during the holiday season. True, no Q.C. was in any real danger of ending life as a Yuletide dinner for some human family, but such was not necessarily true of his less accomplished relatives, and more sensitive creatures (like Judge Owl) had the tact to eschew Christmas goose jokes.

First witness for the prosecution was Dermot Duck. Cinematic slanders to the contrary, he spoke with the clear annunciation of a B.B.C. newsreader, and no interpreter was necessary.

"Mr. Duck, are you acquainted with the prisoner, Bo Budgie?"

"I am indeed."

"How did you meet him?"

"He was a customer at my seaside restaurant."

"A regular customer?"

"No, indeed. I am pleased to say he was there only once. He was a great annoyance to the other diners."

"In what way did he annoy them?"

"By loud talk, chiefly. In a human language. That always makes my customers nervous. I have a very good class of customer, and they were offended by the presence of a former cagebird. They are naturally suspicious of any bird that has been too close or friendly to humans."

"I quite understand," said Sir Graham Goose, and no one in court doubted that he understood very well.

The remaining questions served mainly to underline the prisoner's acquaintanceship with human speech and his reluctance to stem it in the presence of other birds. Presently, Sir Cuthbert Coot rose to cross-examine.

"You identified yourself as a restaurateur, Mr. Duck?"

"That is correct."

"Perhaps you could tell us the name of your restaurant."

"Is that relevant, M'Lord?" the witness implored.

"The witness will answer," Judge Owl ruled.

"It's called Crumbs on the Run."

"I don't think we all heard that," Sir Cuthbert snapped. "Could you repeat that a bit louder?"

"Crumbs on the Run."

"Is yours the only establishment of that name?"

"You know it isn't."

"Is it not a fact that Crumbs on the Run is a franchise operation, what is called in the vernacular a 'fast-food' chain, that there is one at every seaside or lake or pond, and that indeed Crumbs on the Run, specializing as it does in soggy stale bread crumbs, offers the cheapest meals for birds on this whole island?"

"Perhaps. Nothing to be ashamed of in that. They're good nutritious meals."

"M'Lord," said Sir Graham Goose, rising ponderously, "I fail to see the relevance of this discussion of the witness's business . . ."

"It is quite relevant!" replied Sir Cuthbert Coot. "The witness has made his clientele sound too fragile and high-toned to put up with a budgerigar's talking in an unfamiliar language. I submit that Crumbs on the Run customers speak a plethora of dialects, are quite used to the world in all its diversity, and do not need such protection from a colorful and harmless small bird who has had the misfortune of spending some of his early years in a cage!"

"I believe the point is made, Sir Cuthbert," Judge Owl ruled. "Pray proceed."

"Certainly, M'Lord. Was speaking in a human language the only thing that offended your customers about my client, Mr. Duck?"

"He was a bit loud."

"Are loud customers unusual in your establishment, Mr. Duck?"

"Well, we don't mind them having a good time, but . . ."

"Is it not a fact that the other diners shunned Bo Budgie not because of any former association with humans but because they found his Australian accent distasteful?"

"No, certainly not."

"Tell me, Mr. Duck, why do you use the feminine-form surname Duck instead of the masculine Drake?"

"Really, M'Lord!" Sir Graham exclaimed. "What is my learned friend implying?"

"Is this quite necessary, Sir Cuthbert?"

"I don't mind answering," said the witness. "It's traditional, that's all. I come from a long line of Ducks. Why, the most famous drake in the world goes by the surname Duck."

"I daresay," Sir Cuthbert sneered. "I have no more questions of this witness, M'Lord."

Judge Owl shook his head. The poor chap was grasping at straws. He could well understand that Sir Graham Goose, who might have been Sir Graham Gander, took the line of questioning as a personal affront.

The witnesses for the Crown continued. Their thrust seemed to be that Bo Budgie, accustomed as he was to the four walls of a cage, was unable to adjust to free society. He had spent a whole day in a department store, fluttering from mirror to mirror and talking to himself, upsetting other shoppers. He had continued to repeat odd human catchphrases to passing birds. He had had many close calls and appeared to be a danger to himself. Sir Graham emphasized the point that the caging of Bo Budgie would be as much for his own good as for that of society. He called one witness who even intimated that Bo Budgie was a human spy. Judge Owl could understand Sir Graham Goose's fervor, but he feared the advocate might be overdoing things a bit. Were humans so concerned about bird secrets as to resort to espionage?

Sir Cuthbert Coot called only two witnesses for the defense. The first was Colonel Pigeon, a retired army bird who had dined out these forty years on his exploits carrying messages in the last war. Colonel Pigeon was attempting to establish a place in the Guinness Book of Bird Records as the most frequent Law Court witness, and he appeared in the box an average of four times per week, usually for the defense. Normally good for comedy relief, today he left the holiday nerves somewhat frayed.

"Colonel," inquired Sir Cuthbert, "are you acquinted with the prisoner?"

"Righty-ho. Bright-feathered little beggar, ain't he?"

"Um, yes. Tell us, Colonel, how you happen to know Mr. Budgie."

"Round and about. Here and there."

"And have you formed an opinion as to his general character?"

"Generals *are* characters, you know."

"Er, quite so. But the prisoner's general character . . ."

"Don't know his rank. Don't know as he was in uniform at all. Young fellow, though, so I can't imagine he was a general."

"Colonel Pigeon, have you seen any instances of the difficulty the prisoner is reported to have had because of his association with humans?"

"No, sir! That wasn't it at all, y'know. Humans are all right. I worked with humans in the last war and they're okay! Most thinking birds, except for some birdbrains, which is a jolly stupid expression if you've ever thought about it, since we are birds ourselves, and here we are . . ."

"Might you address yourself to counsel's question, Colonel," Judge Owl prompted helpfully. He rather liked the old fellow, but in the waning hours of Christmas Eve he could be a trial. (The fleeting mental pun was unintended.)

"Er, what was the question?"

"The problems Mr. Budgie had with other birds . . ."

"Oh, yes. It was his accent, that's all. And you can't blame a bird for his accent, can you? He's a Down Under bird, and Down Under birds have got a rather unfair press in this country, I think, goonies and boobies and all. Some people have a thing about Aussies. Think they have funny accents. Not so different from cockney as far as I can see, and there were some brave Aussie birds in the last war, but there it is, eh?"

To the relief of all, Sir Graham Goose waived crossexamination, and Sir Cuthbert Coot called to the box the prisoner himself, Bo Budgie.

"Mr. Budgie, is it true that you have had difficulty providing for yourself as a free bird?"

"No it isn't. I have eaten well enough and kept my feathers tidy, as my appearance will show."

"How would you respond to the charge that you disrupted the department store by flying from mirror to mirror?"

"I believed and still do believe that they were public mirrors, and I should be allowed to look at myself in them as anyone else."

"What of the charge that you are endangered by other birds?"

"The reports are distorted and exaggerated beyond belief. The only real mishap I have had was when a hummingbird made an unexpected turn and gave me a sharp poke with his beak. It was my own solicitor, and he immediately apologized."

"Did you enjoy being a cagebird, Mr. Budgie?"

"It was a job like any job. It was all right really."

"Do you wish to be caged again?"

"No, I have chosen to be free."

"Do you feel you have been corrupted by the society of humans?"

"No. My human family was quite pleasant, and I learned some of their songs and sayings to please them. They treated me well. It was just time to move on, take a change of direction."

"Do you, as has been charged, think of yourself as human?"

"No, I am first, last, and always a bird."

"What have you learned about the attitudes of birds toward humans, Mr. Budgie?"

"I have been very patient M'Lord," said Sir Graham Goose in an aggrieved tone, "but I cannot help believing we are going rather far afield."

"I should like to give the prisoner an opportunity to answer," Judge Owl ruled.

"Very well, M'Lord."

Bo Budgie seemed to choose his words carefully. "Birds seem to think humans quite different, but they aren't really. They're doing the best they can, just as we birds do. They celebrate Christmas, you know, just as we do. And yet I find many of my fellow birds believe humans only have a Christmas goose to ruin the season for birds. It's not so, any more than many of the jurors might have a Christmas worm or a Christmas fish so that the worms and fish would have an unhappy Christmas. The thing is that we're all of us, birds and insects and fish and mammals, part of the food chain . . ."

Sir Graham Goose was now clearly incensed. "M'Lord, I most strenuously protest this distasteful line of testimony. I do not choose to think of myself as part of a food chain, or any other kind of chain. This is very easy for the witness, for after all, no one has Christmas budgie!"

"Please calm yourself, Sir Graham," said Judge Owl. He was rather uneasily contemplating his Christmas mouse, fearing it might not taste quite as good this year. "I'm sure the witness intended nothing personal, Sir Cuthbert?"

"I have no further questions, M'Lord."

Sir Graham rose to cross-examine. His every word dripped with contempt. "You tell us humans keep Christmas."

"That is correct."

"They gave *you* presents at Christmas, did they?"

"Oh, yes. Only things they thought a bird would enjoy, you understand. The odd cuttlebone and all that sort of thing."

"And I supose they sang Christmas songs!" the prosecutor said with a triumphant note. It was an article of faith in the bird world that people were incapable of song.

"Yes, many different ones."

"Perhaps you would sing a few for us," the barrister said sarcastically.

"If you would like." Bo Budgie began a rendition of "On Christmas Day in the Morning."

"M'Lord, I must protest," Sir Graham Goose honked.

"With respect, M'Lord," said Sir Cuthbert Coot, "I must remind my learned friend that my client is merely responding to his own question, to which the defense offers no objection."

"Really, M'Lord!"

"Sir Graham, the bench would welcome argument, but if you can offer only exclamations, I shall direct the witness to continue his reply."

Sir Graham subsided, and Bo Budgie continued his concert, offering renditions of "Deck the Halls," "Silent Night," "The First Noel," and other traditional human carols. Judge Owl enjoyed this exotica, found it oddly soothing, though knowing it was an acquired taste. A cultured bird, he was somewhat used to it, having patronized the annual concerts of the Parrots' and Mynahs' Choir for some years. It was hard to tell what effect it was having on the jury, though jurors number eight (a magpie), number nine (a crow), and number eleven (a cockatoo) looked most sympathetic.

Relieved that the concert had finally ended, Sir Graham Goose continued his cross-examination. "If humans celebrate Christmas, do they then believe that the wellspring of our holiday was a man and not a bird?"

"They do, yes."

"And do you not find that a heresy?"

"No, it seems quite natural to me that they should hold that belief."

"I wonder if your fellow birds on the jury will share that very *enlightened* view," Sir Graham said with facetious emphasis. "And how did you feel about the human practice of eating your fellow birds for Christmas dinner? Did that strike you as in the spirit of the season?"

"I found the annual prospect unpleasant I admit, not so much the idea of it, which I well understood as I've explained. The actual doing of it, though, made me squeamish, and of course I could not speak to them in their language, only repeat what they taught me. But one Christmas season, they seemed to understand my feelings, as if we were communicating by some sort of interspecies telepathy. And they began having roast beef instead of goose or turkey for their Christmas dinner. Had I been a pet calf, I might not have welcomed the change so, but all things are relative."

"And yet you escaped this wonderful, generous, uncorrupting human family, Mr. Budgie. Why was that, pray tell?"

"Many of us make midlife career changes, Sir Graham. I wanted to broaden my horizons, get in a little more flying, smell the flowers, enjoy the world. But I find that many of my fellow birds think once a cagebird, always a cagebird. A narrow view, I believe."

"M'Lord, I have no more questions of this witness."

The day was drawing late, but Judge Owl was determined to see the case to its conclusion. If Bo Budgie was to be free, let him be free on Christmas Eve.

Sir Cuthbert Coot's address to the jury seemed to Judge Owl especially eloquent.

"We birds have much to be proud of. We can imagine no other class of animal having as fair and enlightened a justice system as we do. Though we do have to keep a close eye on our eggs at times, we manage to live together relatively peacefully, regardless of our sizes and strengths and habits: eagles and penguins, robins and woodpeckers, seagulls and pelicans. Indeed even"—with a smile to his adversary—"coots and geese. But do we have the same tolerance and understanding for nonbirds or do we fear them as unknown quantities? Is it not time to stop imagining that Christmas is only for us and to understand that Christmas is for everyone? Is it not time to accept the beauty and sincerity of a human carol as a contribution to the beauty of the season, even if it sounds odd or foreign to our ears? We can symbolize the spirit of this season by setting Bo Budgie free today."

The jury's verdict was not long in coming. Some cynically thought it was hastened by the jurors' desire to dig into the Christmas Eve millet, but Judge Owl thought otherwise. He felt it was a gesture of understanding that well befitted the time of year. For the twelve good birds and true set Bo Budgie free.

In Christmases to come, Judge Owl would many times enjoy Bo Budgie, the new soloist with the Parrots' and Mynahs' Choir. His solicitor hummingbird turned the pages of the music, and Sir Cuthbert Coot invariably perched in the front row. And one Christmas Eve, Judge Owl even thought he glimpsed Sir Graham Goose peering in at the back of the hall and listening to the strange and haunting music.

CRISTEMASSE IS FOREVER

by Dorothy B. Hughes

They sat on the brown-black earth, hard frozen this late in December. The small sharp hooves of the hreinndyr had not scuffed a single small dent upon it. As Nikolaas had directed in his invitation, each of us came with sleigh and team. The dyr had been unhitched and were grazing now for the Arctic lichen, which the Norse people call reindeer moss. Not much of it this cold predawn, but it kept the dyr busy.

Nikolaas had formed a circle of fresh pine boughs on the earth for our seating. He himself may have cut them, as his elves would have been too busy with paintbrush, putting the final touches onto the small, fiery red toy fire engines and tinting the soft golden curls of the doll babies. Before the midnight sky blazoned the message:

CRISTEMASSE A NATALIE DIES.

It was here again, centuries upon centuries since the Old Norse sea captains and the Olde English landrovers had brought its memory to these far Northern shores. All the Santa's Elves had likewise been engaged until the time came to hitch the dyr, gather up the sacks and dash away to meet with Nikolaas.

He himself was now seated at the head of his pine bough circle. If a circle has a head.

It was of course Dom Clausdino, a Bargain Basement helper from the Southernmost Firmament, who interrupted our thoughtful silence. If the Dom was not the most difficult of Santa's associates, it would be nearly impossible to find one more so.

"Are you the chairman of this meeting?" Clausdino

demanded of Klaas, just as if he, not Klaas, was our leader, the strength of our ancient memories.

"This is not a meeting," Klaas stated with civility, doing quite well at restraining himself from growling at the Dom. "Santas do not meet in meetings. We have no need of meetings to communicate with each other. We are not Human Beuns. We are more knowledgeable than they. We are Faery Folk."

"Then why are we here?" Dom persisted.

"You are here because I called you here," Nikolaas answered with emphatic softness. "Not you alone, but each one of us is aware that this is our most busy night of the year."

As he was centuries older than even the most venerable of us, his associates, we listened respectfully. If Dom continued with his insulting harangue, I was prepared to bop him, an expression I've heard small boys say of one or another of their obnoxious friends. For that special purpose I had prepared a small sack of special toys. I had brought that along, not that I expected to use it, but because I thought it might become misplaced among the large sacks of toys.

Or did I think its contents might come in handy in case the invitation from Klaas had been extended to the Southern contingent as well as to us of the High North?

"You should know I would not have called all of you here had I not considered this a matter of importance," Nikolaas spoke without inflection.

Dom Clausdino said nothing, but the look on his face demanded, "Prove it!"

The rest of us expressed open curiosity. But no one echoed the Dom aloud. Sint Nikolaas seemed to be finding it hard to explain. When finally he did put the words together, he said, "I am convinced that we are in danger of losing our heritage."

One after another every one of us in the circle put on a mask of puzzlement. This was momentary, followed almost at once by the reaction of total disbelief. Or as little boys would say of one in their circle, "Has he lost his marbles?" Whatever that is meant to signify.

Dom Clausdino was silenced, at least temporarily, by Klaas' gravity.

It was one of the oldest elders who finally spoke up. He asked the question which the others of us were swallowing with difficulty.

"What under the sky full of stars are you saying, Klaas?"

For a moment it seemed as if Klaas would not or could not answer him. Then he said with quiet import, "I will tell you what. I didn't want to believe it when I first proposed it to myself. Now I will say it for you—each one of you. It has been insidiously underway for some time. Attacks on our identity. A special part of our heritage."

This much explanation engendered a round of jibber-jabber. Obviously each us was saying the same thing if in different ways and different tongues.

His oldest friend's voice lifted above the whole, "What are you trying to say, Klaas? Have you this early partaken of too many steins of winter wine?"

Klaas negated the babble with silence, and then repeated, "I believe we are in danger of losing our identity which will lead to losing our heritage."

"And you believe this will happen tonight?" one of the youngest members asked.

"Certainly not," Klaas told him. "Don't be absurd. Things of this importance do not happen overnight. It is one night, then another, and a hundred more. This happens in a deliberately slow, hence unobtrusive, fashion."

"Then why at this hour on this night are we up here with you when we should be in our workshops making certain that everything is ready for us to set out on our Christmas Eve flights?"

"Because," Klaas began, but was cut off by Dom Clausdino's brassiest echo, "*Because*! Because . . . that is the answer little children give when they have no answer."

All of us listen to little children, especially when

Christmas is nearing. All of us can quote a child's reasons that he invents when he has no legitimate answers.

"Silence!" thundered one of the elders. "Allow Sint Nikolaas to answer us so that we can be up and away."

"Thank you, Santa Claus," Klaas said. "Let me get on with this. I too have a Round-the-World flight, just as do we all." When the hubbub had ceased, Klaas continued, "Surely many of you, if not all of you, must have noticed the changes of Christmas Eve in these last decades. Instead of stopping on a rooftop next to a handsome brick chimney, more often than not our reindeer must rise high, high, higher in the sky even to locate a rooftop.

"A fireplace on Christmas Eve with a chimney through which Santa can come down with his sackful of toys has been left out of most modern dwellings. Some old-time families do create a sort of fire screen from which stockings can be hung for Saint Nicholas to fill. But not many parents care any longer about St. Nick. They just set out the store-boughten toys. Nothing created with love and joy by Santa's Elves. And they have the nerve to say to their children, 'Look what Santa brought you!' That is, the few parents who still honor the belief in Santa Claus.

"I will tell you why I asked you to join me here," Klaas stated. "Because I'm tired of being cast away by these Modern vinegar-mouth teachers and the vinegar-mouth Modern Mums who don't want their little boys and girls to learn of the joy and wonder of our Faery Land. I know this will be a small beginning, but tonight I'm going to fight back."

"And how do you propose to do that?" Santiago sniffed. One of Dom's assistants.

Now Klaas smiled. Just a small smile but creamy. "All of you meet me back here before dawn. I will tell you whether I was successful in my first small attempt to show these destructive pedants and parents what Faery Folk can do. And prove to even one child burdened by such oh-so-modern distortions of Christmas that there is a Santa Claus."

You may be sure that we were all at the Pine Circle after our night out. Even the elders were there, rather more than tired after driving their reindeer around the world until daylight flickered.

Klaas was looking pretty pleased with himself. Which led all of us to reckon he had brought off his plan with some degree of success.

"Get on with it, Klaas," one of his longtime helpers urged. "I have to get my steeds back home before they try again to hoist the sleigh and me on it over the moon! Get on with it. What happened?"

"Well," Klaas began, "I chose Rolfe Hastings' parlor."

"With a fireplace?" An eager neophyte wanted to know.

"Yes. I needed a real one. Rolfe lives in one of the old brownstones in the sixties. All of them have fireplaces, if unused in this era. I also needed his Mum to be there if I was to deliver my complete message."

"And how did you manage that?" Dom, of course.

"Very simple. I twinged her when Rolfe and I were ready for her."

"Did he . . . ?"

"Certainly not. But I knew when it was time. Before he fell asleep and his Mum would insist it was all a dream.

"When the Mum, half-asleep, came in after the twinge, Rolfe was sitting on the floor beside my pack, and I was starting to fill the red stocking hung on the fire screen. I'm sure we surprised his Mum, but she'll maintain she was just dreaming.

"But Rolfe will know better. He'll always remember there is a Santa Claus."

Klaas took a sip from the beaker being passed around to those who were still awake. He then continued, "Like all Modern Mums she'd set a plate of little cookies and a mug of milk on the hearth.

"For Santa . . . ," he growled. "These stupid Modern Mums! As if S. Claus was a factory item that should be fed in each of the hundreds of dwellings which he would visit on Christmas Eve. Really stupid! The Mum who thought up that one only a couple of decades ago. Of course today's Mums don't believe in Santa Claus, so stale cookies and skim milk are good enough."

"And then?" prompted his companion who'd had the antic reindeer trouble. "Did you eat and drink?"

"Certainly not!" Klaas snorted. And then smiled all across his white beard. "She'll never forget, nor will Rolfe." He seemed content. "No matter what she and Miss Vinegar Mouth of Rolfe's school may try to tell him, he will always remember that this Christmas Eve was not a dream."

"And then?" repeated the questioner.

"One of the Princes of Serendip came to help. The Mum has a stupid little white dog which she dotes on and which followed her into the room. He headed straight to me and was starting to gnaw the ermine trim on my red coat. And I accidentally on purpose knocked over the mug of milk on him. I strewed the cookies on the hearth for him to eat."

"And then . . . ?" Again the same questioner. He was a young enough Santa to want to hear all. Even if he was tired.

"And then," said Klaas, "I went up the chimney again."

"You remembered how?" The old friends were disbelieving.

"I wasn't sure if I'd remember, but we in Faery Land don't have to worry about such details. We can't forget." He addressed the entire circle. "I may not have rid this Century of Disbelief of those who choose not to believe in our Magical land. But Rolfe will always remember that Santa Claus is real. Because he himself saw the Santa come down the chimney and fill a little boy's big red stocking. And then go up the chimney again to the rooftop where Rolfe could hear the impatient hreinndyr prancing and pawing as they waited to drive Santa home again to Faery Land."

MUST BE SANTA!

by Matthew J. Costello

The magic business turned bad.

That's how I ended up here. The magic business went belly-up, and presto-change-o, *look at me . . .*

There was a time when I was balancing three, sometimes four gigs during a weekend. I'd do a kiddie party in the afternoon—telling the little brats to stay in their fucking seats—"Or Mr. Magician won't do any more tricks."

While they all squealed, *I know how you did it! You're hiding something.* Of course, I couldn't really tell the rug rats to sit down and shut up. Not when Momma and Poppa looked on, checkbook at the ready. No, I had to smile and say, "Why, aren't *you* clever. Now if you'll just sit down I'll show you something really amazing."

Of course, the real problem is that a lot of the yuppie brats had their own damn magic sets at home. God, and some of them could even read. So they knew about rope tricks, they knew about magnets and steel coins, and more than one afternoon's show was blown completely out of the water by some kid, wearing a shit-eating grin, standing up and saying, "You've got a rubber thumb. That's how you do it."

Haven't heard of the rubber-thumb trick, eh?

Good, well, maybe *you'd* be surprised at one of my shows.

The adults were barely better. Some people booked me for birthdays, maybe as a surprise guest for hubby on his birthday. When actually he'd prefer a visit from Zorina of the singing strip-o-gram. Doing magic to drunks is redundant anyway. It's magic to them how a toilet flushes. Fogged vision, a by-product of alcohol, makes illusions effortless.

Unfortunately, the tricks lack the punch when the audience is in its cups.

But the real problem with magic is *money*.

To keep up with magic costs money. Money for new gags, things people haven't seen before, and not rip-offs from David Copperfield, or The Amazing Randi, or some thirteen-year-old performing at the Hidden Valley Nature Center "Save Our Planet Please!" Festival.

I love magic, really love it. But it wasn't paying my modest bills anymore. And I started looking into other avenues of revenue generation. I had one friend who wrote mysteries. I could do that, I thought, forgetting that it required a discipline that was way beyond me.

Then I thought that maybe I could open a business. A magic shop. Now *that* would be fun. Unfortunately, to start a business you needed capital.

It always came back to money.

I could save, I thought. Save for the magic shop. I had recently turned thirty, and this was a dream, maybe my last shot at a dream. All I needed was a way to make some extra money, something more than what my magic shows brought.

And that's when a friend told me about the Santa biz.

The Santa gig is a low-maintenance field.

Yes, all you need is the costume. Basic red, with white trim, cheap boots, and the beard.

And here's an insider's tip: the beard is the *key* element in the Santa mystique. If it's big and fluffy and white, well, you're halfway home.

Trust me. Nothing spoils the whole St. Nick illusion faster than a dirty-white-turning-brownish beard with strands stuck together and dotted with clumps of hast-ily eaten hot dogs with mustard.

It's a rule. Get a good beard and keep it clean.

It seemed perfect. I could be a Santa. It was sea-sonal work, to be sure, but if you hustled you could rake in a ton of cash between Thanksgiving and Christmas.

(I should also mention a little known, er, quirk. There are women out there who want to get it on with Santa. Must be tied to that song, you know . . . "I Saw Mommy Kissing Santa Claus." Except some of these women, usually love-starved friends of the hostess, want to do more than simply make old Santa's cheeks red.)

So, on some nights I was Santa and on other nights I was Mr. Wonder—and for the first time my bank account took a slight curve upwards.

Life was looking hopeful. Ho-ho-ho, and Merry Christmas.

Then something happened to me. It was like that movie with Jimmy Stewart. You know, *It's a Wonderful Life* . . . where something magical happens to him and it saves his life.

Something magical happened to me.

Except—

Ho-ho-ho . . . It was bad magic.

The name and the address I had for the party where "Santa" was to make his traditional appearance was in Briarcliff Manor, a ritzy enclave in Westchester.

The name was Friethoff, and the address was on Old Horseman Road.

I thought I knew where it was. I barely listened to Mrs. Friethoff's directions.

Old Horseman is a winding country road lined with curved driveways that lead up to some really big estates.

I looked for mailboxes. And didn't see any.

How the hell do these people get their mail? I thought. But all I saw were metal medallions that glowed in the headlights. WARNING: PROTECTED BY RABID DOG SECURITY SERVICES.

I checked the number on the slip of paper. 17, Old Horseman Road.

"This is great," I said, jutting my chin out.

My beard was pulled below my chin, making an

uncomfortable bushy white pillow. It was best to arrive *en costume,* even if the sled and reindeer were missing. There might be people on a porch, bundled up, waiting for old Santa to pull up in his battered Toyota.

Ho-ho-ho, the old reindeer are taking the night off, folks. Ho-ho-ho, and old Santa had to borrow Mrs. Claus's Japanese piece of shit.

I said, "Where the hell is seventeen?"

Then, I saw a mailbox. It was more like a mail*room,* the black box was so big. It said "Kreire." Is that a name, I wondered . . . or an anagram? And there was a number: number twenty-three.

I slowed my car. Twenty-three. Shit, then seventeen had to be back the way I came.

A car took the curve behind me and then stopped right on my tail. He flashed his brights at me. Once, twice.

"Okay," I said. "Let's not rush Santa on his appointed rounds . . ." The asshole beeped his horn. I rolled down my window and stuck my head out, doing my best to glare at the driver behind me while I waved at him to pass me.

Forgetting, of course, how stupid it must look to see Santa glaring at you.

"Go on, jerk," I said. He probably didn't want to pass me since we were at a sharp curve on Old Horseman Road.

"Go ahead . . . live dangerously."

The car gunned its engine and then peeled away. I watched the sleek black Mercedes make a tight end run to my left.

"Santa ain't going to bring you shit," I said.

You kinda get into the Santa thing after awhile.

Twenty-three, I thought. So seventeen was back, three, four driveways. *Three,* I thought. Yeah, that was it. I just have to go back three driveways and we'll be okay.

A wet drop splattered onto the windshield.

Then another. Great. It's raining. I reached down beside the bucket seat to feel for my umbrella. There was nothing worse than getting the Santa costume wet. It gave off this terrible odor, as it had been hermetically sealed with moth balls and dead rats for the past eleven months. The bright red suit became positively *alive* with odors when it got wet.

No umbrella.

The first two wet splats were joined by a giddy chorus of other raindrops, big fat raindrops. I clicked on my windshield wipers and was once again reminded that, hey, they don't work so well anymore. Looking out the windshield was like watching Smear-O-Vision. Everything caught by my headlights was a big blurry glare.

"Okay," I said. "But old Santa's close. I'll park by the front door and hustle in and catch only a drop of rain."

I started to back the car up.

There was a crack of thunder. I thought I saw a flash in my rearview mirror, a diffused burst of lightning from across the river.

Kinda late in the season for a Hudson Valley thunderstorm.

It sure as hell didn't feel like Christmas.

There were no numbers, no mailboxes, so I counted driveways. One, two, and—

"Here we are," I said. I pulled into a blurry black swatch that—I hoped—was the driveway.

At one curve on the way up I nearly plowed into a tree that sat too close to the asphalt. My nearly bald Toyota tires—Oh, what a feeling—started spinning on the slippery mixture of asphalt, fallen leaves, and wetness.

This damned hill kept going, going up.

The Friethoffs lived on a hill, the woman had told me that. And judging from the size of the driveway, the accompanying mansion had to be the size of Xanadu.

Getting ready, I pulled up my beard, tasting the elastic band. I steered with one hand while I adjusted the moustache part so it sat below my nose and I could open my mouth without tasting the white, plasticized hair.

"Ho, ho, ho," I said, lowering my voice to its deepest Santa level. Getting into my part.

Many times I was tempted to pack a few magic tricks in Santa's baggy red leggings. I had a bit of money now and had recently expanded my repertoire with a very impressive disappearing shot-glass trick.

But I didn't. I never heard of Santa doing magic . . . he was always too busy, going from house to house.

It was enough he had a bag filled with toys.

I, of course, had no such bag. The hostess, Mrs. Friethoff, said she'd have a large sack *filled* with party favors for her adult guests.

I did mention that this was an adult party, didn't I? Believe it or not, there are well-heeled grown-ups out there who get dewy-eyed when the man in red appears. These are usually people who've never had kids or whose kids are being watched by some bovine nanny imported from Minnesota.

But grown-up parties were better. No kids sneezing into my face, no wet laps from kids peeing over Santa. And there was never a problem with Santa joining in a toast to the holiday season.

Couldn't do that with the kiddies around.

The driveway made one last turn before a house loomed ahead.

It looked kinda dark, considering that a party was on. There were a few lights on upstairs, and one light below.

"Hell, I'm not that late," I said.

I slowed, since I couldn't see where I should park. There didn't seem to be any other cars around. Must be a parking area around the back, I thought.

"Best check that this is the Friethoff manse," I said.

I pulled up as close to the front door as possible. A giant clap of thunder exploded over my head. A *silent night* this wasn't.

I peeked open the door, and the rain seemed eager to blow in.

There was no way I'd make the ten steps or so to the front door without getting mightily drenched.

I took a breath. A few stray white "hairs" stuck to my lips. I spit them out. I put my red cap on my head. Then, I dashed.

My black boots, which looked water-and-snow resistant, immediately smashed down into a sizeable puddle. There were many indentations in the muddy driveway.

And despite the look of my boots, the water rushed into the seams of Santa's boots. Icy water reached my toes.

"Shit," I said, running to the door. At least here I was beneath an overhang. There was a light by the door, too. I saw a buzzer—with no name on it. I pushed the button. This is wrong, I thought. I counted right but this must be the wrong damn house.

But maybe these nice people in the nice big house will let me use their phone to call Chez Friethoff and tell them Santa got lost. Happens . . . especially when Rudolph isn't taking the lead.

But no one answered the buzzer. The place did look a bit deserted. I raised a white gloved hand and knocked at the door.

Which slid open.

The front door was open . . . as if the people had just come back, or were on their way out. An alarm box to the side was blinking green.

There were probably other things I could have done . . . should have done.

But—for the moment—I simply stood there.

I stood at the entrance.

There was another clap of thunder, loud this time, as if the storm was zeroing in on my exact location.

"Hello," I said. Then, louder, "Hello?"

The foyer, with a tall plant and a painting above a small entrance table, looked beautiful, as—I was sure—did the whole house.

I probably should have turned, gone back to my Toyota, and tried another driveway.

But, I thought, I was already late, and I could end up trying goddamn driveways all night.

"Hello!" No one answered.

But then old Santa heard something.

It was singing . . . coming from . . .

Yes, upstairs. Someone was singing. It was opera. A woman, a high soprano voice dreamily echoing from upstairs.

Hey, somebody *was* home, I thought. Maybe the party was going on upstairs.

I entered the house. It felt good to be out of the cold rain, away from the noisy thunder. I wasn't concerned that I was breaking in. The front door was open. This might even be the right house.

Besides, who could be upset at a visit from St. Nick himself?

Except, I remembered that there was an old *Tales from the Crypt* story about a man who escaped from the Criminally Insane Institution—is there such a place? And he dressed up as Santa and started hacking people up. There were even movies later, crazy Santa movies.

Wouldn't want anyone to think that I was like that. I'm a *nice* Santa . . .

I walked to the stairs, and then up the steps, announcing myself as I went up. "Hello . . . hello . . ." while the soprano's voice grew more and more shrill.

The opera—whose title must remain a mystery to you since the only aria I know is that one they use in the British Airways commercials—was coming from a bedroom.

A light was on.

"Hello," I said one last time.

Thinking how I'd ask to use the phone, explaining the bad weather, the open door, how I would explain that I'm not a crazy, ax-wielding Santa, just a poor slob of a stage magician trying to make some bucks.

More steps. (And you know it's only later that you realize how you sealed your fate, how every little

choice is a step on the road to a peaceful, happy life
or into a deep, doom-filled abyss.)

And then I was in the bedroom, in full costume. I
saw the stereo against the wall. A TV was on, silent.
There were circus acts and TV stars on the tube. Doo-
gie Howser rode an elephant.

All that, and he's a doctor too.

I looked around the room. Everywhere, I guess, but
down to the floor, avoiding the obvious, avoiding the
thunder outside now matched by a painful racket in
my head, the pumping of blood kicking into high
speed.

There was a body on the floor.

Surprise!

Merry Christmas.

My throat went dry. I thought my breathing hole
would shrivel shut, it was so dry.

Because—and here I staggered backward, against the
open bedroom door—this wasn't just a body on the
floor. I mean, I *knew* it was dead from the way
the man's legs curled under him in what had to be an
uncomfortable fashion, from the way he lay so still,
but mostly from the way the eyes were open, one
looking up at—

An eggshell-colored ceiling.

While the other had a long, knifelike project buried
into it.

I gagged.

Not a knife. More like a letter opener.

This was not good.

A small parade of options danced before me. I
mean, it's not every day that you're faced with a dead
body and have to decide what to do.

What do I do?

Is it like a hit-and-run? Can I simply back downstairs, drive down the stupid curved driveway, go back
to looking for the Friethoff's?

(No. Fuck the Friethoffs. I'd call them from my
apartment, tell Mrs. Friethoff that I got lost.)

I saw a phone beside the beautiful brass bed.

Or call the police. I'm in this house, I'd say, and I

found a body. No, I just walked in, right up the stairs, and—

The aria ended.

Then someone else sang, a deep voice, a spooky authoritative voice. A deep voice singing in Italian.

I slid out of the room, my back touching the door. It didn't occur to me to pull down my beard.

The dead body continued to listen to the opera.

"I'm getting the hell out of here," I said, giving my mind the sense of direction it so urgently needed.

Out of the room, to the hallway. Where I then turned and, in my sodden boots, clomped down the stairs and out of the house.

Hoping I could simply read all about this in the next day's papers.

Which I didn't.

But I did learn something else that morning. I had thrown my red costume and beard onto the couch, leaving a careful repacking for the next day.

There had been a message from Mrs. Friethoff on my machine. She was looking for her Santa . . .

I guess you weren't good little girl, Mrs. Friethoff.

There was no news on TV of the mansion, the man with the letter opener stuck in his eye socket.

It's not my problem, I thought. I started to pack up my suit, the leggings, the jacket, the beard, and the—

Now, where was the hat . . . where the hell was my hat? I got down on all fours, searching for the red cap with the fluffy white pompom. Must have fallen to the floor, I thought. Has to be here.

But when I turned up empty-handed, I ran down to my Toyota, the only witness to the past evening's nightmare. I checked under the bucket seats, scratching up old gum wrappers and tiny crystalline grit that got stuck under my fingernails.

But no hat.

No hat . . . because, and here I could picture exactly how it happened . . .

The hat was *back* at the house. Yes, boys and girls, Santa's hat fell off. Probably when old weak-kneed

Santa bumped against the door. And when someone finally finds the body, they'll find the hat.

At that point, I was going to call the police—I really was—when I heard my buzzer ring. It was obvious to me that I was now a good two, or three beats behind whatever was taking place here.

The detectives were nice, friendly, almost too friendly. They knew I was supposed to have gone to the Friethoff's last night. They had interviewed *all* the neighbors, they explained.

And I "explained" why I never showed up. How I had a cold, how I fell asleep. . . .

"Is there a problem?" I asked, trying to sound so casual, feeling like the demented murderer in the "Tell-Tale Heart"—except that I didn't kill anyone.

I had to keep reminding myself of that fact.

"Yes, there's a problem," one of the detectives said. "Mr. Elliot Necco disappeared last night. His wife had been at the Friethoff party. The house was open. It looks as if someone had been there, broke in." The detective paused. My heart thumped loudly. Go on, tear up the boards. There it is! I buried his body *here.*

I was tempted to tell what I knew.

Surely they found my hat. That was the surprise they were going to trip me up with.

HARD-LUCK SANTA KILLS FOR LOOT.

But wait a minute—the detective said that the man, Necco, *disappeared*? What about the letter opener? What about his legs curled under him?

"You wouldn't know anything about that?"

I shook my head. Then, in a pithy attempt to add force to my denial, I said, "No. I never got out last night," I coughed. "I felt too miserable."

The detectives smiled. They said nothing about my hat. They looked at each other, and then nodded to me and stood up.

Then, very sincerely, they said, "Thank you. Thanks for your help."

I smiled back.

And after they left, I sat in my kitchen, wondering
. . . where's Mr. Necco?

I didn't leave my apartment that whole day, nor the
next except to get a six-pack of beer and a Hearty
Man Chicken Pot Pie from the Quik Stop.

I was waiting for the other shoe to drop.

Which it did that night.

The detectives returned to my apartment. Again,
they smiled when I opened the door, as if we were
old friends.

"Could you come with us?" one asked. "We want
to show you something."

*It wouldn't be a man on the floor with a letter opener
in one eye, by any chance?* I thought.

"Sure," I said. "Let me grab my coat."

Again, I wondered what I was about to be shown.

I followed the detectives down to their car. I expected them to talk with me, but they were silent,
almost somber. Inside their patrol car, I heard the
radio, incomprehensible messages back and forth.

One detective drove while the other sat back with
me. Finally, he turned to me and said, "How long
have you been doing the Santa thing?"

I shrugged. "Oh, I dunno. Two, maybe three
years." I cleared my throat. "Actually, I'm a
magician."

The detective in the front, the driver, laughed. He
glanced back at me.

"You like to make things disappear?"

I laughed. "Yeah, sure . . . sometimes."

It was quiet again, and—belatedly—I realized the
implications of what I had said.

The detective next to me said, "Elliot Necco
disappeared."

I nodded.

The car took a turn to the left, off Main Street in
Briarcliff, down to the rustic library, then to a path
into the woods behind it.

They stopped the car.

There was another car there, and I saw people standing in the woods, a circle of flashlights.

When we got out, the small circle of grim-faced people turned and watched us.

The detective who had been sitting next to me took my arm and said, "You're good at making things disappear?"

Alert, I said, "Pretty good."

He had my arm, guiding me to where the flashlights were.

Then, the detective pinched my arm.

He's not allowed to do that, I thought. Though it wasn't quite on a par with Rodney King, still—

"Well, we thought Necco *disappeared*. But it turns out—"

Another pinch.

"Turns out that he was killed. And damned if we don't know who did it."

Now he roughly dragged me to the circle of people, and I could see what they had their lights aimed at.

There was a depression, and a pile of dirt. And sitting in the depression, with specks of dirt still on his puffy face, with dirt covering his one open eye, with dirt sticking to the silver handle of letter opener stuck in the *other* eye, was Elliot Necco.

Someone brought him here. After I had been in the house.

I have to tell them, I thought. I started to open my mouth. I looked at the dead man's neck, his chest, his arms, and then one hand holding—

"Elliot Necco didn't disappear," the detective said, hurting my arm now. "The nice old guy was killed." The detective took a breath. Everyone in the circle was looking at me, studying my face.

Elliot Necco held something in one hand, covered with dirt, but the pale light caught the red, then the dirty white, and—

The detective leaned close to me. "And we know who the fuck killed him."

The dead man held my Santa hat . . . tightly in his claw fist.

Someone put it there. God. I almost said, "That's my hat." Stupidly, as if they didn't know.

Another breath, and the detective leaned close, hissing the words in my ear. "And do you know who killed him?"

I waited.

Staring at my hat.

While the detective said, *"Must be Santa . . ."*

THE MAN IN THE RED-FLANNEL SUIT

by Jan Grape

Christmas was supposed to be a candy-making, turkey-baking time, I thought. With furtive trips to buy gifts to hide, special gifts for someone special. A time of joy and laughter, and singing carols about peace on earth and about the spirit of love.

"Merry Christmas, Zoe," someone called out as I walked out the back door of APD headquarters. I didn't recognize the voice.

"Merry Christmas," I said, but under my breath muttered, "bah, humbug." Christmas was meaningless when your police officer husband was in a coma in a nursing home with no hope of recovery, but there was no sense reminding people about Byron Barrow. Don't think I feel sorry for myself. Sure I did for awhile, but you have to go on. Put the past out of your mind and keep on trucking. It's just that I'd rather forget about Christmas, if no one minds.

It was sixty degrees in Austin, Texas, on the evening of December twenty-second and my ROP unit (Repeat Offenders Program), along with the other members of a special drug task force, had busted a crack house at midnight.

I had volunteered to work all week including the twenty-fourth and twenty-fifth to allow some of my fellow officers to be off with their families for Christmas. It was pointless to let myself think about Christmas two years ago, the last one Byron and I had shared. He was on duty when he was shot in the head and left in his present condition.

My unit was part of the back-up team and we'd hung back letting the other team members take care of their jobs. We arrested three suspects, but the house had been full of people. Four little children belonging to two of the suspects ran around crying, begging us not to take their mamma and daddy to jail.

The other people in the house weren't related to the children or didn't want to be responsible for four kids and we'd had to call Child Services. It was a heartbreaker right here at Christmastime.

After the bust, my unit returned to headquarters to take care of the paperwork. Everyone was still pumped—adrenaline highs—it always happens. You get up for the operation and when the bust goes well, you can stay up for hours.

"Hey, Zoe. Did you see that dude trying to get out the window? I was standing on the ground right beneath it and he nearly climbed out on top of me," said Corky. "Man, he was so surprised he almost wet his pants."

"Yeah, Corky. I saw." Corky was from narcotics and I'd known him for years. He's normally a quiet guy until after a big bust and then he'll talk your leg off.

"Zoe, check out this card," said Brad, one of the DEA agents. The card was a depiction of Santa and his sleigh sitting on top of an outhouse with Santa yelling curses at Rudolph and the other reindeer.

Brad opened the card and read the inside message aloud, "I said the Schmidt house, you fools!"

I'd probably seen the card six times already, but I laughed anyway.

It was after two in the morning when I finished my part of the necessary paperwork. Some of the team was going for breakfast at Denny's, but I begged off, saying I was tired and needed my beauty sleep. They pushed a little, but I reminded everyone I was due back on duty at ten A.M. and they gave up and left.

My adrenaline had already ebbed and, although I wasn't quite as tired as I'd made myself out to be, I was ready to get home.

I entered the parking garage of the old patrol building. It felt good to climb into the '92 Mustang I was driving this month. The ROP unit confiscates vehicles and we use them as undercover cars.

This time of year the ground can still be warm and when the air cools, fog forms, especially in the low-lying areas. A few tendrils of fog clutched at my car and I had to use the wipers to clear the wetness from the windshield. Fortunately the drive south on I-35 was short—exit on East Riverside Drive, cross the bridge, and head west.

The Texas-Colorado River, which meanders across central Texas, has been dammed in numerous places forming a chain of lakes. One of the smaller lakes, known as Town Lake, sits in the midst of downtown Austin. The major portion of the downtown area is on the north shore of the lake and my apartment complex is on the south shore a few blocks west of the Interstate.

Riverside Drive makes multiple curves following the lake's contours. With no traffic to speak of at that hour and because I knew the area like the inside of my mouth, I was driving at a good rate of speed. The moisture and fog in the air made it necessary to keep the headlight beams on low, otherwise I never would have seen the bundle of clothes in the right-hand lane.

I thought I saw the clothing move. My foot tapped the brakes automatically and I came to a complete halt a few feet past the bundle. Then I backed slowly until it was in front of my right fender. I backed up a little more and steered my car into the same lane as the clothes, my headlights bathing the scene in a surreal light.

"Oh shit. Tell me I'm not seeing this," I said, but there was no mistaking the fact that the clothing was a woman lying in an awkward position on the pavement, and a small girl hunkered down almost on top of the woman.

I got out and walked over. The little girl looked to be about three or four years old, her hair was long, curling slightly in the dampness. The woman's neck was in an unnatural position and I knew without even checking that she was dead.

The child was patting the woman's face, blood and all, and saying over and over, "Mommy, wake up. Get up, Mommy."

I did a quick visual check of the child, who didn't seem to have any noticeable injuries. The woman had cuts and abrasions on her face, nothing that looked terribly bad or even life threatening.

There wasn't any doubt in my mind about what had happened. A car had hit the woman, flinging her into the air and her neck had snapped when she hit.

I walked back to the Mustang, switched on the walkie-talkie and reported the accident to Dispatch. I took off my windbreaker and went back to the child. I wrapped it around her unprotesting shoulders and began talking to her. "Honey, I've called for some help for you and your mommy. Why don't you come with me to the car?"

The child kept begging her mother to get up. I don't think she even heard me.

I kept talking quietly to her, hoping to keep her from panicking. She became less agitated, but still didn't answer. The calls to her mother eventually stopped. Moments later, a squad car and EMS wagon pulled up and the medical attendants took over, one picking up the child to examine while the other began his futile attempt to revive the woman. There was nothing they could do, but by law they have to try.

I told them I was Zoe Barrow, showed my ID, and said I had no idea when the accident had happened. "It probably couldn't have been more than ten, fifteen minutes. Otherwise someone else would have found her. Called it in."

"Even if someone saw them, they might not want to get involved," said the EMS guy, who was holding the child.

"Well, it's not too easy to see along here, but how could they leave a child?"

"Go figure," he said.

There was nothing to identify the woman on her

person and from the looks of both mother and daughter, they were probably homeless. Once the medical guy had completed his examination of the girl, I carried her to my car and put her inside. She didn't protest. She just looked back over to where her mother was, soundless.

"My name's Zoe. What's your name, honey?"

"April."

"That's a pretty name." She looked at me and her big brown eyes looked like a fawn's. "How old are you, April? Do you know how old you are?"

She held up four fingers, and said "Four" softly.

"Four. You're a big girl aren't you? What's your mommy's name?"

She looked puzzled and finally said, "Mommy."

"Okay. Do you know where you live?"

April shook her head.

"Where's your daddy?"

She didn't answer. She tucked her head down to her chest and began crying. But in a moment she stopped and looked at me and said, "Santa Claus."

Oh, Lord. For a minute I'd forgotten it was Christmas. "Well, yes. Santa Claus will come to see you soon." And vowed that I would make sure Santa brought April a toy or two.

But as I spoke, April began sobbing again. This time it was worse—not only heartrending. This time I thought I heard fear in her voice. I put my arm around her and tried to hold her, but she pulled back. Was she afraid of me?

Better to let her cry it out, I thought. Maybe she'd tire and go to sleep. Probably be the best thing for her.

Accident investigators (we call them "AIs"), a police photographer, patrol officers, and the medical examiner had all arrived while I was talking to April. I saw several patrol officers making a methodical search of the area, poking in the grassy weeds along the shoulder of the road. I knew they were hoping to find clues about the accident or something that would identify April's mother.

The AI in charge came over. I got out of my car and gave him an account of what I'd seen. Which didn't take long. He asked me to stop by headquarters later and make a formal statement. I assured him I would and started to get back into the car.

One of the patrol officers came over and handed me a teddy bear. "We carry these in the trunks of our units to give to kids. It usually helps if they have a pal."

"Great idea. Thanks."

I got back into the car and April grabbed the bear I held out as if she were drowning and I'd just thrown her a lifeline. Tears still glistened on her face and in a few minutes she started making that funny sub-sub noise kids make when they've cried a lot. I patted her shoulder and she leaned her head back, hugging the bear tightly. Her eyelids were getting heavy. I didn't try to talk to her or hold her. As long as she was quiet, it was probably best to leave her alone.

The mother's body was covered with a blanket. Measurements were taken of skid marks and the probable place of impact. I watched an officer pick up and bag some car headlight fragments.

The EMS attendant I'd talked to earlier came over and motioned for me to get out of the car. "The AI asked me to tell you, they called Child Services for the little girl, but it looks to be awhile. They've had a couple other emergencies."

"That's okay. I don't have any place I need to be and can stay here until they come."

"Uh, well, we still have a problem." He was short, redheaded, and had freckles across his nose. He looked around twenty-five, but his hair had receded back past his ears. "The ME said we could go ahead and transport the woman soon, but I think it's a bad idea to do it in front of the child."

"No problem. I'll drive April to headquarters and wait for Child Services there. We'll go now and you can take care of things."

"Good. I was hoping you'd say that."

I got back into the car and saw that April had indeed cried herself to sleep. I pulled the seat belt around her and fastened it. My car engine started with hardly a sound and I pulled slowly around the crime scene, heading west.

I intended to drive to headquarters with April. Honestly, I did. But my place was just down the road and when I reached the driveway of my apartment complex, I turned in almost automatically and pulled around to my parking space.

"Poor little kid doesn't need any more hassles tonight," I said as I turned off the ignition.

I picked up April. She was so frail, her little body couldn't have weighed more than thirty pounds. Her arms tightened around my neck and she mumbled something that sounded like, "Santa Claus."

"Okay, sweetie. Don't you worry. Santa is coming to see you."

She was dead asleep again and didn't even wake when I put her on my sofa and stripped off her soiled clothes. I got one of my T-shirts and pulled it over her head. I carried her to my bedroom and tucked her in bed. She roused enough to put her thumb in her mouth and then she zonked.

I sat for a few moments thinking it all over before I called downtown. I knew I'd get an argument, but I stuck to my guns and in the end got what I wanted. "I promise," I said. "She'll be there on the twenty-sixth."

I slept for about three hours and April didn't move or turn over. After I had showered, I called my mother because I desperately needed her help. There was no way I could take off work as we were down to a skeleton crew already.

My parents, Helen and Herbert Taylor, live in West Lake Hills, a section of Austin noted for canyons, hills, and homes with breathtaking views.

My parents aren't rich, but they could be considered comfortable. Dad has his own engineering firm and Mom retired from the University of Texas Chancellor's office last year. They built their home years ago when prices were still reasonable. It's worth a small fortune now.

I knew my mom would say she was busy with her final preparations for a big family dinner on Christmas Eve, but I also knew everything was already done.

My mom is the great goddess of organization and never procrastinates. She just likes to make us feel sorry for her by making us think she's harried at the last minute. She complained a bit, but agreed to come over about nine.

When Helene Taylor came in, she said exactly what was on her mind. "Zoe, I don't think this is a very good idea."

"It seemed like a great one at four o'clock this morning. Mom, it's just until after Christmas."

April woke up and started calling for her mommy and that was the end of the discussion.

When I got to work, I called the traffic division to see what the latest word was on the hit-and-run. I was glad to discover the investigator now in charge was Trey Gerrod. He had been one of my training officers and he was a first-rate officer. After we exchanged pleasantries, he clued me in on what they'd found.

"We've got paint samples and headlight fragments, Zoe. The car was identified as a 1991 Buick. Metallic blue."

"I suppose there are only ten thousand of those around."

"Yes, but we got lucky. It had been repainted recently and that means it was probably in an earlier accident. We'll be able to narrow it down soon."

He said they'd not identified April or her mother yet and I mentioned my plans about calling a news reporter friend to help. He said he'd been considering that idea, too, and for me to go ahead if I had a connection.

"Keep me posted, would you?" I asked.

"Okay. Hey, is it true the little girl is staying with you?"

"Well, just until after Christmas."

"Great. Is it okay if a few of the guys around here get her some Christmas presents?"

Tough cops? They're the biggest bunch of old softies when it comes to kids. "Sure. Y'all want to stop by tonight?"

"It's a deal," he said and we hung up.

My newspaper friend worked at *The Austin American Statesman*. Mildred Warner and I had been in some classes together at Austin Community College about a hundred years ago. She might be off for the holidays, I thought as I dialed, but she answered her phone. "Millie, Zoe Barrow. Merry Christmas."

"Zoe? Long time no hear from. Ho, ho, ho to you too."

When I explained the situation, she was more than willing to photograph April and run a "Do You Know This Child" article on her. We set up a late afternoon appointment at my house.

Paperwork kept me occupied for the next two hours and then it was time to hit some parties. Christmas is when each department at APD holds open house. Food, I never saw such good food: cookies, candies, spice and fruit cakes, banana nut and cranberry breads and muffins, huge trays of ham, turkey, shrimp, roast beef homemade tamales and, cheeses, dips, chips, veggies, relish trays, no-nog eggnog, and punch. It was pig-out time—just for the holiday, you understand—I ate until I nearly got sick.

When I got home, Mom and April were getting along like old chums. April, brown hair brushed and curling a bit on top and with an occasional smile on her face was a totally different child. Although there was still a trace of a haunted look in her fawnlike eyes.

Mom had taken the child shopping and bought a whole wardrobe of clothes, shoes, underwear, and to top it off, a small Christmas tree. April spent five minutes telling me how much fun they had decorating.

"She's a sweetie," Helene said. "She's been brought up right." That was the highest praise my mother could bestow.

My mom is great with little ones. My brother, Chip, and his wife, Pat, have two—Kyle, three and Alicia, six. They stay with my folks on occasion and always have the greatest time.

Millie Warner came by and got the information for the article she planned to run on Christmas Day. Then her photographer showed up and we had a small crisis when April decided she didn't want her picture taken. Mom finally convinced April by showing her photos, in an album, of me at age four and five.

My younger brother and I always played pranks on each other. One picture showed me all dressed up in Easter finery and my brother sneaking up behind the chair and, just as the picture was snapped, Chip stuck his fingers up and it looked like I had horns on my head. Mom said it was entirely appropriate, because I often was a little devil, and April got so tickled she forgot she didn't want to sit still and pose.

Millie and the photographer left and my mom took off soon after, getting my promise that April and I would spend tomorrow night with her and my dad.

The doorbell rang a few minutes later and when I answered, Santa Claus stood on the front stoop with five uniformed police officers instead of elves, each holding a gaily wrapped present.

"April, look who's here. Someone special has come to see you."

I saw her out of the corner of my eye as she edged across the living room, but when she caught sight of the man in the red suit, April suddenly began screaming and ran down the hall to the bedroom.

"Why is she having such a fit? Is this kid strange or what?" I looked at the group, two women and three men, and said, "Sorry, guys. Come on in and sit. I'll go and see what I can do with her."

Santa, or rather Trey Gerrod dressed in the suit, said, "Take it easy, Zoe. Lots of little kids are afraid of Santa."

"Younger kids maybe, but a four-year-old?"

"Kids are all different. My five-year-old daughter still cries when she sees him—she doesn't scream, but she cries. My son, who is three, runs to him laughing, all excited to sit in Santa's lap."

"Okay, maybe I should just leave her alone a minute." I poured coffee and got some of my mom's fudge-and-divinity candy out for my guests. They put the presents they'd brought around the tree.

I told Trey about Millie's article and he said he hoped it worked. They sure didn't have anything on April's mother. All the while we talked, her screams grew louder. I finally gave up and walked down the hall to the bedroom.

"April, honey? This isn't a very nice way to act. Come to the living room with me, we'll have some candy and talk to Santa."

"I no want any canny," she said, between sobs. "I want my mommy. Where's my mommy?"

It wasn't going to be easy. My mom had told April this morning that her mommy had gone to live in heaven and that we couldn't go there right now. I tried to explain things again, but as she was too young to understand, I felt totally inadequate.

Since I'd never had children I knew much less about kids than most women my age. I couldn't help wondering if I'd made a big mistake by bringing this little girl home with me.

Finally, she stopped crying and stuck her thumb in her mouth. She still didn't want to go out to see Santa, so I left her on my bed, watching *Sesame Street*, and hugging the teddy bear she got last night.

When I returned to the living room, the little group had already left, all except Santa. Trey Gerrod made a great St. Nick, as he was on the roly-poly side, with round cheeks and blue eyes. He didn't have a beard though and had to wear the false whiskers.

He filled me in on the progress they'd made in identifying the hit-and-run vehicle. "We've narrowed it to three cars. All have been in the shop in the past eight to ten months for paint jobs. We've talked to the owners and each has a good alibi."

"What about the cars? What about damage?"

"No damage to two of them, but the third car has

left town. Which sounds a little suspicious to me. The owner, a Mr. Randall Lack, says his son took the Buick this morning to drive to Fort Worth to visit his mother. The parents are divorced and the son lives with his father."

"And you think this could be the one?"

"It's only a guess. However, Lack does have the strongest alibi. He was at a Christmas party and seen by about fifty people." Trey smiled. "He played Santa and wore a suit and everything. Can you imagine a grown man acting that way?"

I eyed Trey and realized his tongue was planted firmly in his cheek. "No, I can't imagine it. So, Lack was there all evening?"

"He supposedly left around midnight to go home and we haven't proved otherwise yet."

"So there's not . . ."

"We haven't given up, Zoe. I'm not called 'tenacious' for nothing." He smiled and I'd have sworn his blue eyes twinkled. "I need to head on down the avenue. We're taking our kids to my mom and dad's tonight. Tomorrow we go to Sara's folks."

I walked with him to the door, "Thanks, Trey. Tell the others they were sweet to come and I appreciate the presents. I'm sorry April didn't get into the spirit."

"No problem. She's been through a lot and it's going to take a bunch of love to get her back on track."

As I closed the door behind Trey, I thought about what he'd said. He was right. April would need a lot of love. Someone to care for her unconditionally. Someone to love her as much as their own. I knew her immediate fate was to be sent to a foster home. Would they be capable of giving the love she needed?

I grilled a couple of chicken breasts, made a salad, cooked some rice, and opened a package of brown gravy mix. My mind kept walking around the idea of what it would be like to be a mother. It did have a certain appeal, I admitted, but a kid with so many problems would be a handful. Even I could figure that one.

Byron and I had talked about having kids. Sometime in the future, maybe, we'd say, not yet. We'll get around to it. We hadn't known then his future was limited. The doctors say he'll never wake up from the coma he's in and I will never have the family we talked about. Now I'd never be a mother.

When I went to see if April was ready to eat, she'd gone to sleep. It didn't surprise me. She'd worn herself out with her emotional outburst. She'd not slept much last night and since she and my mother had run around half the day shopping, sleep was inevitable. No wonder the little thing got the screaming-meemies. She was worn to a frazzle.

After all the stuff I'd eaten earlier at the office, I realized I wasn't hungry either, so I wrapped things up and put them in the refrigerator. I decided to take a warm bubble bath and afterward, climb into bed to read. I'm not too crazy about police and crime books—they're usually either too realistic or not realistic enough—but I'd recently discovered a writer who writes about a female police chief in the fictional town of Maggody, Arkansas, who has the knack of tickling my funny bone. I'd just bought a recent paperback and was looking forward to it.

Around nine P.M., April woke up wanting something to eat. We raced to the kitchen. I let her win, and on the lower shelf of the pantry, I found a can of chicken noodle soup. Mom must have bought it because it wasn't anything I usually stocked. I heated the soup in the microwave and April got a spoon and some crackers out, even though it wasn't too easy, seeing as how she had a teddy bear in one arm. I dished up some of the salad I'd made earlier for myself.

"Are you feeling better now?" I asked as she began eating.

"Jey-es." She almost smiled and took a drink of milk, leaving a mustache of white above her lip.

"I'm glad. Did you and Mo . . ." I broke off. I knew what my brother's kids called Mom, but didn't know what she'd told April to call her. "Did you and Mamma Lene go to the grocery store today?"

"Jey-es."

"Good. Can you say yes?"

"Yes," and, this time she did smile, lighting up her whole face.

"Very good, April." She was a cutie and would be even cuter with a little meat on her bones. "After you finish eating, we'll go turn on the Christmas tree lights. Would you like that?"

"Yes." She finished the soup and asked for more.

It was good to see her eating so well, even if it was an odd time for dinner. While April ate the additional soup, I looked in the refrigerator and pantry to see what extra goodies Mom had bought. I found a carton of Blue Bell Ice Cream—butter pecan—my favorite. April and I each had some.

We finished the ice cream, I washed her face and hands and then we walked to the living room where I turned on the tree lights. When the lights started blinking off and on, April clapped her hands in glee.

"You're a lucky little girl, April. Look at all these presents with your name on them. Look at what Santa Claus brought for you."

April started screaming again, but this time she ran to me and put her arms around my legs, almost toppling me. Not easy when you're five feet nine like I am. She's frightened, I thought. "Honey what's wrong? What are you afraid of?"

"That Santa Claus."

"You're afraid of Santa?"

"Jey-es."

Maybe if I was used to little kids I'd have snapped to it sooner. But now, at least, the light was beginning to dawn. "Why are you afraid of Santa? Did Santa hurt you?"

"No, he hurt Mommy."

"How did Santa hurt your mommy?"

"Mommy said, 'No, no.' He pushed her. Mommy fall out. Mommy cried."

"Santa pushed your mommy out of the car?" I

needed to know if they had been inside the car. If they had it would open up the possibilities and help make the case.

"Jey-es. Mommy told me run. I run. Mommy run. Santa's big car hit Mommy." Tears welled up in her eyes.

I changed the subject. I didn't want her thinking about the bad part right now. "Santa took you for a ride in his car?"

"Je—yes. We go to Old McDonald's. And I got french fries."

"Do you like french fries?"

"Yes, with ketchup."

"I like french fries and ketchup too. Maybe we can go to McDonald's tomorrow and get french fries. I think it's time now for us to go to bed."

"Okay." She took my hand and led me down the hallway.

We held hands until she went to sleep. Maybe being a parent wasn't so difficult after all.

Thinking over my talk with April, I began to get a mental picture of what must have happened to her and her mom. The picture was still fuzzy, but it was a likely scenario that explained why April was afraid of anyone dressed as Santa.

A man dressed in a Santa suit had picked them up someplace. Trey Gerrod had mentioned that one of his metallic-blue car owners had dressed as Santa— that connected. Maybe he offered to buy them food and took them to McDonald's. Maybe he offered money for sex too, beforehand, and April's mom said okay, but feed us first. After eating maybe she wasn't so eager to go along with the sex part and refused to give him whatever he wanted.

That refusal made him angry and he shoved them out of his car. Maybe she taunted him or mouthed off at him. Whatever, his anger exploded and he ran the mother down. The idea was feasible and the best part, from the police point of view, was that April and her mom were in that vehicle. Some trace of hair or fiber could turn up in the car.

I'd thrown away the clothing April had worn—nothing had been worth salvaging. Tomorrow I'd dig them out of the garbage can and take them to the forensics lab for testing.

First thing the next morning, I called my sister-in-law to ask if I could bring April to her house while I was at work.

"No," said Pat. "Helene said for me to tell you to bring April to her house. She knew you'd hesitate to ask her help today."

"But she's got . . ."

"You know she's got everything done."

"I just thought April would enjoy playing with Alicia and Kyle."

"I'll be at your mom's most of the day and we can manage the three between us."

"Sound like you two have things all arranged."

Pat and Helene get along well since Pat is almost as good an organizer as my mom. They gave up on me a long time ago. I'm okay at work but in most everything else, I'm usually disorganized. Sometimes I envy Pat her relationship with Helene, but she will often side with me, keeping Mom off my back. Besides, I liked her.

"Okay," I said. "I'll take April over there and thanks for your help."

A Canadian cold front had moved down across the Texas plains and into central Texas overnight. Made it feel more like Christmas to be able to put on a jacket. Mom had bought a coat with a hood for April and she got so excited I wondered if the kid had ever had one before.

After I dropped April at Mom's, I dropped April's clothes at the lab at headquarters and headed to the East Station patrol building off East 7th to talk with Trey Gerrod. I found him in his lieutenant's office finishing up a telephone call. When I told him what April had said, he got a funny look on his face.

"I just talked to the ME," Trey said. "April's mother had had sex as recently as an hour before her death. I was getting ready to start looking for a boy-friend or a pimp."

"Or a customer?"

"That too. It had occurred to me she was killed by some weirdo or a disgruntled john." He leaned back in the chair and looked at me through narrowed eyes. "If she had sex with the guy, why did he get mad and run her down?"

"Who knows? Like you said, a weirdo with a weirdo reason."

"We do know Mr. Lack was dressed in a Santa suit."

"Right," I said.

He picked up the Austin telephone directory. "Do you want in on this?"

"You bet your buns."

Gerrod handed me the directory. "Look up the locations for all the McDonald's and we'll go talk to some civilians."

I contacted my boss, who gave me a green light to stay with the case. "Nothing except more parties going on around here," he said.

"Save some goodies for me."

He promised he would and when I'd hung up the phone, I flipped open the directory. "Good grief, Trey. There are seventeen McDonald's here. I had no idea there were so many."

"We only need the ones within two to three miles of East Riverside Drive."

I studied the addresses a moment. "That leaves four: East Ben White, East Oltorf, Barton Springs, and East Riverside Drive. But the Riverside one is probably too far east."

"Let's try the first three," he said. "We can move farther out if nothing turns up in one of those."

After a brief argument about who was going to drive, Trey and I left in my Mustang. It was his case, but I remembered riding patrol with him years ago. He drove like a little old country farmer and that made me crazy. We reached I-35 and headed south. "If you had to guess, Trey, where do you like best?"

"I like the Barton Springs location. He probably picked them up in the downtown area or near Zilker Park."

I had thought the Ben White location for the easy access to I-35, but Trey had made a good point. "Okay, let's go there first."

"You're driving," he said.

"Yeah, I remember Santa and the little girl," the young man said. "They pulled up to the window around twelve-thirty that night."

The hamburger emporium's night manager was working again this fine Christmas Eve morning. Guess McDonald's was on a skeleton crew, too. Trey and I ordered coffee and sat in the booth nearest the counter. The manager, Bob Cortez, was in his early thirties, short and thin, and had an Adam's apple that looked like he'd actually swallowed an apple. He sat beside me, keeping an eye on his three other workers.

"That's the same little girl in today's paper, isn't it?" he asked. "I was pretty sure it was her." One of the girls from the kitchen called for Cortez, sounding like it might be a major calamity and he said he'd be right back.

"April's in the paper today? I thought it was going to run tomorrow—Christmas Day." Trey shrugged and I said, "I didn't have time to even look at the newspaper this morning."

"Have a little trouble being a mother, did you?"

"It's not easy getting a kid and yourself bathed, dressed, fed, and out the door on time. Especially when you're not used to it." I could smile now, but this morning I wanted to tear out my hair. "April didn't want to wear the blue jeans I put on her. She wanted to wear the red corduroy pants today."

Trey laughed, "So, who won?"

"She looked cute in the red. It seemed too trivial to fuss about, but I had to take off the jeans and put on the corduroys because we were going to be late if I let her do it."

"You'll soon figure out how to work it."

"You're talking like she's going to stay with me. This is only temporary."

"I hear you. I just don't believe you." Trey pulled the front-page section of the paper out of his jacket pocket and handed it to me.

While I was reading the article Millie had done, Cortez came back, apologetic.

"No problem," said Trey. "Tell us what you remember."

Cortez remembered the car, the woman, and the child, but especially he recalled the man. "Someone dressed like Santa is hard to forget."

"Did he have on the full costume?" I asked.

"Everything except the whiskers."

"Did you get a good look at him?" asked Trey.

Cortez nodded. "Dark hair, young, maybe about twenty. That struck me as a little odd. I figured he was the woman's younger brother and had done this for the little girl."

When Cortez had nothing more to add, Trey and I walked out to my car.

"None of my blue Buick owners were young," said Trey.

"But one of them had a son old enough to drive."

"Mr. Lack," said Trey. "Let's go see old Randall Lack. Maybe he'll tell us why his son really drove up to Ft. Worth the next morning after a hit-and-run."

It was routine after that. Mr. Lack didn't want to cooperate until Trey Gerrod mentioned the Fort Worth police had Randall, Jr., in custody. A search warrant had been obtained for the car.

Lack finally admitted his son had told him he'd put on the Santa suit and had gone out to play a joke on his friends. Lack denied any knowledge about the hit-and-run.

I let Trey handle things from that point and drove over to my parents' house. Millie Warner called to say several people had called the *Statesman* saying they knew April and her mother. No one knew of any other family. April's last name was Collins and her mother's name was Reba. The newspaper was starting a fund for April and was also donating a funeral for Reba Collins.

My family, including aunts, uncles, and cousins, had all fallen for April and she was responding to their care and concern. Everyone kept asking me what was I going to do? Hell, I didn't know.

Later that evening, I slipped away from all the family festivities and drove to the nursing home to visit Byron. As I sat in the car outside the building housing my comatose husband, I was still unsure that what I wanted to do was the right thing for me or for April.

The night was clear and you could see millions of stars, bright and twinkling in the black sky. High wispy clouds were visible against the inky velvet, looking as if an artist had painted them there only a few minutes earlier.

Christmas is a time for giving and receiving love. Love was something a child could bring into my lonely life. I got out of the car and automatically looked upward to see if I could spot a miniature sleigh or Rudolph and eight tiny reindeer.

"Byron," I said aloud in the crisp night air, "guess what Santa brought me for Christmas?"

MAD DOG

by Dick Lochte

The guy who said April was the cruelest month must not have spent much time alone in Hollywood during the Christmas season. There's all that smog-filtered sun shining down. Neon trees. Elves with tans. Reindeer with chrome sidewalls. And the street decorations are flat-out cheesy—sprigs of wilted holly with greetings that are so busy being nondenominational they might as well be serving some other purpose, like telling you to keep off the grass. If there was any grass.

As you might guess from the foregoing, I was fairly depressed that night before Christmas Eve. My few friends were scattered to the winds and the holidays loomed so bleak that I was at the end of my tether. So I agreed to appear on *The Mad Dog Show*.

Mad Dog, last name unknown if it wasn't "Dog," was the latest thing in radio talk hosts. He was rumored to be young, irreverent, glib to the max, and funny on occasion, usually at the expense of someone else. As I discovered by listening to his show the night before my scheduled appearance, he was also brash and self-opinionated and he had an annoying habit of pausing from time to time to let loose with a baying noise. But his coast-to-coast audience was not only charmed by such behavior, it was large and loyal. And, as my publisher's publicity agent informed me, Mad Dog actually read books and was able to sell them.

Even stranger, much to the agent's surprise, the self-described "howling hound of America's airways" specifically requested that I appear on his pre-Christmas Eve show to talk about my latest novel.

His station, KPLA-FM, was in a no-man's-land just off the San Diego freeway, nestled between a large lumberyard, apparently closed for the holidays, and a bland apartment complex that looked newer than the suit I was wearing, if not more substantial. The station would have resembled a little white clapboard cottage except for the rooftop antenna that went up for nearly three stories. It was situated in the middle of a shell-coated compound surrounded by a chain fence.

Security was a big thing at KPLA-FM, apparently. A lighted metal gate blocked the only road in that I could find. I aimed my car at it, braked, and waited for a little watchman camera to spin on its axis until its lens was pointed at my windshield.

"Hello," an electronically neutered voice said, "have you an appointment?"

"I'm Leo Bloodworth," I replied, sticking my head out of the side window. "I'm guesting on the . . ."

"Of course," the voice interrupted me. "Mad Dog's expecting you. Please enter and park in the visitor section."

There weren't many cars. I pulled in between a black sedan and a sports convertible, got out without dinging either, and strolled to the brightly lit front door, my current novel under my arm.

The door was locked.

I couldn't find a bell, so I knocked.

A little peephole broke the surface of the door, through which an interior light glowed. A shadow covered the light and the door was opened by a pleasant woman in her senior years, rather plump and motherly. There was something familiar about her intelligent, cobalt-blue eyes. Had she been an actress on one of those TV shows my family used to watch? Aunt Somebody who was always baking cookies and dispensing comfort and advice?

"I'm Sylvia Redfern, the assistant station manager," she said. "I'm not usually here this late, but we're very short-staffed because of the holidays. Come, I'll show you to what passes for our greenroom."

She led me to a small, pale blue and white, windowless space furnished with thrift-sale sofas and chairs, a large soft-drink machine, and a loudspeaker against a far wall, from which emanated music that sounded vaguely classical.

There were two people in the room. The man was a reedy type whose lined face and sparse white hair made me place his age as somewhere in his mid-sixties, at least a decade older than me. The woman, tall and handsome with good cheekbones and short black hair, I figured for being at least twenty years my junior.

"Another fellow guest," Sylvia Redfern announced cheerily. "Ms. Landy Thorp and Dr. Eldon Varney, this is Officer Leo Bloodworth."

"Just Leo Bloodworth," I corrected, nodding to them both.

Sylvia Redfern looked chagrined. "Oh, my," she said, "I thought you were with the police."

"Not for twenty years or so. I hope our host isn't expecting me to . . ."

"I'm sure his information is more up to date than mine," she replied, embarrassed. "Please make yourself comfortable. I'd better go back front and see to the other guests when they arrive."

Dr. Varney's tired eyes took in the jacket of my book. He gave me a brief, condescending smile and returned to his chair. Landy Thorp said, "You're the one who writes with that little girl."

It was true. Through a series of circumstances too painful to discuss, my writing career had been linked to that of a bright and difficult teenager named Serendipity Dahlquist. Two moderately successful books, *Sleeping Dog* and *Laughing Dog,* had carried both our names. This was the newest in the series, *Devil Dog.*

"May I?" Landy Thorp asked and I handed her the novel.

She looked at the back cover where Serendipity and I were posed in my office. "She's darling," Landy Thorp said. "Is she going to be on the show, too?"

"No. She's in New England with her grandmother." And having a real Christmas, I thought. "So I'm here to flog the book. What brings *you* to *The Mad Dog Show*, Miss Thorp?"

She frowned and returned *Devil Dog* as she replied, "I'm not sure I know." Then the frown disappeared and she added, "But please call me Landy."

"Landy and Leo it will be," I said. "You don't know why you're here?"

"Somebody from the show called the magazine where I work and asked for them to send a representative and here I am."

"What magazine?" I asked.

"Los Angeles Today."

"Los Angeles Today?" Dr. Varney asked with a sneer twisting his wrinkled face. "That monument to shoddy journalism?"

Landy stared at him.

"The magazine ruffle your feathers, Doc?" I asked.

"I gather they're in the midst of interring some very old bones better left undisturbed."

Landy shrugged. "Beats me," she said. "I've only been there for a year. What's the story?"

"Nothing I care to discuss," Dr. Varney said. "Which is precisely what I told the research person who phoned me."

I strolled to the drink machine and was studying its complex instructions when the background music was replaced by an unmistakable "Ahooooooooo, ruff-ruff, ahoooooooooo. It's near the nine o'clock hour and this is your pal, Mad Dog, inviting you to step into the doghouse with my special guest, businessman Gabriel Warren. Mr. Warren has currently curtailed his activities as CEO of Altadine Industries, to head up Project Rebuild, a task force that hopes to revitalize business in the riot-torn South Central area of our city. With him are his associates in the project, Norman Daken, a member of the board at Altadine and Charles 'Red' Rafferty, formerly a commander in the LAPD, ahooooo, ahoooooo, and now Altadine's head of security.

"Also taking part in tonight's discussion are Victor Newgate of the legal firm of Axminster and Newgate, mystery novelist slash private detective, Leo Bloodworth, journalist Landy Thorp, and Dr. Clayton Varney, shrink to the stars."

Varney scowled at his billing. I was doing a little scowling, myself. Red Rafferty had been the guy who'd asked for and accepted my badge and gun when I was booted off the LAPD. I suppose he'd had reason. It all took place back in the Vietnam days. Two kids had broken into a branch of the Golden Pacific Bank one night as a protest. The manager had been there and tried to shoot them and me and so I wound up subduing *him* and letting the kids go. The banker pushed it and Rafferty did what he thought he had to. But I never exactly loved him for it. And I was not pleased at the prospect of spending an hour with him in the doghouse.

A commercial for a holiday bloodbath movie resonated from the speaker. Dr. Varney stood suddenly and headed for the door. Before he got there, it was opened by a meek little guy carrying a clipboard. He looked like he could still be in college, with his blond crew cut and glasses. "Hi," he said, "I'm Mad Dog's engineer, Greg. This way to the studio."

"First, I demand a clarification," Dr. Varney told him. "I want to know precisely what we're going to be discussing tonight."

Greg seemed a bit taken aback by the doctor. He blinked and consulted his clipboard. "Crime in the inner city. What's causing the current rash of bank robberies. The working of the criminal mind. Like that."

"Contemporary issues," Dr. Varney said.

"Oh, absolutely," Greg replied. "Mad Dog's a very happening-now dude."

Somewhat mollified, Dr. Varney dragged along behind us as the little guy led us down a short hall and into a low-ceilinged, egg-carton-lined, claustrophobic room with one large picture window which exposed an even smaller room with two empty chairs facing a soundboard.

The men in the room looked up at us. They occupied five of the nine chairs. In front of each chair was a microphone. Mad Dog stood to welcome us. He was a heavyset young guy, with a faceful of long black hair that looked fake, and a forelock that looked real bothering his forehead and nearly covering one of his baby blues. He was in shirtsleeves and black slacks and he waved us to the empty seats with a wide, hairy grin.

Since I was locking eyes with Red Rafferty while I located a chair across from him, I didn't spot the animal until I was seated. It was a weird-looking mutt nestled on a dirty, brown cushion in a far corner.

"That's Dougie Dog, the show's mascot, Mr. Bloodworth," Mad Dog explained. "We use him for the Wet Veggie spots. He's not very active. Kinda O-L-D. But we love him."

"Is this for him?" I asked, indicating the empty chair next to me.

"No," Mad Dog smiled and settled into his chair. "The D-Dog prefers his cushion. That's for . . . someone falling by later."

"Sir?" Dr. Varney, who was hovering beside the table, addressed our host.

"Please, Doctor. It's Mad Dog."

"Mad Dog, then." Dr. Varney's lips curled on the nickname as if he'd bitten into a bad plum. "Before I participate in tonight's program, I want your assurances that we will be discussing issues of current concern."

"Tonight's topic is crime, Doctor. As current as today's newspaper. Or, in Ms. Thorp's case, today's magazine."

"Sit here, Clayton," the dapper, fifty-something Gabriel Warren said, pulling out a chair next to him for the doctor. "Good seeing you again." He looked like the complete CEO with his hand-tailored pinstripe, his no-nonsense hundred dollar razor cut, his gleaming white shirt, and red-striped power tie. His voice was

clear and confident, just the sort of voice you need if
you're planning on running for the Senate in the near
future, which everyone seemed to think he was. "You
know Norman, don't you?" he asked Varney.

"Of course." The doc nodded to the plump, middle-
aged man in a rumpled tweed suit at Warren's left
hand, Norman Daken.

"What are you doin' here, Bloodworth?" my old
chief asked unpleasantly. Never a thin man, he'd
added about six inches around the middle and one
more chin, bringing his total to three.

"Pushing my novel," I said, pointing to the book
on the table.

He glanced at it. "Beats workin', I guess," he said.

"It takes a little more effort than having somebody
stick a fifty dollar bill in your pocket," I said. That
brought a nice shade of purple to his face. There'd
been rumors that he'd made considerably more money
as a cop than had been in his bimonthly paycheck,
especially in his early days.

"Aaoooo, aaoooo," Mad Dog bayed. "Gentlemen,
lady, I think Greg would like to get levels on all of
us."

While each of us, in turn, babbled nonsense into
our respective mikes to Greg's satisfaction, the woman
who'd greeted me at the door, Sylvia Redfern, entered
the engineer's cubicle and positioned the chair beside
him—the better to observe us through the window.

Mad Dog asked innocently, "Any questions before
we start? We've got one minute."

There was something about his manner, the edge to
his voice, that made me wonder if we weren't going
to be in for a few surprises before the show was over.
The empty chair at our table was added intimidation.
I think the feeling was shared by the others. They
asked no questions, but they looked edgy, even lawyer
Newgate whom I had observed in the past staying as
cool as a polar bear under tremendous courtroom
pressure.

Seated at his console behind the glass window, Greg
stared at the clock on the wall and raised his hand,

the index finger pointed out like the barrel of a gun. Then he aimed it at Mad Dog, who emitted one of his loud trademark moans. As it faded out, Greg faded in the show's theme (a rather regal-sounding melody that Landy later identified for me as Noel Coward's "Mad Dogs and Englishmen").

Then our host was telling his radio audience that they were in for a special show, one that people would be talking about through the holiday season.

Dr. Varney's frown deepened and even the smooth Gabriel Warren seemed peeved as Mad Dog blithely continued his opening comments. "Thirty years ago tonight, before I was even a little Mad Puppy, a terrible crime was committed in this city." Gabriel Warren leaned back in his chair. Norman Daken edged forward in his. Rafferty scowled. "Two crimes, really," Mad Dog corrected. "But the one people know about was the lesser of the two. The one people know about concerned the grisly death of a man of importance in this city, the father of one of our guests tonight, Theodore Daken."

Norman Daken's face turned white and his mouth dropped open in surprise. He had a red birthmark on his right cheek the size and shape of a teardrop and it seemed to glow from the sudden tension in his body. Mad Dog rolled right along. "Theodore Daken was then president of Altadine Industries, which in the early 1960s had developed one of this country's first successful experimental communications satellites, Altastar."

"Excuse me," Gabriel Warren interjected sharply. "I understood we were here to discuss urban violence."

"If Theodore Daken's death doesn't qualify," our host replied, "then I don't know the meaning of 'urban violence.' "

"Please," Norman Daken said shakily. "I don't really feel I want . . ."

"Bear with me, Mr. Daken. I'm just trying to acquaint the listeners with the events surrounding that evening. Both you and Mr. Warren were young executives at Altadine at the time, weren't you?"

"Yes, but . . ."

"You were the company's treasurer and Mr. Warren was executive vice president, sort of your father's protege. Is that right?"

"I suppose so." The birthmark looked like a drop of blood. "I handled the books and Dad was grooming Gabe to assume major responsibilities."

"Yes," Mad Dog said. His blue eyes danced merrily. "Anyway, on that night you two and other executives—and their secretaries, that's what they called 'em then, not assistants—had your own little holiday party in a large suite at the Hotel Brentwood. A good party, Mr. Warren?"

"As a matter of fact, Norman and I both had to leave early. Theo, Mr. Daken, was expecting an important telex from overseas that needed an immediate reply. It concerned an acquisition that we knew would involve a rather sizable investment on our part and Norman was there to advise me how far we could extend ourselves."

"And you didn't return to the party?" Mad Dog asked.

"The telex didn't arrive until rather late," Warren said. "I assumed the party must have ended."

"Not quite," Mad Dog said. "You missed what sounded like, for the most part, a very jolly affair. Lots of food and drink. Altastar had gone into space and it had taken your company's stock with it. Each guest at the party was presented with a commemorative Christmas present—a model of the satellite and a hefty bonus check. And everyone was happy.

"Daken, very much in the spirit of things, presented the gifts wearing a Santa Claus suit. He didn't need a pillow. He was a man of appetite. For food and for women."

"Please," Norman Daken said, "this is so unnecessary."

"Forgive me if I seem insensitive," Mad Dog said. "But it *was* thirty years ago."

"And he *was* my father," Norman Daken countered.

"True," Mad Dog acknowledged. "I apologize. But the fact is that he did set his sights on one of the ladies that night. Isn't that true, Mr. Newgate?"

"I'm not sure what point you're trying to make," lawyer Newgate said.

"Simple enough," Mad Dog replied. "On that night of nights, after all the food had been consumed, the booze drunk, and the presents dispersed, everyone left the party. Except for Daken and his new office manager. While they were alone together . . . something happened. Perhaps you can enlighten us on that, Mr. Rafferty."

Red Rafferty was living up to his nickname. He looked apoplectic. "Sure. What happened is that the woman went crazy and bashed . . . did away with poor Mr. Daken. Then she dragged his body down to her car and tried to get rid of it in a Dumpster off Wilshire."

Mad Dog's lips formed a thin line as he said, "The woman's name was Victoria Douglas and because the story about her and Theodore Daken was all anybody talked about that holiday season, she became known as 'The Woman Who Killed Christmas.' She was tried and eventually placed into a hospital for the criminally insane. And, after a while, she escaped.

"She was at large for several years. Then fate caught up with her and she was discovered driving her car on an Arizona road, tripped up by a faulty brake light. She was put back into another facility and again she escaped. Five times over the past three decades did Victoria Douglas escape. She was found and brought back four times. And yes, my math is correct. The last time she escaped from a hospital, eleven years ago, she remained free.

"But The Woman Who Killed Christmas has never been forgotten. Even now, thirty years after the fact, her 'crime' remains one of the most infamous in this nation's history. And, all of you dog lovers out in radioland, here's something to chew on during the next commerical: It's entirely possible that the worst crime that took place that night wasn't the one committed by Victoria Douglas. Of that greater crime, *she* was the helpless victim.''

Mad Dog leaned back in his chair, let loose a howl, and surrendered the airways to a commercial for soybean turkey stuffing.

Gabriel Warren stood up and turned to his associates. ''Our host seems to have made a mistake inviting us here tonight. I suggest we leave him to contemplate it.''

Red Rafferty knocked over his chair in his hurry to stand. Victor Newgate was a bit smoother, but no less anxious. The same was true of Dr. Varney. Norman Daken stood also. He said to Mad Dog, ''I can't imagine why you're doing this terrible thing.''

''How can you call it 'terrible' until you know what I'm doing?'' Mad Dog asked. He turned to me. ''You going, too, Bloodworth?''

''To tell the truth, I never was certain justice triumphed in the Daken case. So I'll stick around to see what's on your mind.''

''Good,'' he said.

Since he didn't bother to ask Landy if she was staying, I figured she was in on his game, whatever it was.

The others were having trouble with the door, which wouldn't budge. Warren was losing his composure. ''Open this goddamn door, son, if you know what's good for you.''

''You'll be free to leave when the show is over in a little under an hour,'' Mad Dog informed them. ''In twenty seconds we'll be back on the air. Whatever you have to say to me will be heard by nearly a million listeners. They love controversy. So feel free to voice whatever's on your mind. It can only boost my ratings.''

Red Rafferty lifted his foot and smashed it against the door where the lock went into the clasp. The door didn't give and Rafferty grabbed his hip with a groan of pain.

"Not as easy as they make it seem in the police manuals, is it, Rafferty?" I asked.

"You son—" Rafferty began.

He was cut off by Mad Dog's howl. "We're back in the doghouse where some of my guests are milling about. Something on your minds, gentlemen?"

The others looked to Warren for guidance. He glared at Mad Dog and slowly walked back to his seat. The others followed. In the engineer's booth, Sylvia Redfern was viewing the proceedings with a rather startled expression on her face. In truth, I was a little startled myself at the way Mad Dog was carrying on.

"O.K., Mr. Bloodworth," he said, "why don't you tell us what you know about the eve of Christmas Eve, three decades ago?"

"Sure." And I dug into my memory bank. "I was barely in my twenties, the new cop on the beat in West L.A. My partner, John Gilfoyle, and I were cruising down Santa Monica Boulevard when we got a Code Two—that's urgent response, no siren or light. Somebody had reported a woman in distress in an alley off Wilshire.

"We arrived on the scene within minutes and found a tan Ford sedan parked in the alley with its engine going. The subject of the call was moving slowly down the alley, away from the car, a small woman in her mid to late thirties. She was in a dazed condition with abrasions on her face and arms. Her party dress was rumpled and torn.

"She didn't seem to understand who we were at first. I thought she might have been stoned, but it was more like shock. Then she seemed to get the drift and said, 'I'm the one you want, officers. I killed Theo Daken.'

"Around that time, John Gilfoyle poked his nose into her car. He shouted something to me about a big Santa Claus dummy on the backseat. Then he took a better look and saw the blood. He ran back to our car to call in the troops."

"Did Victoria Douglas make any effort to escape?" Mad Dog asked.

"No. She was too far out of it. I don't know how she was able to drive the car."

"Did she say anything?"

"Nothing," I answered. "I had to get her name from the identification cards in her purse."

"What happened then?"

"Gilfoyle and I were helping her to our vehicle when the newspaper guys showed up. I don't know how the heck they got there that fast. I put Miss Douglas in the back of our vehicle and helped Gilfoyle pull the photographers away from the body. But they got their pictures. And the people of Los Angeles got their dead Santa for Christmas."

Norman Daken opened his mouth, but decided against whatever he was going to say. I remembered what he was like back then, sitting in the courtroom, in obvious pain. Thinner, more hair. Women might even have found him handsome. Not now. Unlike Warren, to whom the years had been more than kind, Daken resembled an over-the-hill Pillsbury doughboy.

Mad Dog turned to Rafferty. "You took charge of the Daken case personally, Mr. Rafferty. Care to say why?"

"Because it was a . . . " he began, shouting. Then, realizing that his voice was being carried on an open radio line, he started again, considerably more constrained. "Because it was a circus. There was this crazy woman who'd used a blunt instrument on Santa Claus. Not just any Santa, but a Santa who was an old pal of the governor's. And a damn fine man." This last was said with a glance at Norman Daken. "And my chief wanted action. That's why I took charge."

"Even though there was this tremendous pressure, you feel that the police did all that they could in investigating the murder?"

"Absolutely. It was handled by the book."

"Mr. Bloodworth." Mad Dog shifted back to me. "According to an account printed at the time of Victoria Douglas's trial, you felt that maybe the detectives on the case had missed a few bets."

"Bloodworth was a cop on the beat," Rafferty squealed. "His opinion is worth bupkis."

"It wasn't just my opinion," I said. "Ferd Loomis, one of the investigating officers, agreed with me."

"Ferd Loomis was a soak," Rafferty growled. "That's why he took early retirement and why he wound up eating his Colt."

"I wouldn't know about that," I said. "All I know is what he told me. He said that the officers sent to secure the crime scene were greener than I was and they let reporters in before the lab boys got there. Not only that, a hotel bellboy was collecting tips to sneak curious guests into the room.

"All the evidence—the glass statue that was the supposed murder weapon, wiped clean of fingerprints, the dead man's clothes, the bloody pillow—was polluted by a stream of gawkers wandering through."

"But the evidence was allowed, wasn't it?" Mad Dog asked with the assurance of a man who'd read the trial transcripts. He wanted to lay it out clearly for the radio audience. When no one replied, he specified, "Mr. Newgate, you were Miss Douglas's lawyer."

"Judge Fogle allowed the evidence," Newgate said flatly. "I objected and was overruled. It was highly irregular. I don't know what made Fogle rule the way he did. Since he's been senile for nearly fifteen years, I don't suppose I ever will."

"What was the motive for the murder?" Mad Dog asked, like a man who already knew the answer.

Rafferty didn't mind responding. "According to our investigation, Victoria Douglas had been having an affair with Daken. We figured he broke it off that night."

"Sort of a 'Merry Christmas, Honey, Get Lost' approach?" I asked.

"Yeah. Why not? He dumped her. And then made the big mistake of falling asleep on the bed. She picked up one of those satellite statues and beaned him with it. Then she hit him a few more times to be sure and lugged him down to her car."

"Without one witness seeing her," I said.

Rafferty shook his head as if I were the biggest dufus in the world. "She took the freight elevator or the stairs. My God, Bloodworth. The suite was only on the third floor."

Mad Dog was vastly amused by our interchange. The others were expressionless. Landy Thorpe winked at me.

I realized that I probably wasn't going to be plugging my book that night. But maybe this was better. As I said, I'd never felt right about the trial. And even if nothing came of this re-examination, it was getting under Rafferty's hide.

I said, "When we found Victoria Douglas, she looked like she'd been roughed up. But that wasn't mentioned at the trial."

"You can muss yourself up pretty bad swinging a heavy statue fifteen or twenty times with all your might," Rafferty explained.

"Then there's her size. She weighed about one hundred twenty-five pounds. Daken weighed twice that. How'd she get him down the stairs?"

"Maybe she rolled him down." Rafferty's little eyes flickered toward Norman Daken, ready to apologize for his crudeness. But Daken seemed to have adapted a posture of disbelief that the discussion had anything to do with him. He stared at his microphone as if he were waiting for it to suddenly dance a jig. The fingers of his right hand idly brushed his cheek where the birthmark was.

"Anyways," Rafferty said, "crazy people sometimes have the strength of ten."

"Which brings us to you, Dr. Varney," Mad Dog announced, getting back into the act. "The defense used your testimony to legitimize its insanity plea. But was Miss Douglas truly insane?"

"That was my opinion," Dr. Varney said, huffily.

"You came to this conclusion because of tests?"

"She refused to take part in tests," Dr. Varney said.

"Then it was her answers to questions?" Mad Dog inquired.

"She wouldn't answer questions. She wouldn't talk at all, except to repeat what she'd said to the police, that she'd killed Daken."

"Then how could you form a definite conclusion?"

"My God, man! All one had to do was see pictures of the corpse. It was determined that she'd hit him at least twenty times, most of the blows after he was dead."

Norman Daken closed his eyes tight.

"Ah," Mad Dog said, not noticing Norman, or choosing to ignore him. "But suppose she'd hit him only once? One fatal blow?"

Dr. Varney frowned. "I decline to speculate on what might have been. I was faced with what really did happen."

"So now we've come to the beauty part of the story," Mad Dog said, blue eyes sparkling. "What really *did* happen?" He lowered his hand to the floor and snapped his fingers. The ancient cur, Dougie Dog, rose up on creaky bones and padded toward him. "But first, a word from Mad Dog's own mutt about Wet Veggies."

Mad Dog lowered the mike and Dougie Dog gave out with a very laid-back but musical bark. Greg, the engineer, followed the bark with a taped commercial for a dog food that consisted of vegetables "simmering in savory meat sauce." I was getting a little peckish, myself.

Gabriel Warren tapped Victor Newgate on the arm and asked, "How many laws is our friend Mad Dog breaking by keeping us here against our will?"

"Enough to keep him off the radio for quite a few years, I'd think," Newgate replied.

"C'mon, guys," Mad Dog told them. "Aren't you even the least bit interested in where we're headed?"

Norman Daken's eyes moved to the picture window where Greg was staring at the clock and Sylvia Redfern was looking at us with concern. His fingers continued their nervous brushing of his cheek near the birthmark. "Where *are* we headed?" he asked, so softly I could barely hear him.

"Thirty years ago, I would have been interested," Warren said dryly. "Today, I couldn't care less. It's old news."

Dougie Dog put his paws on his master's leg and made a little begging sound. Mad Dog reached into his jacket pocket and found a biscuit that he placed in the animal's open mouth. "Good old boy," he said.

"Family dog?" I asked.

Mad Dog smiled at me and his clear blue eyes didn't blink. "Yes," he said. "Fact is, he was given to me by my mother when I moved out on my own."

"You can sit there and talk about dogs all you want," Dr. Varney said. "But I am definitely not going to let you get by with . . . "

"Awoooo, awoooo," Mad Dog interrupted. "We're back again, discussing the thirty-year-old murder of industrialist Theodore Daken. You were saying, Dr. Varney?"

"Nothing, actually."

"We were getting to a description of what *really* happened in the murder room that night."

"What happened is public record," Rafferty said. "The verdict was in three decades ago. Case closed. Some of you guys like to play around with stuff like this, but you can't change history."

"Things do happen to make us doubt the accuracy of history books, however. Look at all the fuss over Columbus. Or the crusades. Or maybe a murder case that wasn't murder at all."

"What the devil's that mean?" Rafferty asked.

"This really is quite absurd," Gabriel Warren said flatly. "Why Victoria Douglas killed Theo Daken three decades ago is an intriguing question, but its answer will solve none of today's problems. We should be discussing the murders that take place every seven hours in this city, or the bank robberies that take place on an average of one every other day."

"That's what I thought we were here to talk about," Victor Newgate added.

"We can discuss crime in L.A. for the next year and not come up with any concrete answers," Mad

Dog said. "But tonight, it's possible that we will actually be able to conclude what really happened to Theodore Daken. Isn't that worth an hour of your time?"

"You're going to solve the Daken murder?" Rafferty asked sneeringly.

"Actually, I was hoping to leave the solving to Mr. Bloodworth."

"Huh?" I replied. "Thanks for the vote of confidence, Mad Dog. But I'm not exactly Sherlock Holmes. I'm just a guy who plods from one point to another."

"Plod away, then."

"The world turns over a few times in thirty years, and its secrets get buried deeper and deeper. Too deep to uncover in an hour."

"Suppose we make it a little easier?" Mad Dog said.

I thought I knew where he was headed. I pointed at the empty chair at the table. "If Victoria Douglas were to come out of hiding and join us, that might make it easier."

The others didn't think much of that idea. They eyed the chair suspiciously. "She's still a wanted woman," Rafferty said. "And it'd be my duty to perform a citizen's arrest and send her back where she belongs."

"Don't worry," Mad Dog said. "The chair's not for her. Is it, Miss Thorp?"

We all turned to Landy expectantly. "Victoria Douglas is dead," she stated flatly. It was the first sentence she'd spoken since we all sat down and it more than made up for her silence. "She died of a heart attack nearly six months ago in the Northern California town of Yreka, where her neighbors knew her as Violet Dunn. Knew and loved her, I should add."

The others seemed to relax. Then Landy added, "But before she died, we had many long talks together."

"What kind of talks?" Gabriel Warren asked.

"Talks that I'm using in an article on Victoria Douglas for my magazine."

Dr. Varney exclaimed, "I told you about it, Gabriel. Someone phoned my office."

"N-nobody called me," Norman Daken said.

"You're on my list," Landy told him. "We're just starting the major research. I'll be calling each of you."

Warren stared at her appraisingly. Rafferty seemed amused. "So, honey, on these long talks you supposedly had," he asked, "did she happen to mention anything about the murder?"

Landy stared at him. "She told me that she killed Theodore Daken in self-defense. It was she who fell asleep that night. She was not used to alcohol and had had too much champagne. When she awoke, Daken was beside her on the bed in his underwear, trying to remove her clothes.

"She called out, but everyone else had gone. She tried to push him away and he slapped her across the face. Struggle seemed useless. He was a big, powerful man. Her hand found the statue somehow and she brought it down against his skull. Then she blacked out. She doesn't remember hitting him more than once."

"Doesn't remember? That's damn convenient," Rafferty said. "No wonder she didn't try that yarn on us at the time."

"She might have," Mad Dog informed us, "if she'd taken the stand at her trial."

Newgate waved a dismissive hand. "She would have hurt her case immensely. It was my feeling that, in light of the grisly aspects of the situation, she was better off with an insanity plea. She could only have hurt that defense by taking the stand."

"She told me she did mention self-defense at her first parole hearing," Landy said.

"And, alas, as I feared, they didn't believe her," Newgate said. "I suppose that's what pushed her into making her initial escape."

"How did you come to be her lawyer, Newgate?" I asked.

He stared at me as if he didn't feel he had to waste

his time responding. But we were on radio, so he replied, "I'd met her socially."

"You mean you'd dated her?" I asked.

"No. But, from time to time, I had lunch with her and . . . other employees of Altadine. The firm I was working for did quite a lot of business with the company."

"Did Daken sit in on these lunches?" I asked.

"The old man? Hardly," Newgate replied with a smile. "He was the CEO. We were a few rungs down."

"Who else would be there?" Mad Dog wondered.

Newgate brushed the question away with an angry hand. "I don't really know. An assortment of people."

"Mr. Warren?" I asked.

"I was part of the crowd," Warren said. "Eager young execs and pretty women who worked for the company. Victoria Douglas included. There was nothing sinister about it. Nothing particularly significant, either."

"According to testimony from a woman named Joan Lapeer," Mad Dog said, "Miss Douglas had been Theodore Daken's girlfriend. Did she confirm that, Miss Thorp?"

"Victoria told me that Joan Lapeer had been Altadine's office manager before her. Theodore Daken fired the woman and hired Victoria. Joan Lapeer was so bitter that she spread the word that Daken had wanted to hire his girlfriend."

"Then there was no truth to it?"

"None," Landy said. "Victoria told me she'd only met Daken once or twice before she went to work for Altadine."

"Met him where?" I asked.

"Joan Lapeer was a very lazy, very incompetent worker," Gabriel Warren suddenly announced. Norman Daken looked up from the table at him, without expression.

"So she lied about Victoria Douglas's involvement with Theodore Daken," Mad Dog said.

"Miss Douglas said he asked her out a few times," Landy told us. "But she always refused."

"Because he was her boss?" Mad Dog asked. "Or a fat slob, or . . . ?"

"Because she was involved with someone else," Landy said.

"Who?"

Landy shook her head. "She wouldn't name him. She said it was the one oath she would never break."

"She used the word, 'oath'?" I asked.

"Precisely."

"Is he our mystery guest?" I asked Mad Dog, indicating the empty chair.

"No," he said, turning toward Greg in the booth. "But this might be a good time to cut to a commercial." He nodded, let out one of his wails and Greg responded to the cue with a spot announcement for a holiday lawn fertilizer, "The perfect gift for the gardener around your home."

"How much longer are you going to hold us here against our will?" Warren demanded.

"The old clock on the wall says another nineteen minutes."

"This is going to turn into a very expensive hour," Warren said.

"Why don't you just make your point," lawyer Newgate said to our host, "and be done with it? Why must we put up with all this cat-and-mouse routine?"

"That's how radio works," Mad Dog replied. "We have to build to a conclusion." He leaned toward me. "Are you willing to give us a wrap-up, Mr. Bloodworth, of what you think happened that night?"

"I wouldn't want to go on record with any heavy speculation. You don't seem to care about these litigious bozos, but I personally would just as soon stay clear of courtrooms."

"No need to mention any names," he said. "Just give us . . ."

He paused, some sixth sense informing him that the commercial had ended and he was about to go back on the air. He let out a howl and said, "Welcome back to the doghouse. Private Detective Leo Bloodworth is about to give us his version of what happened back at that hotel thirty years ago."

"Well," I said. "I'll take Victoria Douglas's word for it that she acted in self-defense. That would explain her battered condition. But if the guy attacked her and she repelled him, why wouldn't she just stay there and call the cops?"

"Because she panicked?" Landy speculated.

"When you panic, you run away. But Rafferty and his detectives tell us she didn't do that. Their scenario has her hanging around the suite and finally taking the body with her when she left. Why would she do that?"

"The dame was *crazy*." Rafferty was almost beside himself.

I replied, "She's just killed a man. She's confused. She decides to take the dead guy with her? Nobody's that crazy. Wouldn't it have been much more natural for her to just run away? Probably down the service stairs?"

"That's your trouble, Bloodworth," Rafferty said. "You refuse to believe what your eyes tell you. You saw her with the stiff . . . ah, the poor guy's body."

"That was later. What I think is that she ran away to the one person she trusted—the guy she was in love with. She told him what had happened in the hotel suite. He told her he'd help her, but she had to promise to keep him out of it, no matter what.

"They went back to the hotel in her car, parking it near the service exit. Maybe they went up together. Maybe he told her to stay in the car. He, or the both of 'em got Daken's body down in the service elevator. They put it in the back of Victoria Douglas's car. By then, she was in no condition to drive. So the boyfriend drove to the alley off Wilshire. And here's where it gets a little foggy. For some reason the boyfriend ran out on her and left her to face the music all alone. And true to her promise, her 'oath,' she refused to name him. Even though it made her look like a crazy woman."

"Wait a minute, Bloodworth," Rafferty blustered. "If it didn't make sense for *her* to move the body, why did *he* decide to do it?"

"Because there would be less scandal if Daken were found beaten to death in an alley wearing a Santa Claus suit than if he turned up dead in a hotel room in his skivvies."

"You're saying that Theodore Daken was moved to salvage his reputation?" Mad Dog asked.

"And that of his company's," I said. "I assume Douglas's boyfriend was an executive at Altadine . . ."

"Why?" Mad Dog asked.

"That's one way Victoria Douglas would have met Daken once or twice before he hired her. It's also how she would have known about the job opening. For all we know, the boyfriend could have closed the deal with Daken for her to come aboard. Anyway, he was the one who was trying to downplay any scandal."

"Only it didn't work," Mad Dog said.

"And I bet the guy next in line to the presidency, Gabriel Warren, had quite a job on his hands keeping Altadine's investors high on the company." I looked at him.

"You're right about one thing," he said. "It would have been quite a lot easier if Theo's death had been minus the sordid details. But as bad as it got, I managed."

"I'll bet you did," I said.

"Wait a minute!" Landy interrupted. "This was a company Christmas party. If Victoria's lover had been an Altadine exec, would he have just gone off, leaving his girlfriend passed out and easy prey for Daken?"

"I think the guy left the party early, before she was in any danger," I said, looking at Warren.

"Would you care to take a guess at the name of Victoria Douglas's lover, Mr. Bloodworth?" Mad Dog asked.

I continued staring at Gabriel Warren. "Like I said, somebody who left the party early. Somebody who wanted to squelch the scandal. But when that didn't happen, he was shrewd enough to know when to cut and run. Somebody smooth and savvy and well-connected enough to know how to push enough buttons, once Victoria Douglas was on the spot, to keep himself clear of the fallout."

"How would he do that?" Mad Dog asked. Warren glared at me.

"By pressuring a high-ranking police officer to disregard a few facts that didn't jibe with the official story of how Daken died. By getting a defense lawyer to plead his client insane and keep her off the stand, just to make sure his name didn't come up in testimony. By convincing a judge to bend a few rules. All to keep one of America's great corporations flying high. Because, surely, if one more guy at the top of Altadine had got caught by that tar baby, the company might never have recovered."

"You're not going to name him?" Mad Dog asked.

"He knows who he is," I said, nodding at Warren.

I was hoping to get the guy to do something. Like snarl. Or show his fangs. When he didn't, I said, "It just occurred to me that maybe Victoria Douglas didn't really kill Theodore Daken at all. She told Miss Thorp that she didn't remember hitting him more than once. Suppose that wasn't enough to do the job, though she thought it was. Suppose the boyfriend went up to that hotel room, saw Daken on the bed sleeping off that nonfatal whack and picked up the statue and finished the job, wiping the weapon clean. Then he had an even stronger reason for wanting Victoria Douglas to keep quiet about his participation in the removal of the body. What do you think, Warren?"

"You're making a big mistake," he hissed.

I shrugged.

"This may be the perfect time to bring in our mystery guest," Mad Dog said. And almost at once, the door opened and a wizened old man entered. He looked like he was a hundred-and-one, his khaki pants flapping against his legs, his bright red windbreaker hanging on his bony frame. A plaid cap with a pom-pom covered his bald pate at a jaunty angle.

The door slammed behind him and he turned and looked at it for a second.

"We've just been joined by Mr. Samuel J. Kleinmetz," Mad Dog informed his listening audience, which included me. "Mr. Kleinmetz, would you please take this chair?"

As the old duffer shuffled to the chair, Mad Dog said, "Mr. Kleinmetz was working that night before Christmas Eve, thirty years ago. What was your occupation, sir?"

The old man was easing himself onto the chair. "Eh?"

"Occupation."

"Nothing," he said, louder than necessary, sending Greg jumping for his dials. "Been retired for fifteen years. Used to drive a cab, though. Beverly Hills Cab. Drove a Mercedes. Leather seats. Wonderful radio. Worked all the best hotels . . ."

"Good enough," Mad Dog said, stemming the man's flow. "You were working the night . . . "

"The night the woman killed Christmas?" the old man finished. "Sure. I worked six days a week, fifty-two weeks a year. I was working that night, absolutely."

"In the Wilshire district?"

"That's where I used to park and wait," the old man said. He squinted his eyes in delight, staring at the microphone. "This is working?" he asked.

"I hope it is," Mad Dog told him. "On that night, you picked up a passenger not far from where they later found the body of Theodore Daken?"

"The guy in the Santa Claus suit, yeah. I guess it was minutes before. The paper said they found the guy at about ten-thirty. I picked up my fare at maybe ten-twenty . . ."

"How the devil can he remember that?" Gabriel Warren snapped. "It was thirty years ago."

"There are days you remember," the old man said. "I can remember the morning I woke up to hear the Japs bombed Pearl Harbor. I can tell you everything that happened that day. And the day that great young president John Fitzgerald Kennedy was assassinated by that Oswald creep. And the night the woman killed Christmas."

"We showed Mr. Steinmetz photographs of the members of the executive board of Altadine taken that year," Mad Dog said. "He identified his passenger. We then showed him a photograph of that same man today. Would you tell us if he's in this room tonight?"

"Sure." Sam Steinmetz looked across the table in the direction of Gabriel Warren, and I could feel a smug grin forming on my face. "That's him right there."

My smug grin froze. Steinmetz was pointing a bony finger at Norman Daken. "You didn't have to show me all those pictures. He's changed a lot, but I'd have known him right away, as soon as I saw that red dot on his face. Never seen one quite like it before or since."

Daken looked more relaxed than he had all evening. "So many years ago," he said, almost wistfully. "I'd almost forgotten. As if anyone could."

"Don't say a word, Norman," Gabriel Warren cautioned.

"No more, Gabe. I don't want to hold it in any longer. My father and I . . . we had our disagreements. He thought I was weak. I suppose I am. I loved Victoria."

I looked from him to the engineer booth. Both Greg and Sylvia Redfern were totally caught up in the tableau in the studio. Her expression was impossible to read, but her blue eyes looked kind and sympathetic.

"I think that's why he felt he had to have her," Norman continued. "Because I loved her. And he ruined it all for us. I never blamed her. It wasn't her fault, poor woman. She fought him and knocked him unconscious. She didn't hate him, you see. Not like I did."

Warren was scowling at him. "What the devil are . . ."

"Bloodworth was right. I killed him, Gabe. I thought you knew that."

"You thought I . . . How could . . . ?" Warren was having trouble articulating.

Norman Daken gave him a pitying smile. "He wanted you to be his son. I guess you felt that way, too."

"I would never have . . ."

"That's what was so beautiful about it, Gabe. You fixed it so that I stayed clear of it."

"I was trying to save the company," Warren said. "But if I'd known . . ."

"Well, now you do," Norman Daken told him. "You did everything you could to keep Altadine going. I, on the other hand . . ."

He didn't finish his sentence. I said, "I always wondered who reported Victoria Douglas to the police that night. And who called the reporters. That was you, wasn't it, Norman? You left that poor woman in the alley and went off to call the cops."

"I'm sorry I hurt Vicki so," he said. "I told her that she would never go to prison and I lived up to that. Thanks to Gabe's influence."

"But she wasn't exactly free," I said.

"No," Norman agreed. "But I had to make that sacrifice, if my father's reputation was to be thoroughly destroyed." He looked at Mad Dog hopefully. "Maybe now, thanks to you, he'll be dragged through the mud again."

Station KPLA-FM went off the air early that night, even though the police made short work of their task. They came, they saw, they escorted Norman off to be booked. As they explained, there was no statute of limitations on murder, not that he really wanted one.

As for the crimes Warren and his associates may have committed, the police were less certain of their footing. So that foursome left on their own recognizance. Even if it turned out to be too late to nail them for railroading Victoria Douglas, they probably wouldn't be suing Mad Dog or myself. And I doubted I'd be seeing Warren's name on any ballots in the near future.

When they'd all departed, leaving only Mad Dog, Landy, Dougie Dog, and myself in the main studio, I asked, "Are you both her children?"

"Just me," Mad Dog admitted, grinning. "What tipped you?"

"Dougie Dog, for one," I said, looking at the drooping mongrel. "The family hound, you said. Dougie. Douglas. And then, there's your nickname. Mad Dog. Madison Douglas?"

"Nope. Just Charlie Douglas. The 'mad' is, well, they said she was mad and what happened to her made me pretty angry. My dad worked at the hospital where Mom spent her first three years. He helped her escape. When she was sent back, I was raised by my paternal grandparents."

"And you kept her name?"

"It's mine, too. They never married officially. How could they? Anyway, figuring out that I was her son, that was good detecting."

"It's the least I could do after picking the wrong murderer," I said.

"We didn't know about the murder," Landy said. "Poor Victoria always thought she'd killed Daken."

"Who are you?" I asked. "Just a friend of the family?"

"As I said, I'm a journalist. I happened to rent a house next door to Victoria's a few years ago. We became friends and eventually she opened up to me about who she was. I think she hoped Charlie and I might get together."

"And you did."

They both smiled.

The dog rose to its feet, yawning, and dragged itself to the door and out of the studio.

"And you two decided to clear Victoria's name," I said.

"Right again," Charlie "Mad Dog" Douglas said. "Thanks for the help."

I stood up and picked my book from the table. "I didn't sell many of these tonight," I said.

"Come on back," he offered.

"It's too bad your mother passed away without ever learning the truth about that night. But I guess it's just as well that she won't have to go through the ordeal of Norman's trial."

They both nodded solemnly.

I left them and wandered out into the corridor. A light was on in the greenroom. As I passed, I saw Sylvia Redfern sitting on the couch, reading a book. Dougie Dog was curled up at her feet, sleeping peacefully. Her eyes, blue as a lagoon, blue as Mad Dog's, suddenly looked up and caught me staring at her. She smiled.

"Goodnight, Mr. Bloodworth," she said. "Thanks for everything."

I told her it was my pleasure and wished her a very merry Christmas.

"It will be," she replied, "the merriest in years."

NEVER ON SANTA

by Mark Richard Zubro

"I'd go, but I've got a previous commitment," Scott said for the fifty-seventh time. After the first couple times he said it, he began sounding distinctly peeved. After the twentieth repetition, he hit extremely angry. Now we were to the edge of an overblown fight. What's worse is, the angrier he becomes, the softer his voice gets until it's almost inaudible. He's a hurricane under strict control.

Scott said, "Meg understands. Why can't you?"

I didn't want to understand, and I didn't want to do it.

That afternoon Meg Swarthmore, the librarian at Grover Cleveland High School, had called and asked Scott if he would fill in as Santa Claus at the River's Edge Community Center Annual Christmas Pageant, billed as the largest holiday extravaganza of its kind in Chicago's south suburbs.

The original Santa, the mayor of River's Edge, whom Meg had lined up for months, had canceled late the previous night. He probably needed to be about his duties accepting graft and bribes from the good citizens of River's Edge.

Meg wanted my lover, Scott, to fill in. Scott works wonderful magic with the younger set. From squalling babies to screaming toddlers, through crabby four-year-olds and on up, he can perform miracles. Silence and calm envelop him and the kids as soon as he puts forth his powers, but he had a previous commitment, and I didn't. So Meg had come to my classroom between seventh and eighth hour, and I was dragooned into service.

Don't get me wrong, I enjoy Christmas and I love kids. Watching my wide-eyed nephews and nieces rip open presents on a crisp Christmas morning is a delight. I'm just not good with kids. Hand me a sleeping baby, and seconds later it is bellowing louder than the *1812 Overture*. Put me in charge of a group of toddlers, and they rush for the nearest deadfall or busy street to play in. Stick me in the middle of a crowd of four-year-olds, and they will begin plotting the overthrow of western civilization.

But Scott couldn't go, and Meg was a good friend, and so I was stuck. All day I prayed for a blizzard to start. The stupid weathermen predicted down to the last smarmy syllable that for the next three days the weather would be perfect for the last half of December and would get even more perfect with a gentle snowfall on Christmas Eve.

In the living room I tossed the Santa suit onto the couch. "It won't fit," I said.

"I'll help," Scott said. "We'll stuff it with pillows. You could really have fun with this." I hate it when he's angry and reasonable.

I grumbled persistently for the forty-five minutes it took to fit me into the suit comfortably. I refused to go through the nonsense of getting into it twice, so I ate dinner in the outfit.

At one point Scott suggested some rubberized protection for my lap in case of accidents by the kids. That nearly tore it for my going. He dropped the subject.

When he mentioned that he thought I should practice a few "ho, ho, hos," I used my entire repertoire of teacher glowers on him. He didn't bring it up again.

On the drive over I had visions of getting a flat tire and helping to change it while I wore my costume. When we arrived at the Community Center, I glowered at the stream of cars flowing into the parking lot. People were flocking to the event.

Other years I've gone to the Pageant and enjoyed myself immensely, but I'd never done it as Santa. Scott kissed me through the fake beard, said an encouraging word, and sent me on my way. I wanted to strangle the traitor.

I lurked to the appointed door so I could make my entrance unseen by the awaiting hordes. Meg found me in the chaos behind the stage, and smiled while patting my newly crafted substantial bulge.

"You look wonderful," she said. She burbled enthusiastic thanks for my being a good sport. People hurried by and said kind words and wished Santa well.

I began to lose some of my grumpiness, and I didn't want to disappoint Meg. Maybe I could get through this with no major disasters.

At seven I made my grand entrance on the seat of a glitter-encrusted, four-wheeled carriage pulled by six puffing elves. We made a circuit of the entire gymnasium through a path amid the throng. Against three walls and around the center of the gym, booths overflowed with all manner of crafts, toys, ornaments, games, and stuffed animals. The red-faced sellers hawking their wares and equally red-faced buyers paused to wave sweaty hands at Santa, call out happy remarks or, in the case of a few, make nasty cracks. I thought of yelling "up your chimney" back at these last, but I didn't want to scandalize the youthful believers in the crowd.

The slim hope that no one would recognize me was broken when three of the seniors in my Honors English class from Grover Cleveland High School waved and screamed, "Hi, Mr. Mason." Meg had asked me just before my last period class, and for some insane reason I'd blurted out the news to eighth hour that I'd be playing Santa tonight at the fair. If they were high school seniors why weren't they out doing sex, drugs, or rock and roll instead of being at a kids' pageant? The three of them got swallowed by the throng. Maybe they'd leave me alone. I hoped no other kids from school recognized me.

At the far end of the community gymnasium was a stage, upon which sat a Santa's village complete with nodding reindeer, under whose feet existed a menagerie of small furry animals with little glittering lights for eyes. A regiment of mechanical snowmen and snowwomen danced and twirled at the left of the stage, while on the right an equal number of them continuously bellowed out carol after carol. The din from the crowd echoed from the rafters.

Kids and their parents had formed long lines in anticipation of Santa's arrival. As I ascended the stage, the kids oohed and aahed for a few minutes. The parents beamed and applauded. I assumed my throne, center stage. The elves took up positions to ensure the orderly procession of kids into Santa's presence. The elves were bureaucrats from the mayor's office. This was their yearly volunteer duty for the occasion, and they took great pride in it. I thought they needed to get a life.

Six-foot-high pillars surrounded the throne, along with trellises festooned with garlands, leis, and flowers. Someone had cut up greeting cards and stuck the pictures to surfaces the other decorators had missed. Pots of poinsettias encircled the throne. The overly cheerful elf on my left leaned over and said, "Do you like the decorations? Every year the mayor gives us an afternoon off to do them."

Perhaps he should give them a week. I smiled and said they were delightful.

I turned and faced my first child. Scott and Meg had briefed me on the drill. Ask their name and what they wanted, inquire if they'd been good or not, smile for the picture, and keep all promises noncommittal.

The first kid was a nervous little dear of about three. He or she (with all the winter clothes on, I couldn't tell which it was) whispered in my ear that he or she had been good, and could I bring a big stuffed dog for under their Christmas tree? The kid was kind of sweet, and it didn't barf all over me, so I figured I was a step ahead.

The second kid was definitely a little girl, who gave me the most charming smile and asked for a job for her daddy. I felt like a heel for all my complaining. I wanted to hug her forever. I adjusted my attitude, perked up, and got into it.

By seven-thirty I was beginning to think I'd gotten the hang of the operation. By seven-forty-five I started to feel almost comfortable. At seven-forty-eight a four-year-old in a pink snowsuit lost control of a bodily function. Unfortunately modern science had made neither her nor my suit waterproof. At first I felt a slight dampness, glanced down and then realized a veritable Niagara had been let loose on my pants. I squawked, jumped up, and thrust the child at a disgusted elf who flung the bundle of leaking humanity at its mother.

The parent said, "Milly, we should never do that on Santa."

I looked down to check the damage. I heard a thunk over my left shoulder and craned my head back to see what it was. I felt a searing pain in my left leg just above the knee. I collapsed to the ground, landing between two rotating bunny rabbits.

The next little kid in line pointed at me and said, "Santa's bleeding."

I looked down and saw blood rapidly soaking through my pants leg. One elf fainted. Several screamed.

The next few minutes were kind of a blur to me. I tried pulling myself up, but the pain was too intense. I heard shouts and screams all around me. Meg appeared from somewhere and grabbed a microphone. Her voice boomed through the whole crowd. Whatever she said prevented a general panic in which a lot of people would have been trampled. I barely noticed. I tried gritting my teeth through my agony while attempting to stop the bleeding.

Two hours later I was back from the hospital and sitting on a folding chair in the gym. My left leg was outstretched. Its entire knee area was heavily bandaged. I could barely bend it. They'd given me a shot for the pain, and I couldn't feel anything for the moment. Meg sat in a chair next to me.

Eight feet away the mayor of River's Edge, Bill Blodgett, held court for a cluster of reporters and two minicams. He broadcast his theory that the shots had been meant for him since few knew he'd backed out of his starring role. The police mostly ignored me and followed up on the mayor's suggestion.

The gym had been cleared of pageant attendees. A minute before, someone had finally turned off the forty-third repeat of "Little Drummer Boy," my formerly favorite Christmas carol.

At the hospital they had told me I'd only lost a small piece of skin and less than one hundred CCs of blood. I thought it was more like a gallon. They told me I was fine, and Meg had driven me back to the auditorium to talk with the police.

The first bullet, the thud I'd heard, had stuck in the back of the chair I'd been sitting in. A third bullet, which I hadn't heard, had whizzed past me and decapitated a rotating wiseman. I glanced at a mob of cops on the stage, still doing all the minute things cops did at times like this.

It hadn't been difficult finding the weapon or where the shot had come from. A rifle had lain where the shooter dropped it, on a catwalk at the opposite end of the auditorium. I'd watched a cop walking out with the thing in an enormous plastic bag a few minutes earlier. Having been a marine twenty years ago, I knew a little about guns. I recognized the rifle they found as a Ruger Mini-14.

Frank Murphy, a detective on the River's Edge police force and a buddy of mine, stopped by to tease me a little bit. Frank and I worked together with some tough juvenile offenders, trying to keep them out of prison. We had a few successes. He'd been assigned to homicide several years ago. He was a good friend.

Unlike the other cops assigned to the investigation, Frank asked who I thought might try shooting at me. I had no idea.

When Blodgett finally finished his self-aggrandizing tirade, Fred Clark, a reporter for one of the big Chicago television stations asked, "Who would want to kill you?"

"I have many enemies," Blodgett said. "I've tried to clean up and reform this town."

This was true. He'd tried his best to modernize, computerize, realign, and reform the government of River's Edge, the second oldest southwest suburb of Chicago.

Blodgett's biggest fights had been with the police department and its police chief. The mayor puffed out his chest and continued, "Many of you have chronicled the heroic fights I've had. I've always been on the side of right and truth and good government. You know how progressive my administration has tried to be. Naturally I have enemies, fiends of the lowest order."

Blodgett did have lots of enemies, but probably not for the reasons he stated. The man was notorious for antagonizing those who supported him, much less infuriating his enemies, who at this point were legion. The kindest thing his few friends said about him was that he needed a vacation. His enemies thought he was a raving lunatic. If there was an easy way or a conciliatory way to alter something or a difficult, unpleasant path to follow, Blodgett always took the hard way.

Art Hampton, the River's Edge chief of police, joined the mayor at the microphone. Blodgett with his snow-white hair was a head shorter and fifty pounds heavier than the photogenic police officer.

Chief Hampton didn't have an extra ounce of weight on his six-foot-five frame. He had iron-gray hair in a brush cut and reminded me mostly of a marine drill instructor.

"Caught anybody, any suspects, is this a political assassination attempt, do you have any leads, is this gang related, does this killing mean the gangs have taken over River's Edge?" were all questions shouted at Hampton in the first few seconds after his arrival.

Hampton held up his hand palm out, like a bishop preparing to give a blessing to a crowd of pilgrims. The reporters hushed. Blodgett looked red to bursting.

"We have no leads at the moment," Hampton said.

"We are looking into every possibility including that this could have been politically motivated."

"Isn't it true," Fred Clark asked, "that the rifle used is the kind issued to the River's Edge police department?"

"Why wasn't I told that?" Blodgett shouted into the microphone.

Hampton sneered down at his nemesis, leaned into the microphone, and said, "Yes, it is the same type of rifle. No, we don't know if it actually came from the department. We're checking all the possibilities."

"What if it did come from the department?" Clark asked.

"We will pursue every lead," Hampton said.

Blodgett shook a finger at the police chief. "You don't have something in twenty-four hours," Blodgett said, "heads will roll." He turned to the reporters. "There is not a doubt in my mind where this assassination attempt originated. I'm calling in state agencies immediately to coordinate the efforts in the investigation. We can't have the fox questioning the chickens."

In Blodgett's own convoluted way this last statement almost made sense.

Meg whispered to me, "Why aren't they talking about what a horrible tragedy this could have been? Hundreds of people might have gotten hurt."

"Blodgett's a fool," I said.

"I'm sorry I got you involved," Meg said.

"Don't be," I said. "Until that last kid let loose, I was starting to get into it." Mercifully someone had found an old pair of painters' pants from somewhere for me to put on. I still wore the Santa suit top without padding, but I'd changed out of the stinking pants.

A commotion at the door drew our attention. A uniformed cop emerged from a knot of people and rushed to the police chief.

"What?" Hampton asked.

The cop, who barely looked to be out of his teens, muttered in the chief's ear. Blodgett tried to edge his way between them. The reporters huddled closer.

Hampton said, "Are you sure?"

The young cop nodded.

Reporters joined Blodgett in a chorus of, "What's going on?"

Hampton turned a face, pale now even through his winter tan, to the crowd. Camera lights flicked on as he said, "We just found a dead body."

Pandemonium.

By the time Scott arrived to take me home, Frank Murphy had told Meg and me the following facts: As part of their service to the community, a cadre of National Honor Society students from Grover Cleveland High School had agreed to act as marshals for the event. Some would provide babysitting. Others would watch entrances so no one would try to sneak in. Some would do cleanup, or in general be gofers for any of the small things that needed to be done. They'd been trained to call for help from security personnel, rather than confront anyone breaking the rules.

In an unused portion of the auditorium kitchen they'd found the body of Tim Lorenz.

I knew Tim slightly from helping out with the school newspaper last year. He'd been a stringer working on occasional sports stories. He was a thin kid, just growing out of mild acne. He had a soft voice and never caused anybody any problem.

Frank said, "We found a broken window. Probably how the killer got it. The Lorenz kid heard or saw something, went to investigate, and lost his life."

"Poor kid," I said. "Anybody talk to the parents?"

"We sent somebody to bring them in. The scene in the kitchen was pretty grim. Looked like the killer took Lorenz by the front of his sweater and pounded his head against the wall."

"Someone should have noticed a guy covered with blood waltzing around," I said.

Frank said, "There wasn't as much blood as you would think, and most of that came from the back of his head. Whoever it was, probably concealed the rifle under a winter coat. It's not surprising nobody saw anything."

I gave my official statement, and they told me I could go. Scott showed up and escorted me toward the doors. He's one of the highest paid baseball players around and often recognized in public. Unfortunately the reporters and then Blodgett spotted him. The mayor tried to get in close for a photo opportunity, but Meg, despite being in her late sixties, stepped neatly in front of Blodgett and placed a strategic elbow in his ribs. The mayor tumbled back into the reporters, and we scuttled away.

Frank stopped over late the next afternoon to see how I was doing. I'd managed some Christmas shopping in the morning, but my knee was sore and I spent most of the afternoon lying on the couch reading.

The first thing he told me was the rifle was definitely from the River's Edge police station. "Somebody somehow managed to switch one of our regulation Ruger Mini-14's with one not registered to us. They look alike and we wouldn't have noticed, if we hadn't been checking the registrations because of the murder."

"One of the cops did it?" I asked.

"Could be, but we haven't had any break-ins and only authorized personnel have access to the rifles. All proper procedures for signing any of them out were taken. The last time the gun was checked was during its monthly inspection three weeks ago. We test fire and clean all firearms once a month. The switch could have happened before that. We don't examine the registrations each time. Hampton has been going nuts all day."

"Why didn't the killer just run back to the police station and switch it back?" I asked.

"He'd have had to carry the rifle out through the crowd and pass a gauntlet at the station," Frank said.

"Who's in charge of the weapons?"

"Guy named Kramer. Has a clean record for fifteen years in the department. We have absolutely no proof he had anything to do with the shooting. We also don't know for sure who the killer was trying to nail," Frank said. "You, the mayor, or someone else."

"Why shoot at me?" I asked. "And there have to be a zillion less risky ways to try and take a shot at the mayor. The Lorenz kid was unlucky, but the killer took some pretty big risks."

"So far, it was the perfect time. We've got no witnesses, and until now he or she has gotten away."

"Are the cops in the department really that fed up with the mayor?" I asked.

"Hard to tell. A few people might be losing their jobs because of cutbacks, and a couple years ago we had all that trouble with the police strike when he hired replacement cops, but you'd think somebody would try and harm one of the scabs, not the mayor. But we're checking every angle more than usual."

"Fingerprints on the gun?" I asked.

He shook his head no. "I'm fairly unpopular at the station at the moment," he said. "I still want to work on this from the angle that someone was after you. Everybody else wants it to be political. Makes a bigger splash for them."

"I can't imagine the point of killing a high school English teacher," I said.

"You know anybody who might have a grudge against you? I admit that the mayor might be right and somebody was trying to off him, but just in case it wasn't, give it some thought."

I promised him I would.

He pulled out a roster. "Here's a list of all forty-five employees in the department. I want you to check for names you might recognize for any reason, especially former students."

I ran my eyes down the list. I've taught nearly two thousand kids in my teaching career. At this point I could barely remember most of their names. While out shopping or going to dinner in the local area, when a kid said, "Hi, Mr. Mason," I smiled and nodded back. If they pushed it, I simply asked them their names. Then I'd say something like, "I didn't recognize you because you're quite the adult." Mildly dumb, but the only socially acceptable way I knew to handle the situation.

I saw five names on the list that I recognized. Frank asked me about them.

Wayne Davello guffawed through a couple semesters of sophomore English nearly twenty years ago and was now a sergeant in the department. I remembered his distinctive laugh, but I couldn't picture him.

Another was Rita Jasinski from around seven years ago. I remembered her as petite but with a nasty tongue for any of her classmates who crossed her.

A third was Phil Kroll, an honor student, who had wanted a career in baseball. I'd heard he'd had a bad case of nerves at the minor league level, so he'd come back to town and become a cop.

The last two were a couple of prizes.

For the past ten years, besides my Honors English classes, I've had all the remedial readers for their senior year English requirement. In that time I've given Fs to four students. Giving them an F in senior year is a major deal for me. I don't like to do it. I want these kids to meet their graduation requirements. I work with the social workers, psychologists, the special education department, and their other teachers in trying to get them their diplomas. I also try to meet with the parent and about half the time I had some success in getting them to come to school so we could talk.

One of these four former students, Roderick Livingston, was currently in jail. While working with Rod, I spoke with his mother once on the phone. Before I called I found out that she'd been married several times and had a passel of kids, all with different last names from several different marriages. The social worker had added that he thought Rod's mom had a live-in boyfriend at the time.

Keeping track of which kid belonged to which parent could get complicated in these days of high divorce and remarriage. It was easier to remember them by their kids' last names.

Rod was a kid from her first marriage. I didn't remember what her last name was then. I just remembered her as Rod's mom. On the phone she blamed me for her kid's failure. She never showed up for the conference I set up, and she refused to cooperate with any of the social agencies. Currently, Rod was doing five to ten years in Stateville Prison for armed robbery.

Another kid, Jack Marco, had moved out of state and worked on a fishing boat on Puget Sound. The other two were on the River's Edge police force.

One was Edward Overgaard, a huge kid who claimed he'd lost the possibility of playing for a major college football program because of the grade I gave him. The other, Sally Slocum, couldn't produce a diploma so she lost the chance at a fantastically well-paying job she might have gotten right out of high school.

I wasn't the only one who flunked them their senior year, but I'd become involved in their lives, and I could see why they might blame me for their problems.

When I finished, Frank said, "The obvious thing is to figure out if any of these people hold a grudge against you and then find out where they were the night of the murder."

"Won't it be kind of tough getting them to talk?" I asked.

"All the cops in the department are being questioned. We've all had to come up with alibis for the time. I can check the paperwork and see what it says about these five. Right now everybody else is searching for who hates the mayor. I'll be able to dig deeper in a new area."

"Won't you get in trouble for not concentrating on the political?" I asked.

"We've got a huge team of federal, state, and local people working on this. I should be able to slip through the cracks."

"I hope it wasn't me the killer was aiming at," I said, "because he or she is still out there."

Frank reassured me as much as he could then left.

The next day, Christmas Eve, I had a lot of last-minute rushing around to do. We were scheduled to be at my parents that night. I spent the morning limping from store to store, while Scott stayed home and wrapped packages. I got home a little after two. Frank Murphy had left a message asking me to come down to the station as soon as I could. Scott didn't know what it was about. I left for the station around three.

On the way there I passed River's Edge Park with its gargantuan Christmas display. The red nose of the ten-foot Santa was big enough to signal airplanes with.

From its outward appearance, you'd guess the police station was the first building erected after the founding of River's Edge. Dirty faded bricks—probably originally yellow—crept around the two-story disaster area. Gutters along the north side of the building hung at crazy angles. Around the outside of the building, shattered glass, broken bottles, and crumpled beer cans decorated the swatches of dirt and waited for the snows of winter so they could hide their ugliness. Warped shutters nailed haphazardly closed over the first-floor windows added appropriate touches of dreariness. I managed to find a parking spot in the back. Two out of the three nearest street lamps were burned out. They probably didn't fix them because they figured nobody would get mugged with all the cops only a few feet away.

Inside, the musty old station had been given some festive cheer by sprigs of evergreen plastered to the old mahogony counter and three of four red and gold ornaments dangling from the ceiling.

Phil Kroll sat behind the reception counter. He stood up and smiled in recognition. I remembered Phil because he'd only graduated a few years ago and because he was probably the smartest and best-looking kid we ever graduated. He was still lithe, handsome, and muscular in his blue uniform.

We barely had time to exchange hellos when Frank appeared down the corridor. He joined us at the desk.

"I want you both to meet with the rest of us in the second conference room down the hall," Frank said.

"What's going on?" I asked.

Frank said, "Hang on for a minute."

I wanted to know what was up, but I trusted Frank, so after arranging a replacement for Phil, we trooped after him down the hall.

The second conference room was painted a hazy shade of gray. It was filled with metal folding chairs, grouped haphazardly around two eight-foot-long folding tables.

People filled four of the chairs. I recognized Sally Slocum. I was reintroduced to Edward Overgaard, Rita Jasinski, and Wayne Davello. Ed had blossomed from a two-hundred-fifty-pound left tackle into an immense bulk.

"What's going on?" Rita asked. "I have to get home. I've got kids to pick up and shopping to finish."

From her first word I remembered clearly the high-pitched grating whine that had so often asked in the immortal words of a thousand different students, "Why do we have to do this stuff?"

Seeing Wayne Davello brought to my mind the picture of a tiny kid who had a laugh that boomed from his diminutive frame. What I saw now was a man in his early thirties, with light brown hair, a trim mustache, freckles, and a small smile that hinted at his sense of humor.

Frank began the conversation simply. "We're looking into who on the department might have reason to be shooting at Mr. Mason."

"I thought it was political," Rita said.

"You think because we were his students, we had some reason to shoot at him?" Phil asked.

"That's stupid," Slocum said. "Who cares about an English teacher? Who even remembers? I can't believe you think we're suspects."

"I still hate you, Mason," Overgaard said. "I can say that because I was at a Christmas party with fifty people that night. I have a great alibi with lots of people to back me up."

"And I never had access to the rifles," Davello said. "Plus I've got no reason for a vendetta against Mason. His class was funny, and I was playing Santa myself that night at my youngest kid's Christmas pageant at school."

Frank insisted that they talk about their movements on the night of the shooting. Only Overgaard and Davello had solid alibis for the time of the murder.

"Does this mean the rest of us are suspects in the murder?" Rita asked.

"It means," Phil said, "that we've got no witnesses to where we were, but Frank has no way to prove that we were there, or we'd have been accused already. He's got a connection of us with Mason, but that's not much. He wants us to get tense enough to make a mistake."

"I don't even think I want that much," Frank said. "I'm just asking a few questions."

"You can't bluff us," Slocum said. "We're cops and we know all the tricks."

"Did any of you have access to the guns?" I asked.

Phil pointed at me. "He doesn't know?" he asked.

Frank said, "I haven't had time to mention it. They found a bunch of counterfeit pass cards to the equipment room. Only five people are supposed to have them. Everybody who has one swears they never left it out of their sight."

Frank explained that they passed these credit-card-sized identifications over an electronic scanner to let them in. "We found them in this week's trash," Frank said. "As if the killer left them there to throw us off. If there were that many fake cards around, then almost anyone could have switched the guns any time."

"We're wasting time here," Rita said. "Either charge us with something, make an accusation, or ask a sensible question, or I'm out of here. If there's a problem, you can take it up with the union. I know my rights."

A few minutes later Frank told them they could go. We walked to the door of the station. "Sorry for wasting your time," he said. "I thought if I could get you all together maybe something would break."

Through a pane of glass in the door, I gazed out

at the gathering darkness, saw the first flakes of the promised Christmas snow gust past on the rising wind.

"It was worth a try," I said.

"The way I see it," he said, "is we've got two major problems. How'd they get the gun and who knew you'd be Santa at the pageant?"

"Unless you find somebody who saw them take a gun, you're stuck there," I said.

He nodded in agreement. "Just to make sure, I checked," Frank said. "None of them has kids who go to Grover Cleveland High School. Most aren't old enough to have kids in school, but I wanted to be sure they couldn't have found out about the switch from school."

"The younger cops could have friends who are seniors," I said.

"I suppose," Frank said. "Having a friend doesn't make you a murder suspect."

We talked for a minute or two, then he walked back into the station, and I made my way to my truck. Snow swirled at my feet but, because of the wind, it hadn't begun to stick yet. I hesitated for a moment before climbing in. The glow from the distant street lamp cast shadows through the barren tree branches and lit the flakes of whiteness to a shimmer. I looked down and saw the mounds of trash around the police station. I realized I was the only person on this side of the building and except for the street light and a feeble glow from the police station windows, it was dark and slightly eerie.

I pulled out my keys. I heard the click of the safety lever on an automatic pistol. I dropped to the ground. Began to look wildly about, but a second later the feel of cold, round steel against my temple stopped me.

"In the truck, Mason," a gruff voice said.

Out of the corner of my eye I could see a lean frame and make out the handsome features of Phil Kroll. I could feel the tremble in the pistol held against my head. I obeyed slowly and carefully. If the safety was off, this guy meant business.

Seated in the truck, me behind the wheel, he with the gun pointed at my head, he ordered me to drive.

"Where to?" I asked.

The gun lifted higher.

I started the engine and eased the truck into gear. I made sure my seat belt was on, because I knew I'd try something with the truck. I let the engine idle at the edge of the driveway. I waited for him to give me directions.

"Why?" I asked.

"You know your encouraging me was a big part of the reason I screwed up in baseball," he said.

"That's why you're trying to kill me?" I asked. I felt sweat cascading down my armpits.

He didn't seem to hear me as he continued. "You told me I could be anything I wanted and I believed you. You said I could cope with stress and play baseball. You introduced me to Scott Carpenter and held him up as an example. But I couldn't handle the pressure. Every time I tried to bat, I'd start thinking. You told me there were smart baseball players, but I found out it's better not to think. Your advice ruined me."

"Come on, Phil. I just wanted the best for you."

"Yeah, well I got nothing."

"That's not enough reason to kill somebody," I said.

"Drive," he ordered and pointed to the left.

I pulled out. "Why?" I asked again.

"Remember Rod Livingston?" he asked.

I nodded.

"He was my brother."

I stopped at the light at the corner. I glanced across the seat at Phil. "You don't look much like him," I said.

"We had the same mom," Phil said. "I grew up listening to stories about how rotten you were. Every time I saw you, I hated you more and more. I didn't tell my mom you were my teacher. She'd have gone ballistic and taken me out of your class, but I wanted to get my revenge on you for Rod's sake. I waited for my chance that year, but I was too scared, and you were too nice. I knew you lived in town, so when I came back from the minors, I became a cop on the department so I could try and keep an eye on you."

"How'd you know I was playing Santa?" I asked.

"I'm friends with a couple of the kids in your Honors English class. I saw them before I came on duty. They told me."

"How'd you get the gun?"

"I made the switch a couple of months ago after Rod's sentencing. I threw the extra computer cards in the trash today to throw suspicion on everybody."

"How will killing me help Rod?" I asked. I had driven slowly through River's Edge. I hoped my unexpected visit had prompted him to act without prior planning.

"You ruined his life," Phil said. "Killing you will be a message to all over-zealous teachers to back off, and my mom will feel better knowing that you're dead."

By this time I was half a block away from the River's Edge Park Christmas display. I jammed on the brakes, and he lurched forward. The gun exploded in the cabin. The noise was incredible. I stomped on the gas pedal and aimed us for the display. Phil's arm swung wildly. I swatted at the gun. The front of the truck bashed into Santa. Fortunately I hadn't had that long of a run, and I had my seat belt on, but Phil wasn't as lucky. His head banged against the windshield. I grabbed the gun and put the safety on, then looked out the windshield. Santa's nose was a foot from mine.

THE SEASON OF GIVING

by Richard T. Chizmar
and Norman Partridge

I was still thinking about the deuce of hearts when the little girl with the face of an angel yanked on my coat sleeve.

It was the first weekend of December, six inches of new snow blanketed the city, and we were already pulling double shifts at Parker's Department Store. Management had settled on the usual preholiday security setup—four guards spread out over each of the three floors; one man per floor in a regulation United Security uniform, the other three working plainclothes.

Only one of us had to wear the suit.

Earlier, as per our new daily routine, we'd cut a deck of cards in the guard lounge. I'd felt pretty confident when Eddie Schwartz, who had worn the suit three days running, pulled the black three. And I'd gone on feeling pretty confident until I turned up the stinkin' deuce of hearts.

Eddie ho-ho-hoed like Santa when he saw it—something he hadn't done once during his tenure in the suit. The others had a good time with it, too. Cracking wise, speculating about my relationship with the reindeer as they watched me dress. Giving me a standing ovation as I left the lounge, my middle finger extended as stiff and proud as the candy-striped pole in front of Santa's workshop way up north.

I wasn't laughing, though. I'd avoided wearing the suit since the season started, and after hearing the complaints from my co-workers—"God, that thing's hot. It smells like an old closet. Christ, it's embarrassing."—I'd been hoping my luck would hold.

Well, I'd never had much luck. But now, a few hours into my shift, I could almost see that the whole thing was pretty funny. *Almost.* Me, of all people, dressed up as Santa Claus. Me, a bearer of gifts, when my usual commodity was misery. Mr. Sunshine in a bright red suit and cap. Shiny black boots. Pillow stuffing for a belly. Fluffy white beard. Everything but the red nose, which I'd lost for good when I stopped drinking.

On top of all that, the guys were right. The suit *did* smell like an old closet, and it *was* hot and heavy as hell. But it also had its advantages. Working the front of the store was a relatively easy job. Not much to do, actually. Stand behind an old Red Cross kettle, smack dab in the middle of the mall's main intersection, just south of a North Pole display featuring jungle gyms disguised as Victorian houses, slides, and plenty of not-so-inconspicous toy advertisements. Ring a rusty old cowbell every few minutes; but mainly keep an eye out for trouble on the North Pole, because Parker's didn't want to handle any personal injury suits involving kids at Christmas. Still, compared to chasing shoplifters and pickpockets up and down the clothes aisles and arguing with irate holiday shoppers, the Santa gig was a cakewalk.

Anyway, that was the setup. Back to the little girl.

I'd noticed her as soon as I returned from my break. A little angel moving slowly through the crowd, head down, getting bumped and nudged with every step. She looked about seven or eight, a tiny thing wearing a faded winter jacket at least two sizes too big for her. The frayed collar was flipped up, and you could just see the top half of her pale face as she bobbed and weaved, eyes telling anyone who bothered to look that she was on her own.

The crowd swept her along like a strong wind pushing a tiny leaf, and I feared that she might be trampled. Instead, as if sensing my concern, she looked in my direction and our eyes locked momentarily.

Thinking for an instant that I was wearing my security uniform instead of the Santa suit, I mistook the look of glee in her eyes for desperate relief. I could play the rest of the scene out in my head. She was going to tell me that she was lost; could I please help her find her parents or her brother or sister?

That happened all the time, but sometimes the scene took a scarier turn. Plenty of parents these days used the mall as a free baby-sitter—dropping off their underage kids for a few hours while they ran errands. In these tough times, too many people thought it was cheaper and easier to give a kid a five-spot for pizza and video games than to spring for a sitter. They were the kind of parents who thought everything would always be okay. With them, with their kids, with their spouses.

I used to think that way, but now I know better. We all do a hundred little things every day, without even thinking about them. But one thing I've learned—little things have a way of becoming big things before you even have a chance to notice.

As the girl approached me, I decided she was a definite candidate for a drop-off. Reason number one: her eyes told me that she was alone. Reason number two: she looked scared. Reason number three: her appearance—clothes that were hand-me-downs or garage sale bargains; the pale, unhealthy cast of her otherwise beautiful face—spoke of a family that couldn't afford a baby-sitter, let alone three squares a day.

The girl stopped in front of me, her eyes lonely but somehow still as blue and bright as a summer sky. She smiled suddenly, and my own mouth twitched into a grin.

I was unused to that particular expression.

"You have to sit down," she said, very seriously.

"Huh?"

"You have to sit down so I can sit on your lap."

The Santa suit. Of course. I crouched down to her level. "Sorry, sweetie," I said. "You're looking for the real Santa. He's over on the second floor, sitting next to the carousel."

"I *know* you're not the real Santa." She rolled those lonely eyes, branding me a first-class dope. "And neither is the other one. But you work for Santa, right?"

The only thing I could do was nod.

"Then you can tell Santa what my wish is."

I had to laugh then, and the thick elastic band on the fake beard knifed into my cheeks. It didn't matter though. I didn't care. I mean, it wasn't a raucous ho-ho-ho worthy of good old Eddie Schwartz, but it came from a part of me I thought I'd forgotten about. There was something special about that, just as there was something special about this serious, sad-eyed little girl.

Change rattled into the kettle, and I waved my thanks to a shopper, but the little girl didn't have patience for my manners. "Well?" she asked. "Are you going to sit down, or what?"

"Here's the deal." My voice was low, conspiratorial. "You're right about me being on Santa's payroll. But I still think you'd better talk to the other Santa." I crossed my white-gloved fingers. "He and the big guy are just like *this*."

I expected a smile out of her, but what I got was a frown. Her blue eyes puddled up, and the brightness leeched from them. "You don't understand. I can't wait. The line for the other Santa is way too long." She pointed over her shoulder, and her tiny finger was actually shaking. "M-my mom will be done shopping any second. And then we gotta go home."

Okay, I thought, *now we're getting somewhere.* "Your mother is in this store? Does she know where you are?"

"Yes . . . Well, kinda. I told her I was going to the bathroom and that I'd meet her by the North Pole." She pointed over to the playground where other kids were sliding and charging around and having a good time.

"Sure about that, sweetheart? You know, it isn't nice to fib to one of Santa's stand-ins."

She nodded furiously. "Can't I please tell you now?

Can't I, please?" Her eyes were beyond desperate. *"Pleeaazzze . . ."*

God, she was a cutie. Fragile as the expensive dolls in Parker's toy department, and with the same porcelain complexion. I watched her tiny lips move as she talked. Noticed the patch of freckles on her nose, the perfect shape of her ears, the way her hair was tied back with a long red ribbon.

Realized with a sudden jolt why the girl had captivated me so.

Realized exactly who she reminded me of.

I hadn't seen my daughter in almost seven years. Not since she was eight years old. Not since that rainy December morning Sheila had chosen to make their break for freedom. Talk about your basic holiday hell. Divorce papers had followed a week later. Merry Christmas. Not that I noticed at the time.

It was an easy decision for the judge. I was a drunk then, didn't care that I had a wife who needed me, a daughter who needed me even more. Didn't care that the alcohol was killing my spirit and turning me into a man my family genuinely hated. And then when I finally did realize what I had lost, and what I had become, it was much too late.

I spent a full year in a stupor, trying to forget the look on my daughter's face when she summed the whole thing up so beautifully: "You're not my daddy anymore," she said the last time I saw her, "because you're a bad man."

I emptied hundreds of bottles in her memory after she spoke those words, savoring the simple truth of that baldly elegant statement. And when I finally got tired of emptying bottles, I broke one and carved up my wrists with a sliver of glass. Pathetic, if you want to sum it up bald and elegant.

The little girl tugged my sleeve again, and I jerked away, imagining her fingers brushing across the scar tissue on my wrists, imagining that the red material of the Santa suit was stained with my blood.

"Please let me tell you my wish."

"Okay." I pushed away my memories, feeling a

strange combination of sorrow and glee. "But you have to tell me something first. Have you been a good girl this year?"

Her forehead wrinkled in deep thought—and my heart melted a little bit more because I'd forgotten all the perfectly genuine expressions that kids have—and then she gave me a very serious nod. "I think so. Mommy says that I'm a good girl all the time."

"I'm sure your mom wouldn't lie," I said. "Now, you give me the word, and I'll give it to the big guy at the North Pole."

She moved closer, and her voice became a whisper. "I don't want any toys." She paused and looked around, as if someone might be listening to her little secret, as if an eavesdropper could render the wish null and void in Santa's eyes. "I just want Santa to bring me a brand new daddy for Christmas. And I want him to make my real daddy go away."

My heart skittered, then started beating faster. I looked at the little girl and suddenly saw my daughter, and a hot sheen of sweat dampened my face.

You're not my daddy.

My mouth was running before I knew what to say. "Now, sweetie, I'm not so sure that Santa Claus can bring you that type of present. Wouldn't you rather have a pretty new dress?" *Or a coat that fits?* I thought, looking again at the tattered things she was wearing.

She didn't say anything, but that didn't keep me from hearing the other voice in my head. *You're not my daddy, because you're a bad man.*

And then I was apologizing, alibiing for a man I didn't even know. "Look," I continued, "I'll bet your dad will get you something nice. I'll bet he already has a great big present for you right under the tree. I'll bet—"

"No!" A tear rolled down her cheek, and she wiped it away before anyone else could see it. "I don't *like* my daddy's presents. I want a new daddy, someone to make me and mommy happy. I just have to get one. You gotta help me."

Suddenly the Santa costume felt as heavy as a suit of armor; all the weight centered on my chest and stomach. And for the first time since going straight three years before, I thought of just how lucky my little girl was to have a real father now, someone to watch over her and protect her and love her. Someone who wasn't a *bad man* . . . even if he was a damn chiropractor.

My eyes misted over and I closed them. I didn't know what to say. I sent my own wish to Santa, Fed Ex. All I wanted for Christmas was the right answer for this little girl.

"Julie, what in the world have you done to Santa?"

I opened my eyes. The girl's mother was younger than I would have guessed, late-twenties probably. A mirror image of her daughter, another waif in faded jeans and a worn jacket, carrying a single Parker's shopping bag.

I grinned. This time it was reflex. I really didn't know what to do.

"I sure hope Julie hasn't been bothering you," the woman said. "I got held up in line and—"

I waved her off. "She was no trouble at all. We had ourselves a nice time talking."

The woman smiled and tousled Julie's hair. She was every bit as beautiful as her daughter, and every bit as tragic. Her eyes held the same sadness, but they never flashed bright the way her child's sometimes did. They were the eyes of a woman who had faced too much pain in her time and had given up the fight. Someone who was merely existing, not living.

Someone just like me.

"Well, I'll apologize anyway," the woman said. "Julie's a good girl"—Julie nudged my leg, as if to say *I told you so*—"but she can be a bit headstrong." The woman made a polite show of checking her watch. "Julie, honey, we really have to get going. We're already an hour late. You know how your father gets when his dinner isn't waiting for him."

"Okay. In a minute, Mom."

I smiled at the friendly mother-daughter battle waging before me, recalling the occasions when my wife and daughter had done the same.

But those days were gone.

You're not my daddy . . .

"Well, thanks again for being so nice to Julie," the woman said. "And have a Merry Christmas." She took Julie's hand. "Let's go, honey."

They were swallowed by the crowd and, just like that, the incident was over. Or so I thought.

A few seconds later, the little angel reappeared. "I almost forgot," she said, panting. "Please tell Santa this is where I live."

She handed me a piece of paper. The lined kind you tear from a small tablet. Three short sentences in careful block print. A street address that wasn't far from the mall.

Her hand drifted away slowly. Brushed my big black belt. Brushed the front of my red pants.

Her fingers lingered for just a second against my crotch.

She looked at me with those lonely eyes. "I'll do anything," she said. "Tell Santa I'll do anything if he gives me what I want."

Then her hand was gone, and she was gone, and everything was very clear.

I just want Santa to bring me a brand new daddy for Christmas. And I want him to make my real daddy go away . . .

You know how your father gets when his dinner is late . . .

I don't like my daddy's presents . . .

Tell Santa I'll do anything if he gives me what I want . . .

I stared at the slip of paper with Julie's address on it, thinking about the fierce determination on the little angel's face and the sad quiet beauty of her mother, knowing with complete clarity how life had molded them.

Understanding, for the first time, how life had molded me.

I called in sick more than I should have, made use of my days off, didn't sleep much. You can always find time to do things if you really want to, and I found that I wanted to do something for the first time in years. Besides, it wasn't like I had a ton of unfinished Christmas shopping or invitations demanding my presence at holiday parties hither and yon. No airplane ride to visit the relatives out west. No drive in the country to visit friends. No Christmas in Connecticut for me.

No, my social schedule was clear. I spent my time with Julie and her family, though they never knew that I was around.

The rusted mailbox in front of the house said COO-PER. The house itself looked like any other in the neighborhood, just another old ranch-style thing that needed work—new gutters, energy-efficient windows, some paint. There were no Christmas lights hanging from the eaves, no tree in the window. That wasn't unusual—more than a few of the Cooper's neighbors seemed to be getting along without the prescribed signs of seasonal cheer. The neighborhood was definitely not upwardly mobile, more like *we're-holding-on-by-the-skin-of-our-teeth*. But Julie's was the only house on the block where the snow mounded unshoveled on the walk, the only house where a television antenna stood in for a cable hookup.

None of that really surprised me, not at first. I'd seen the way Julie and Tina—that was her mom's name—dressed. I'd followed them to enough discount markets and cheap gas stations to know that things were tight with them.

I wasn't really surprised until I saw Julie's father for the first time. He glided past my parked car late one evening, lounging behind the wheel of a black Cadillac Seville that shone like a new eight ball. He parked next to the rattletrap Datsun that Tina drove, a hunk of Japanese metal that looked like Godzilla had had his way with it.

A couple days passed before our schedules meshed. Then I followed Mr. Cooper instead of Julie and Tina.

I hated him instantly. For one thing, he worked for the phone company. He was a big enough fish to warrant his own parking space, and he made a habit of

taking the bigger fish to lunch and picking up the tab.
I followed him into places where I could barely afford
the price of a Diet Coke and a bowl of soup. I
watched as he left generous tips for the waiters, and
I don't think I'll ever forget the satisfied little smirk
that crossed his lips when he gave his boss a pen-and-
pencil set from Parker's, a shoplifter's favorite that
would have set me back several day's pay. After work,
Cooper stopped off for drinks at a bar near the highway, a dive called the High Hat Club. Dropped more
tip money, though he kept to himself. Didn't spare
the booze, either. He was always pretty well tanked
by the time he headed home.

All this while his wife and daughter lived like
paupers.

That wasn't the only reason I disliked Julie's dad,
though.

His first name was Adrian. That went right along
with the little smirk.

And Adrian Cooper liked to rape his daughter.

It happened on weekends as far as I could tell. Tina
actually had a job on Saturday and Sunday at a run-
down florist shop over by the mall, but I knew the
job was just a ploy to get her out of the house.

I wondered if Tina even knew what was going on.
I figured she would have to be blind not to see it
somehow, but, then again, I'd specialized in being
blind for several years myself.

I sat in my car on two consecutive weekends, trying
not to be noticed on that gray little street. Four days,
and every one of them was the same. Tina would leave
for work. Shortly thereafter, the drapes would whisper
closed, and the lights would be extinguished. The last
drape to close and the last light to dim were always
in Julie's bedroom.

Several hours passed each time. Then the lights
came on and the drapes were opened, after which
Adrian packed the sullen little girl with the porcelain
complexion into his big black car and treated her to
an ice-cream sundae at the mall. I'm sure that in his
sick little mind that trip to the mall made everything

okay with him. The son of a bitch couldn't even see it. Slurping up his ice cream, fingers drumming so innocently on his pale daughter's knee.

Four days of that, and I saw everything as if I had X-ray vision. I sat there in my old car, watching the minutes tick by on the dashboard clock. It was all I could do to stay behind the wheel while it happened.

And then the last Sunday came, the Sunday before Christmas, and suddenly I realized I was done sitting.

The Caddy pulled out and headed for the mall. I made a U-turn and parked in front of the rusted mailbox that said COOPER. I got out and walked up the drive, and I didn't even bother to knock because no one who lived on the gray little street was paying attention.

I kicked in the door. Like I said, there wasn't a Christmas tree, but there were a few presents. It didn't surprise me that most of them were addressed to "Adrian" or "Daddy." I collected a stack, took them out to the car, and dumped them in the backseat, just to make it look good. I waited to hear the sirens, but there was no sound at all.

I returned to the house, and this time I closed the door behind me. Adrian and Tina had separate bedrooms. Adrian, of course, occupied the largest in the house.

It was a fairly boring room. Dull—if tasteful—furniture, stupid little Sharper Image gadgets, uninspiring prints on the wall, and a bed with a very hard mattress.

A stout, masculine dresser stood to the right of the bed. I searched the drawers and found stiff pin-striped shirts and argyle socks and other clothes that seemed designed especially for a phone company fast-track kind of guy. Other drawers housed Ralph Lauren clothes for fast-track-kind-of-guy weekends.

In the bottom drawer, beneath Adrian's Polo sweaters, I found a pistol.

So, the bastard was smart enough to be a little paranoid.

I figured the pistol was a sign that I was getting

close. I pulled up the lining paper glued to the bottom of the drawer. A large envelope was hidden underneath, along with a few kiddie porn magazines.

I dumped the pictures on the hard bed and saw the little girl with the face of an angel doing the things her daddy made her do.

But I only looked at her eyes.

After I left the house, I drove over to the florist shop and parked next to the battle-scarred Datsun with four balding tires.

Tina was inside, busily misting some ferns that hung near the cash register. I thought that she looked good in the cheap pink blouse with her name stitched over the pocket, and then our eyes met and I found myself remembering Julie's eyes in Cooper's secret pictures.

"Can I help you?" she asked, and it sounded like she'd break apart if I refused the offer.

"I hope you can." I tried to make it light, but I was a bundle of nerves. "I guess I'm just not a white Christmas kind of guy. I want something green. You know, something nice. Not a fern or anything. Something with flowers."

Her eyes narrowed. "I don't mean to sound weird or anything," she said. "But your voice—it sounds really familiar. Have we met?"

"Picture me with a long white beard."

"What?"

"Santa Claus." I smiled and found the expression was becoming a little more comfortable. "Parker's Department Store version, at your service."

She laughed, and it was a good sound. "I thought we'd met."

"Yeah. I guess there's something about a man in red that makes a lasting impression."

We stood there for a moment, staring at each other, and then she went into florist-shop mode. "So," she said, looking around, "we've established that you're not a fern kind of guy. Is this for a gift?"

"No. It's for me. I just want a little something to, y'know, brighten things up."

"If you want bright, maybe you should get another string of lights for your tree."

I shrugged. "I don't have a tree. I live alone." The statement sounded too blunt, so I tried to lighten it. "It's a really small apartment. I need all the oxygen for myself."

That fell flat.

"Sorry," Tina said. The word slipped out as a sigh, and she left it at that. I recognized the ploy. She didn't *ask* any questions because she didn't want to be *asked* any questions.

"So?" I said.

"How about this." She was smiling now, holding a little pot with some kind of miniature bush in it.

"I don't know," I said. "I'm looking for something with flowers. And this looks like one of those Japanese bonsai things—"

"No." Her voice brightened. "It blooms. It's a miniature rose."

"What color?"

"White."

I nodded, and we moved over to the cash register. The top button of her blouse was undone, and I could still see the porcelain skin of her neck . . . and the bruise that began at her collarbone and ran God knows where.

She cringed a little, raising her arm, working the register buttons. I didn't say anything, even though the picture of her husband's little smirk was locked up tight in my head without possibility of parole. *Fair trade,* that smirk said, *a little pain for a late dinner.*

She took my money, and I started for the door. Then something inside me switched gears, and I stopped short. "I've got a question for you," I said.

"Shoot."

"Miniature roses—if you treat them right, do they grow up to be regular roses?"

She shrugged. "I really don't know."

I stood there a moment, just to let a beat pass, and then I shrugged. "Well, I guess I'll just have to wait and find out for myself."

"You'll let me know?" Tina asked.

"I'll let you know," I said.

I didn't realize then, but it was the first promise I'd made in years.

The black Caddy with the billiard ball shine pulled away from the parking spot marked A. COOPER, and I followed it into the night.

Adrian had worked late—three hours overtime by my estimation—but that didn't matter to me. Now that his day was over, everything was going to go smoothly. Adrian was going to hit the High Hat Club. I was going to join him. Belly up with Mr. Fast Track and strike up a conversation, if that was possible. Order a beer, my first in three years, and hold myself to just one, if *that* was possible (and I prayed that it was). Maybe we'd talk about the kind of magazines that came in brown paper wrappers, or trade tips about how to find camera shops that were willing to print pictures of naked children if you were willing to shell out some of the cash your wife and kid never saw. In short, I wanted to watch old Adrian sweat a little bit, just so I would know what that looked like. I wanted to see him loosen his expensive tie, and I wanted to sniff the air and learn just how effective his expensive deodorant was.

But if he was all chatted out after a tough day shilling 800 numbers, that was okay too. I could wait. I could bide my time. Either way, when Adrian left the High Hat, I planned to be right behind him, closer than he could imagine. Closer even than his own shadow.

The Caddy eased onto the freeway and dipped into traffic. I followed. I was signaling for the exit near the High Hat when Adrian changed lanes and headed south. Sweat beaded on my forehead, and a hole seemed to open up in my guts. This wasn't right. This wasn't supposed to happen.

And then Adrian's turn signal was flashing. He took the Briarwood exit, traveled a road I knew by heart, and made the same turn I'd made morning after morning for the last three years, ever since I'd gotten sober.

There weren't many empty parking spaces, it being the Monday before Christmas, so Adrian Cooper parked his Caddy in a handicapped spot near the big glass doors of the mall that housed Parker's Department Store.

I started to worry when closing time came and there was no sign of Mr. Adrian Cooper. Then I remembered what kind of guy he was. Cooper certainly thought he held a paramount spot in the universe. Such an important personage wouldn't think anything of holding up a few working stiffs so he could get what he wanted.

The thought got under my skin and stayed there. As if on cue, Adrian exited the mall's smoked glass doors. A slash of bright light knifed across my feet, and then the door whispered closed and the light was gone. I stood to one side of the door, just some nobody Adrian had to step around, and I welcomed the shadows and the soft green light that painted the snow-covered parking lot.

Adrian's expensive loafers crunched over the fresh snow. He balanced a stack of boxes which were wrapped in the signature silver-foil wrap of my employer.

The Caddy was one of two cars parked in the first row.

Adrian noticed what I'd left for him quicker than I'd expected.

"Shit," he muttered, setting the boxes on the hood of the Caddy and snatching something from under the windshield wiper.

It wasn't what he had expected. It wasn't a parking ticket.

His knees actually quivered. He nearly went down. I enjoyed seeing that.

I walked over and took the little picture of Julie out of his hand.

"This is what it feels like," I said.

He didn't seem to hear me. I took the keys out of his hands, opened the door before he could protest.

"We have to talk," I said, lowering a leather-gloved hand on his shoulder, pushing him into the car.

The first thing Adrian did was loosen his tie. Then he started to sweat, and the Caddy was choked with a scent both raw and spicy.

We were parked at the edge of the mall lot, next to a chain-link fence that rimmed a Christmas tree lot. The hour was late and the lot was closed. All I could see was a sprinkling of dim white Christmas lights; a giant inflatable Santa, arms bobbing under the weight of fresh snowflakes; and the stark, spindly silhouettes of the cheap, dead trees.

"I bet Julie would like a tree," I said.

Adrian Cooper nodded.

I laughed, kicked at the silver paper around my feet, and shifted the boxes so my hands were free. "You know, she still believes in Santa Claus."

Adrain sputtered, "I—I didn't realize that."

"And you know what else?" He didn't reply, but our eyes met, and it killed me that even in this moment his blue eyes held more spark than either Tina's or Julie's. "No," I continued, "you don't know, so I'll tell you. Julie knows something most seven-year-olds don't know. She knows how to come on to Santa Claus. She's a little kid who had to learn how to whore just to survive. And you taught her that. You're the one who twisted her."

Cooper's hands were tight on the steering wheel. He didn't say a word.

"Aren't you going to offer me money?" I asked.

"I . . . I don't think . . . you want money."

"You're right about that." I reached into my coat, and my fingers closed around the pistol I'd taken from Adrian's stout, masculine dresser. "You know, I had a wife and kid once. A little girl, just like Julie. A woman just as pretty as Tina. I blew it with them. Oh, not as bad as you. Not nearly as bad as you. But I blew it. See, I was a smash-up-the-family-car kind of guy, a come-get-me-out-of-jail kind of husband. A sorry-I-missed-Christmas kind of dad.

"With me it was the bottle. That's a sickness. But I woke up and saw it. I faced it down until I memorized every ugly scale on the monster's hide. And I learned how to control it. Things are better now."

Adrian's voice was very quiet. "Maybe I can . . ." He hesitated, searching for the right word.

I found it for him. "Change? Maybe you can. I'm not saying it's impossible. But I don't think that it's going to happen. And I don't think Julie and Tina can count on the odds you'd give them."

One hand stayed on the pistol. The other hand drifted over one of the boxes from Parker's Department Store. My gloved fingers brushed the wisps of red silk nestled in tissue paper. I hooked the spaghetti straps, lifted the teddy, and watched it dance in the shadows. It didn't seem any bigger than a handkerchief, really.

"Amazing," I said. "I didn't know that they made these things so small. What did you tell the salesgirl, anyway? You tell her that your wife was Vietnamese?"

"Look," Adrian said, "if you're going to do something—"

I slipped the gun from my pocket. I could hardly feel it with my hands sheathed in heavy gloves.

"Wait a minute." His blue eyes were focused on me instead of the gun. "I know this is going to happen. I know I can't stop you. But I think it would be easier on both of us if you give me the gun. I'd rather do this myself."

I thought it over. I really wanted to believe him.

But I couldn't, and that was sad. "I can't play those odds, Cooper," I said.

He closed his eyes. I stared down at the Christmas card which had been covered by the skimpy teddy. On the front, a cartoon man wearing a goofy grin, saying, "You're invited to trim my tree." On the inside flap, same man, naked and grotesque. "All it takes is two red balls."

Under that, scrawled in expensive ink from a Parker's Department Store pen:

LOVE MY LITTLE GIRL,
DADDY

Adrian Cooper said, "Are you sure—"
He never finished the sentence.

When they lowered the coffin into the grave, I was thinking that it should have been wrapped with a big red bow.

Tina and Julie buried Adrian Cooper on Christmas morning. I interpreted that as a good sign, a sign that Tina wanted to lay the past to rest and move on. No one else attended the funeral but the minister, and he was in and out in a matter of minutes. Everyone's busy on Christmas.

Everyone but me.

I stayed in the shadows, standing over the grave of a man I didn't know with flowers in my hands. It looked like Adrian's death would be ruled a suicide. I had been pretty careful—I'd worn gloves when I pulled the trigger, and then, after Adrian was dead, I'd twisted his fingers around the weapon and fired a shot through the open window. And if there wasn't a suicide note, the ripped up greeting card, torn photos, and lingerie seemed to stand in pretty well in the minds of the homicide detectives.

Still, I wasn't willing to take any unnecessary chances by getting too close to the ceremony. Cops love to watch funerals, I'm told. So I viewed the proceedings from a distance, and I saw a little girl and her mother standing over a dirt grave rimmed by a meadow of snow, their faces showing nothing, but their fingers interlocked.

I guessed it was as good a start as any. God knows there have been worse. But the real start came a moment later, when the two of them turned and walked toward Tina's Datsun.

I had to stop myself from chasing after them, and it was probably the hardest thing I've ever done. I stood there in the cold, flowers gripped in my gloved hands, remembering the deuce of hearts I'd drawn on the day I met Julie. I thought of her father and his black heart, and I wondered what color my heart was after all done.

The Datsun took off under a cloud of smoke. Four bald tires left black lines in the snow.

And everything was very quiet.

Snow dusted the gravestones, so very white. I thought about the white rose sitting all alone in my apartment, and the gray little neighborhood where Tina and Julie lived. All those houses that no one seemed to care about. Maybe one of them was waiting for someone to come along and give it some special attention.

I found, to my surprise, that I was making plans again, but this time they were the kind of plans that were meant to be shared.

And standing there in the snow, I began to wonder how soon my miniature rose would flower.

FULL-BODY SANTA

by Terry Beatty and Wendi Lee

Detective Jack Buell was convinced this had to be the stupidest case he'd ever been sent on. A missing box of candy containers? Come on. There were only a few days left until Christmas and he was still trying to scrape together enough money to buy the damn video game system his kid wanted, and he didn't have a clue what to get for his wife. He thought the blender last year was a good idea, but she'd just looked at him like he'd given her a lump of coal. Oh well, at least this would be better than trying to track down the Christmas decorations that had been reported stolen out of yards all over town. Last year it was hood ornaments, this year it's big plastic snowmen. What'll kids think of next?

Jack pulled his unmarked car up to Marjorie Palmer's house and got out. He stood and blew on his cold, gloveless hands for just a moment as he looked at the house, a big yellow-brick, art deco affair. There were a few strings of tastefully small Christmas lights blinking in the windows, and the walkway to the door (on which hung a gold-colored artificial wreath) was carefully shoveled of any trace of snow. Whoever lived here could probably afford all the video game systems they wanted.

Jack pressed the doorbell and was treated to the ringing of chimes playing the first few notes of that religious Christmas song he could never remember the name of. He'd have to ask his wife what it was called.

"Oh thank goodness you're here!" Marjorie Palmer exclaimed as she opened the door and ushered Jack into her home. "It's gone. My mint box of full-body

167

Santas is just gone!" She was a large, plump woman in her late forties, with short dark hair and a youthful air about her.

"Full-body Santas?" Jack asked, not sure he wanted to know the answer.

"From my Pez collection. Didn't they tell you? I told the officer over the phone," she said nervously.

"I was told there was a box of candy containers stolen. Why don't you tell me the whole story?" Jack took a small notebook and a pen from his inside coat pocket.

"Let me show you," she said as she led Jack through a house full of antique furniture he could never begin to afford. One piece particularly caught his untrained eye: a softly lit green globe, held aloft by a bronze statue of an elegantly posed nude woman. The figure stood on an otherwise empty and sharply angular blond-wood table. It was a dramatic contrast. Jack followed Marjorie down a hall to a room that in most houses would have been a bedroom, but in this one was something else. "This is the Pez room," she said.

Jack stepped inside and looked at shelf after shelf, all of them covered with little plastic candy dispensers, brightly colored rectangles, each topped with the head of some cartoon or TV character. Tweety Pie and Mickey Mouse shared shelf space with Zorro and the Frankenstein monster. So far Jack was right—this was the stupidest case he'd ever encountered. Who the hell would want to collect these, let alone steal them?

"This is the most complete collection of Pez candy dispensers in the country. At least it was until the Santas went missing." There was pride and hurt in her voice at the same time.

"Can you describe the missing item or items?" Jack asked, ready to take notes.

"It was a mint-condition box of twelve full-body Santa Claus Pez dispensers, still sealed in its original cellophane wrapping, yellow and white with the Pez logo on the side."

"What do you mean by 'full-body Santas'?"

"Oh, most Pez are just a molded plastic head on top of the standard candy dispenser, but these are early rare examples of a full-figure dispenser. And as you can imagine, to turn up a sealed box, well it's just unheard of."

Actually, he couldn't imagine—the only thing he cared about collecting was his paycheck. "Are these items valuable?" Jack asked, not believing that the answer could possibly be yes.

"Oh goodness, yes!" Marjorie clasped her hands together. "A single full-body Santa typically sells for one hundred to a hundred twenty-five dollars. The contents of the box alone would be worth from twelve hundred to fifteen hundred dollars. And the fact that it's a sealed mint-condition box on top of that, who knows what it could be worth?"

Jack hoped that his jaw hadn't dropped open too far, afraid he'd look like one of the cartoon characters staring at him from the shelves. "Fifteen hundred, ma'am?"

"Or more," she replied.

"Are there other collectors in the area?"

"Not that I know of," she replied, her brow furrowing in thought. "And I've had dealings with most of the Pez collectors in the country. We're a relatively small group, compared to, say, comic book collectors."

"And this is the only item missing? Aren't any of the other pieces valuable?"

"That's what I don't understand," she replied, a mystified expression on her face. "The Santa box is the most desirable piece in the collection, but many of these individual dispensers are quite valuable on their own. Maybe the thief just didn't have time to take more." Marjorie raised her eyebrows and shrugged.

"Have you noticed any sign of forced entry—any idea how a thief could have gotten in here?" Jack asked.

"Well, no. But I did go out this morning to do some Christmas shopping, and well, when I got home, I realized I'd forgotten to lock the front door. I don't know how I could have done it, I mean I'm terribly embarrassed, but that's when I noticed the box of Santas was missing." Marjorie smiled a nervous smile as Jack wondered what kind of nut, with access to this house full of antiques, would choose to steal only a box of candy containers, valuable or not.

Marjorie told him she had gotten the box about a month ago at a small auction house on the edge of town. She'd paid a little over three hundred for it, but couldn't tell him much about the bidder she was pitted against. Jack hoped the auctioneer kept good records or had a good memory.

Jeff Crown was the owner and chief auctioneer of Crown Auctions Inc. He was tall and lanky, fortyish, with close-cropped salt-and-pepper hair and a full mustache. The auction house, a large metal building, was empty except for row after row of metal folding chairs—no auction today.

"Oh sure, I remember that auction. Couldn't believe that little box of Santy Clauses would bring so much money. Three hundred thirty, I think," Jeff said, smiling and shaking his head. "Crazy, huh?"

"Would you have a record of the bidders?" Jack asked.

"Everything goes into the computer. Got a full record of who bought what for the past ten years. Don't know how we ever got along without one."

"I know who the winning bidder was, but would your computer records show who was bidding against her?"

"No, they wouldn't tell you that, but I sure can."

Jack looked up from taking his notes. "Really?"

"Sure," Jeff answered with a big smile, "Tom Foster—he's a toy collector. Comes to the auction all the time. He went nuts here last week. Bought a whole bunch of old model kits at ten bucks apiece. Can you imagine?"

After seeing the Pez room, Jack thought he could

imagine just about anything. "Can you get me his address from your records?"

Tom Foster's house was a far cry from Marjorie
Palmer's. Not that it was a dump or anything, just a
modest two-story bungalow, but the place screamed
Christmas. There were large plastic lit-up Santas and
snowmen and elves all over the yard. The house was
covered in multicolored Christmas lights all blinking
in a chaotic jumble that would give an epileptic a sei-
zure. In the window, an oversized poster of a colorful
Santa wished everyone a Merry Christmas while holding a bottle of Coca Cola in his mittened hand. There
was a doorbell, but it was covered with a piece of
tape, so Jack assumed it was broken. He knocked on
the door.

"Merry Christmas! Ho, ho, ho!" The door opened
and there stood Santa Claus. Jesus Christ! The guy
was dressed like Santa Claus. And he was perfect for
the part—short, fat and jolly.

"Are you Tom Foster?" Jack asked, hoping he
didn't have another cartoon look on his face.

"Sure am. What can I do ya for?" he said, a big
smile behind his fake Santa beard.

Jack explained who he was and why he was there.
Foster invited him in and explained he was trying on
his Santa suit for an upcoming event at the local Boys'
Club.

"Geez, I spend so much money on my toy collection, sometimes I feel guilty about it. So when Christmas comes I do the Santa thing and distribute toys to
underprivileged kids. It's not much, but hey, Santa
was always good to me, and I don't want any kids to
miss out on that."

If the prices of Tom's toys were similar to the prices
of Marjorie Palmer's, then Tom Foster had indeed
spent a lot of money on his collection. It seemed that
every room of the house was full of bookshelves, but
the shelves weren't full of books. They were full of
toys. Here there was a tin wind-up Popeye, there a
plastic model kit of the Creature from the Black La-

goon. Stuffed dolls of Little Lulu and her tubby boy-friend (what was his name?) rubbed elbows with Batman, Howdy Doody, and Charlie McCarthy. There were games, puzzles and puppets. There were metal lunchboxes, G. I. Joes, dinosaurs—and standing quietly among the other toys, a few Pez dispensers.

Jack asked about the auction.

"Heck yes," Tom said, "I remember that. Thought I was gonna make a killing by picking up those Pez cheap and sellin' 'em to Marge Palmer."

"So you know Ms. Palmer?" Jack asked.

"No, but I know of her. She's the foremost Pez collector in the whole dang country. Got want ads in all the collector magazines. Been written up in most of 'em. When I realized it was her I was bidding against, I dropped out."

"Why?"

"I wanted 'em for resale. She wanted 'em for her-self. Geez, she's got the money to pay full value for stuff, so I didn't have a chance. Anyway, I think stuff ought to belong to who wants it the most. Let her have a bargain. I've had my share of mine—like those model kits there."

"What about them?" Jack asked.

Tom pointed at a shelf loaded with a half dozen sealed model kits, their colorful logos announcing they contained various monsters and comic book heroes—Bride of Frankenstein to Captain America. "Paid ten bucks apiece for 'em at auction. They're worth hundreds."

Jack, now firmly convinced the world was entirely populated by crazy people, asked, "So you wouldn't want those candy containers enough to steal them?"

"Hey, I'm Santa Claus! I'm into givin', not takin'," Tom replied in a goofy good-natured sort of way.

"So you wouldn't object to a search of your home?"

He shrugged. "I guess not. But you'd have to be careful with the toys. I've got mint-condition stuff here. One little ding on some of this and the value goes kerblooey."

"Anything else you can tell me?"

"Don't think so. Are you going to talk to the other guy who bid on 'em?"

Jack looked up from his notebook. "The other guy?"

"Sure," Tom said, "the skinny guy with the long red hair and beard who dropped out when the bidding hit five bucks. Geez, he was damn near heartbroken he didn't get 'em. Kept comin' over and askin' me questions about what they were worth and who the lady was who bought 'em."

"And you told him?"

"Yeah. A quick look in the *Pez Price Guide* would tell him what they're worth, and in toy collecting circles Marge Palmer is famous. Most of the Pez pictured in the *Guide* are from her collection."

Stifling an urge to ask about the *Pez Price Guide*, Jack asked for a more complete description of the other bidder.

"He was probably in his late thirties or early forties, but he looked older, you know, like he'd had a tough life. And he was skinny, but not scrawny, kind of tough-lookin'. Funny thing, though."

"What's that?"

"When he didn't get those Santa Pez, I think he darn near cried."

After getting some good information from Foster about where to get a good price on that video thing his kid wanted, and telling the guy that the police probably wouldn't need to come search through his toy collection, Jack got back in his car and headed toward the station. He'd go file his report on this thing. But he figured his chances of turning up this scraggly Pez thief were about as good as those of him figuring out what his wife wanted for Christmas.

Except, there he was. Not ten blocks from Foster's house, in an area where the homes started running toward dumps but were covered with Christmas decorations nonetheless, here was a skinny guy with long red hair and a beard, dressed in a T-shirt and blue jeans (despite the cold winter weather), running frantically down the sidewalk with a big, plastic, lawn snowman under his arm. A few houses down, a guy in a bathrobe and slippers stood in his snow-filled yard yelling, "Bring that back, you son of a bitch!"

"Thank you, Santa Claus," Jack muttered as he sped up and then pulled his car over about half a block up from the running thief. He got out of his car and bounded through piles of snow to flash his badge at the guy. But before he could say anything to the nut, who was running right at him, Jack slipped and fell on a patch of ice on the not-very-well-shoveled sidewalk. The guy with the snowman leapt over him and kept running.

"Shit," Jack said as he hauled himself to his feet and took off after the guy. After four blocks Jack nearly caught up with him, but the thief countered, swinging around and clobbering Jack with the plastic snowman, a hard blow right to the face. Jack slipped again on another patch of ice, his feet flying out from under him. He hit the sidewalk hard this time, knocking the wind out of him. Groaning, he silently wished that Marjorie Palmer had had *these* walks cleared.

Jack pushed himself up, slower this time, to see his assailant, still packing his big plastic weapon, turn down Noel Avenue, a one-block street with a cul-de-sac at the end. "Got him," Jack said to himself. Hobbling down the street, Jack was certain that he would find his thief in the house with the most Christmas decorations. This guy was a Christmas collector! But unlike Palmer or Foster, he had no money to buy his toys, so he stole them. This guy was Anti-Claus—stealing from everyone else to put toys under his own Christmas tree.

But when Jack turned the corner to Noel, all the houses were lit up like Christmas. Here in one of the poorest sections of town, every house was decked out like a float in the Christmas parade. Every house but one.

At the end of the street was a little gray place, desperately in need of paint, heavily curtained windows hiding the inside from prying eyes, its sidewalks unshoveled. And there was a trail of newly made foot-prints leading right to the front door.

Jack trudged through the unshoveled snow to knock on the door. "Police. Come to the door, please."

From inside came a pathetic voice. "No. I won't let you in. You're trying to steal Christmas!"

This guy had it backward. "I can get a warrant. I'll be coming in sooner or later," Jack shouted through the door.

The door opened, and through it came a big inflat-able candy cane which bonked Jack on the head. "You're the Grinch! You're the Grinch!" the lunatic shouted as he hit Jack on the head again. Jack, now convinced he was living in a cartoon world, grabbed the candy cane away from the guy. "You're the Grinch," the nut said one more time, and then he sat down on the floor and started to cry.

Later, after the thief had been hauled away, still crying and hollering about the Grinch, Jack and sev-eral uniformed officers went through the house. It was filled to the brim with Christmas stuff, a tree in every room, lawn ornaments where furniture should have been. Most of this stuff was probably stolen property, but Jack doubted they'd ever be able to turn up all the owners and return it all. This guy had been doing this for years, from the look of the place. It took a lot of searching, but among all the decorations and stockings and wrapped packages, they finally found the box of Santa Pez. The thief had opened it, and set the dozen Santas on a shelf, all in a row.

When Jack returned the opened box and the now loose Santa dispensers to her, Marjorie cried almost as hard as the thief had when his Santa fantasy came tumbling down. These were now just ordinary loose Pez figures, she explained, the box's mint value de-stroyed when it was opened.

Jack described the thief to her and her eyes wid-ened. It seems that this was the poor soul she had hired to shovel her walks this winter. He'd knocked on her door and given her a sob story. She couldn't resist helping him out. Well, he cleared her sidewalk all right. Tough luck for him that he didn't bother with his own.

As a thank you, Marjorie gave Jack one of the Santas. Driving home with the plastic figure sitting on the dashboard of his car, he wondered if his wife would like to start a Pez collection.

SOUTHERN JUSTICE

by Billie Sue Mosiman

Bigdaddy hadn't talked about Uncle Raymond since we heard he had died on the shrimp boat in the Gulf of Mexico. Oh, he said a couple of important things when he came back from the morgue in Mobile where he had to identify his son. That night at the supper table he said to Bigmama, "It wasn't an accident."

"What do you mean, Billie? He drowned, they say."

"He didn't drown. His neck was broke."

I sat at the end of the table, forgotten. I pushed a mess of peas and cornbread around on my plate. It was hot, summer, not even a breeze blowing the sheer white curtain at the window. I didn't want to be privy to this conversation. But my grandparents had raised me from a baby, and they didn't keep any secrets from me. They knew of all the grandchildren, I was the one most likely to be trusted. I was so quiet sometimes, I faded into the background of their lives. We all liked it that way. Children were not supposed to speak until spoken to. I had little to say, but quite a lot to think about. Grown-up life seemed endlessly complex and fascinating. Even death had its shadowy crevices and hidden niches. Especially this death.

Every time Bigmama talked about her son, she cried. She was crying now, daubing at the corners of her eyes beneath her glasses with her apron. "I don't want to hear any more," she said weakly.

"I just thought you should know. Someone broke his neck. When I picked up his head, it turned easily side to side. This was no drowning accident."

I almost said, "Did you tell them, Bigdaddy? Did

177

you tell the police?" But it wasn't my place. He must have had his reasons. Mulling it over I expected the reasons had to do with Uncle Raymond being a drinker and carouser that gave the cops of Mobile some grief when he was on shore raising hell after his shrimping trips.

They had called when the body was brought in and said the crew told it this way: Something got caught in the shrimp boat's prop. Raymond was the best swimmer they had on board. He volunteered to swim under the boat and untangle the prop. He got caught some way. He drowned. End of story. It seemed plausible to the police so no investigation was begun. Accidents happened all the time while out at sea. Couldn't be helped.

I went to the funeral and nursed a broken heart while Bigmama cried and Bigdaddy stood over the grave with his fists clenched until the family led him away.

Summer died in a swelter of heat that left us all prostrate before the box fans. Bigmama halfheartedly shelled the peas, shucked the corn for the chickens, worked on a quilt. I read books about fairies and elves, dreaming of far happier kingdoms than the ones on earth. When I remembered, I'd sneak looks at my grandmother's closed face. It held back grief the way a dike holds back the sea. In stalwart fashion, unyielding. Bigdaddy puttered in the field some, but spent most of his time off at the Blue Hole with a fishing pole. I don't think he fished much. He hardly ever brought anything home. A few blue gill. A catfish. Not enough, Bigmama said, to cause her to want to warm a skillet.

School days were full of ennui. I couldn't wait for the Christmas holidays. Finally they came, fabulous freedom from dull teachers teaching duller subjects. I could hardly recall the summer heat, the funeral, but I keenly felt Uncle Raymond's absence when Bigdaddy and I went into the woods to find a thick round cedar tree to decorate. He always came home for Christmas.

In town Bigmama gave me five dollars to use for buying gifts. I found a box of embroidered handkerchiefs for her and a little pocketknife for Bigdaddy. He might whittle me a slingshot if I asked nice.

Outside Woolworth's the sidewalk was packed with shoppers, children begging, lights twinkling from store windows. As Bigmama and I tried to make our way to the drugstore for an ice cream soda, we were forced to the edge of the sidewalk and right up against a barrel-bellied man in a Santa Claus suit, a brass bell held aloft in his hand. Bigmama halted in her steps. She stared at the Santa for long seconds. I realized he was taking donations in his big black iron pot for the Salvation Army, but I knew what my grandmother was thinking. Raymond had been the one who dressed as a Santa on Christmas mornings for the grandchildren when we had family gatherings for the holiday. There was even something about this stranger's Santa smile, the shape of his lips beneath the white beard that reminded me of my Uncle Raymond. I looked quick to check Bigmama, see if she noticed. She must have. She had already moved away in the opposite direction and she had a hand up to her forehead to shield her eyes.

All winter long Bigdaddy brooded in front of the fireplace. He didn't fish anymore. He didn't even go into Paul to sit on the store benches with the other old men to gossip. Some of the neighbors came by to see what was the matter, but all they got was a cup of coffee and a slice of cake. Nothing to take back to tell the others.

When spring came again, Bigmama broached the subject they must have been discussing in the privacy of their bed nights when I couldn't hear. "It's time to go." I knew this was a serious pronouncement. I watched them closely. She put her hand on his slumped shoulder where he sat in the rocker before the dead-cold hearth. His dazed gray eyes fastened on her.

"Did you hear me, Billie? I want you to go get the one who took our boy. I want you to make him pay for his evil."

"They might not take me on," he said, rousing himself, a spark coming back to his eyes.

Bigmama made a sound in the back of her throat that denied he had an excuse. "They take on men older than you when they can get them cheap."

I lay on my belly on the floor cutting paper dolls out of a Sears Roebuck catalog. I almost asked who would take him on, where was he going, what was the plan anyway, but patience usually got me the information I wanted so I held my tongue. I put the scissors down and smoothed the page. I already had too many paper dolls anyway. Enough to people five playhouses if I wanted.

"You know which boat took him out, don't you?" Bigmama asked. "You go to them before the season gets started good and you get on the crew. You shrimped before. You know what to do."

"I know I might go to prison for what I'm going to have to do, that's what I know."

Bigmama turned her back and went to the open door. She stood staring out at the dusty road. She shooed a banty rooster from the porch. "They broke his neck," she said simply. "You going to let them get away with it?"

Bigdaddy rose from the rocker like a man older than Methuselah. "No. I never intended they would. You just ought to know if I get caught, I won't be coming back."

She nodded. I saw her nod, but I know it must have been a notion that scared her out of her wits. I jumped to my feet. I wasn't supposed to interfere, but this time it was necessary. "Don't go, Bigdaddy! They might kill you, too." I wrapped my arms around his waist and hugged him so he couldn't move. "Bigmama, tell him. Tell him not to go." He smelled of tobacco and good honest sweat. I could have stood there forever, soaking in his smell, keeping him close and safe.

He clasped the back of my head and pulled me clear. He tilted my chin so I could look into his face. "I'd do the same for you, Sugar Baby. If anyone ever hurt you, I'd go after him. I wouldn't give up until I made him pay a thousand times over. Didn't I drive my old truck all the way to West Texas when your mama called to come get you? Wouldn't I walk through fire to get you if I had to?"

"But why can't the police do it. Why do *you* have to go?"

"Some things don't get done by people in authority. It ain't their fault. They can't right all the wrongs or catch all the crooks and the killers. This is family business. I have to do it myself."

He'd do it for me. I knew that. He was my hero, my dragon-and-troll killer, my wise, gentle, and best-loved grandfather. He taught me to blow songs on a peach leaf; he let me ride on the cow's back while he led her with a rope; and he bought me penny candy, two-for-a-penny sugar cookies, and chocolate ripple ice cream cones. He loved his children and adored his grandchildren. He protected what was his and avenged the pain visited upon them.

Once, long before I was born, they said he worked a crew of men cutting timber on a WPA project. One of the workers sneaked off and, knowing my grandmother was alone, came to the house. He tried to attack and rape her. She had narrowly escaped by the back door, taking off for the cover of the dark woods behind the house. She cut her arms and legs on brambles; she was terrified to come home until after night had fallen. The next day Bigdaddy called his team of men together. He had them line up. "Now, one of you tried to rape my wife yesterday. I want the one who did that to step forward. Or better yet, why don't the innocent among you step back and leave the culprit out front on his own. I promise you, if this ain't done right away, everybody's going to get punished."

He glared them down and suddenly, it was said, two dozen men all stepped backward leaving one shaking, frightened man standing alone facing my grandfather.

It was the Depression. In South Alabama it was still a frontier justice kind of place. They say Bigdaddy walked the offender into the woods and the man never returned. It wasn't known if he just left the area for good or if he was shot and buried deep. I wouldn't want to make a bet either way.

With Bigdaddy gone shrimping, Bigmama and I fell into a silence that was thick as sorghum syrup. I kept pretending to be sick in order to miss school so I could be home if we had word from Mobile. Bigmama took up her husband's place in the rocker before the blackened fireplace. She was normally an energetic farm woman, used to hard work and never idle. That she was so still now worried me terribly. I tried to read to her from my storybooks, but she shushed me and cocked her head as if she was listening for something. The old black phone to ring. Or a car to turn into the drive.

"Will he really kill someone?" I asked one day out of sheer frustration and mounting trepidation.

She felt in her apron pocket and took out a can of sweet snuff. After depositing a bit just behind her lower lip she said, "I hope so."

"Isn't it a sin to kill people, Bigmama?" After all, she had taken a correspondence course on the Bible, Old and New Testaments—there was a diploma hanging on her bedroom wall to prove it—and she had to know the rules.

"That's right."

I waited. I knew she'd say more. There had to be some reasoning for murder that had escaped my youthful mind.

"An eye for an eye," she said finally. "The way of sin is death."

"Will Bigdaddy go to heaven?"

"I don't know. I don't think he cares. He's always been an old reprobate."

"But what if you go to heaven and he doesn't? Won't you miss him?"

"I don't know if I will," she said. "I don't know if

we remember anything in heaven. Besides, I told him to go to Mobile. If St. Peter won't let him enter the pearly gates, I 'spect he'll say the same to me."

I thought about that for a long time. I pretended to read again about toadstools and fairy princesses, but I was thinking about heaven and the man who was left standing alone in the work camp, and my Uncle Raymond, that smile of his that crinkled up his eyes and how he always brought me those big red-and-white peppermint sticks that lasted forever, bending over his pillow-belly in the Santa suit, ho-ho-ho-ing like the real thing. I thought about going under a boat where seaweed floated from a propeller, and then the seaweed turning into long strands of Raymond's hair, and Bigdaddy bearing down on the man who did it while the night was dark, a gaffing hook in his hand, and Bigmama standing on a big fluffy white cloud with St. Peter arguing the responsibility of family and avenging the death of the innocent because that's what the Good Book said: you take an eye, you lose an eye, you break a neck, you get yours broken, and that's a fact, just simple justice anyway you look at it.

The first we knew it was over, it was done and there would be no repercussions, was when Bigdaddy came home in the middle of the night late in the summer, trailing a scent of fish and dead sea things. Bigmama and I got up from bed, turning on all the lights, and I watched while she put a pot of coffee on the stove. We sat at the dining table, unable to keep our eyes from the doorway where he would enter and talk to us. We could hear the shower running. By the time the coffee had dripped and Bigmama had a saucerful cooled and already drunk, Bigdaddy came to the table in clean clothes, his bald head shiny, reflecting bold white glints from the overhead light.

"It was over a card game," he said, sipping at his coffee.

"They killed Raymond because of cards?" This was incredulous to my grandmother.

"He won too much. This one fellow's whole month's pay. They'd all been drinking, which was no excuse. There wasn't anything wrong with the prop. Raymond was jumped while sleeping. The other fellow was a big guy, very strong. When the nets got stuck, he was the one who hauled them in. He was on the crew again and I got into a card game with him once I found out the story."

"Did you cheat, Bigdaddy?"

He gave me a wink. "Of course I did. I took everything he had. Even his daddy's pocket watch. Even his shoes. But I gave them back. I wanted to hear him if he came into the cabin. Then I went to bed."

I held my breath. What if he'd actually gone to sleep? What if the huge man had killed my Bigdaddy, too?

"Well, what happened?" I asked, forgetting how quiet I always was, how I never butted into conversations. The entire time Bigmama sat with her hands in her lap, listening quietly.

"Let's just say that fellow's fish food on the bottom of the sea now. When we got into Mobile the captain reported he . . ."

"Drowned!" I finished for him.

"Good," Bigmama said, weeping softly and steadily now. "That's a fine thing. A very fine and decent place to end up."

That summer things finally returned to normal at my grandparents' house. Bigdaddy plowed under the field and made a tidy profit selling sacks of dry peas to surrounding farmers who envied his long purple-hull pea crop. Bigmama finished a quilt and gave it to me for the coming winter. My parents reconciled—the way they were always doing for short spurts of time—and came to get me for the next school year. I didn't want to go. I liked the smell of Alabama jasmine, the comfortable quiet nights on the porch swing between my grandparents, the sound of crickets outside my bedroom window.

Long years later, after Bigdaddy was taken to rest in the same cemetery where more of his children besides

Raymond had already been buried, I asked Bigmama about the man on the shrimp boat. Did she think Bigdaddy really killed him? Did he also kill the man during the Depression who threatened to rape her? Was Bigdaddy one of those old-time vigilantes who took the law in his own hands, or could it all have been imagination and untruths—or half-truths?

She put her old hand over mine. I remember it was cool as stream water in a dappled forest. And soft like tissue paper. She was so old I could see the purplish veins showing through the top of her liver-spotted hand and wrist. She gave me a wistful smile.

"Your Bigdaddy was a man to be reckoned with," she said. "I never saw the death certificates. I never saw the bodies, but I 'spect if you dig long enough out in the woods, you'll find a few stray bones, and if you scrape the ocean bottom awhile, you'll find some more. Who's to say who put them there?"

And in the end, what does it matter? That's what I decided. Like my Bigdaddy said, sometimes you can't leave it up to the proper authorities, you have to do what's right.

I just hope St. Peter knows how to handle all the gray areas of human relations. I'd like to think my grandparents found their way through the gate and into a heaven where parents know how to care for their own.

THE REAL THING

by Christopher Fahy

The Job Service guy looked up and said, "I just might have something for you."

Albert covered his mouth with his tattooed hand and coughed. "Oh yeah?" he said.

"I might." The Job Service guy was young, about twenty-four, with rosy round cheeks and a flop of dark hair hanging close to one eye. "Did anyone ever tell you you look like Santa Claus?"

"Well what do *you* think?" Albert said.

"Yeah, that's what I figured. Well Nelson's is looking for one. The sooner the better. You know where Nelson's is?"

"Of course."

"Here's the number to call." And he wrote on a pad, tore the sheet off, and held it out.

Albert took it and read, "Mr. Hawkins."

"He called us this morning. One of his Santas got hit with appendicitis yesterday. He's in a fix."

"It's worth a try," Albert said. "Thanks a lot."

At the Palace Hotel he paid for a shower, and now he was down to a dollar—four quarters. He held the coins in his fist as he washed himself. He combed his hair and beard in the broken mirror, put his clothes back on. They were all that he had to wear and smelled pretty bad. He put on his overcoat, checked it for spots, rubbed the obvious ones with his towel till they faded away. The coat had held up fairly well and would hide his frayed, torn clothes.

He walked four blocks to Chestnut Street, stopped in a discount drug, spent a quarter on a trial-size aftershave. In a phone booth he sprinkled his coat with the sweet-smelling liquid, then made the call.

The office was dingy gray, with piles of papers all over the place. A wire-mesh skylight with black blotches on it admitted a weak slice of sun.

"You ever been Santa before?" Mr. Hawkins asked. He was balding, paunchy, neat and trim in a pin-striped suit with vest.

"No," Albert said.

"There's a knack to it, it's not simply sit on my knee and what do you want. You have to relate. You like children?"

"I like them okay," Albert said, coughing into his fist.

Frowning, Hawkins said, "Sure, you can fake it. We've had a few Santas who faked it and did okay, but what we *really* want is a guy who's sincere. Understand?"

"Yes."

"You sure look the part," Hawkins said. "I'll say that much. Even your eyebrows—you'll hardly need makeup. The gloves will cover that tattoo."

"From my sailor days," Albert said, coughing again.

"Mmm. Your cheeks are a little thin, but other than that. . . . Let me hear your hos."

"What?"

"Ho, ho, ho. Let's hear it."

"Ho, ho, ho," Albert said.

Hawkins squinted and shook his head. "From the *gut.*"

"Ho, Ho, HO!"

"Mmm. I'm going to have someone work with you on it."

"I'm hired?"

"No, not till I see you in action. And first, you need to pass a TB test. Take this paper to Dr. Higgins down the street, twelve-forty-two. It'll take a few days to get the results."

"Yeah," Albert said.

"If we do take you on, we pay minimum wage.

You'd work four hours a day every day for the next two weeks—through Christmas Eve. We're open till ten, and you'll do the late shift."

"That's okay by me."

"Of course, if you're not any good—"

"I'll be good," Albert said. "I have a few days to practice."

"Come back when you pass the TB test, and Danny will show you how it's done. He starts at ten, so be here by nine."

"Okay."

"And one more thing. Cut down on that cologne you're wearing. Kids don't go for that."

To Albert's great relief, the TB test was negative.

He'd had the cough for two months now; it was why he was looking for work. On the job application he'd put his address as "Box 0023 Water Street"— which was accurate, though the postal service might quibble. He *did* live on Water Street, in a box, and 0023 was the model number of the freezer that box had once held. Perhaps if it wasn't a *freezer* box it might not be so cold, Albert thought.

Whatever, he had to get out of that box, and soon. To stay in it all winter long would kill him—or put him in City Hospital. He swore he would never go back there again; it was worse than the street, that place.

Albert needed a room away from the cold, away from the heavy wet air of the river. A room until spring and he'd be okay. With a couple of weeks at this job, he'd be able to pay for a room till the end of March and his cough would fade. He knew it would—once he had shelter with heat and a bed off the cold damp ground. Then a year from now his Social Security check would start and he'd be just fine. He wouldn't have to fight for deposit bottles with kids who had knives in their jackets and lacked all feeling in their hearts.

So all he had to do to survive this year was stay sober a couple of weeks. He had gone without drinking for more than three weeks five times in these past ten years, and now, with this job, he was sure he could hold out till Christmas.

He got enough money from bottles to wash his clothes, sat naked under his overcoat in the Laundromat, a legitimate customer, paying for rich steamy heat with no fear of a cop coming up and demanding he leave. When he put on the warm clean clothes in the Palace, after another tepid shower, he felt like a king.

The fellow named Danny said, "You think: Santa Claus, the good guy, right? But to real little kids he's a monster—they're scared to death. And some of them kick and scream and cry while their mamas insist that they talk to the monster, bare their souls. So here you are, stuck with this screaming kid, and the lights shine down, and everyone's looking, and other kids wait in an endless line with their folks. It can get really bad. And you gotta be Santa, Mr. Nice, keep smiling and talking real sweet. Ho, Ho—Hey, you really do look the part."

Albert watched from the sidelines when Danny was Santa and two of the kids backed out and two started crying, and one little girl threw herself on the floor and had something that looked like convulsions. But most of the kids were fine, and sat right up on Danny's lap, and Albert said to himself: I can do this, I really can.

But under the railroad bridge that night, in his freezer box, as a wet snow fell on the river, he couldn't sleep. He hadn't worked in seven years, and had never done anything even remotely like this. It was acting, that's what it was. He had taken an *acting* job. When he'd tried on the Santa Claus outfit he'd said to himself: I'm not *me* anymore—which felt good, surprisingly so. Thinking of this, he lay huddled against the cold, wide awake as the dark wind howled.

In the morning he paced the gray city streets, every cell in his body craving a drink. Just a small one—to ease his coughing and steady his nerves, and then no more. No! He battled the urge, walking quickly past wide windows brilliant with Christmas cheer—the trees, the garlands, twinkling lights—went into a store to warm his frozen face and hands, and there was a Santa, the line of children, the floodlamps. A photographer snapping the kids on Santa's knee. Tonight, that's me, he thought—and the doubts came on strong, and he wanted that drink worse than ever.

The day took forever to pass. He wandered in and out of five-and-dimes and drugstores, cafeterias. He couldn't eat, but God did he want a drink! At last it was five o'clock, and office workers clogged the sidewalks, hustling for buses and trains. Albert went into Nelson's, past glittering counters where perfumes were sold, and handbags, cosmetics. He went to the back, where the offices were.

"You're early. Good," Mr. Hawkins said. "You might as well get your suit on now."

"Right," Albert said, and went to the room where it hung in a metal locker.

As he changed his hands trembled. One small drink would set him up so fine. . . . When he saw himself in the mirror, though, he felt a surge of confidence. This is the best I've looked in years, he thought. And I *do* look like Santa!

He dabbed red circles of rouge on his cheeks as Danny had done, then chewed on a mint. Bad breath is the death of Santas, Danny had said, and while Albert's front teeth were in decent shape (thanks, no doubt, to superior genes), his molars—what remained of them—required attention, and sometimes his mouth turned sour.

He had no watch and there wasn't a clock in the room, so he waited, standing, staring at blue linoleum and mint-green walls, a calendar with a winter scene of Vermont, a row of gray file cabinets. At last a knock on the door—Mr. Hawkins. "You ready?" "I'm ready," said Albert. The door came open, and Hawkins entered. He nodded. "You look quite good. Walter's coming off now and you're on in five minutes."

"Okay," Albert said, and coughed.

And then he was walking, with Hawkins beside him, through tables of towels and quilts to the toy department. Three dozen TV sets showed the same frantic scene. "Okay," Hawkins said, "show time. I'll be watching."

Albert felt numb as he walked past the plastic reindeer, the blinking tree, and sat on the red plush throne. Floodlamps dazzled his eyes, his heart was pounding, and he felt like he had a fever. He looked at the line of parents and kids and swallowed hard and coughed and cleared his throat. Near his foot sat a bulging red sack tied shut with a crisp white satin bow. In the background he saw Hawkins staring.

He focused on the first kid in line, a girl about four years old, and said, "Your turn to see Santa." His voice was a squeak.

He expected to hear some giggles, but no, this was serious business. The girl came up shyly, her hand in her mother's, and sat on his lap, her eyes watchful and wary.

"And what's your name?" asked Albert, hoping his mint had worked.

The girl simply stared. Albert realized that she was shaking.

"Her name's Melissa," the mother said.

"Hello, Melissa," Albert said—and thought of Laura. How many years had it been since she'd sat on his lap? Over fifty. And no other children had sat on his lap since then.

"What would you like for Christmas, Melissa?" His voice was not right, but better.

Melissa looked close to tears. Her mother said, "Tell Santa, honey."

"I . . ."

"What, darling?" Albert said.

"A . . ."

"What?"

"Go on, sweetheart," the mother said. "Santa's busy, he has lots of children to see."

"A . . ."

"What?" Albert said. He was clammy and burning.

"A troll."

"A troll," Albert said with immense relief. "A troll. And what else?"

The girl hung her head.

"A troll," Albert said. "Good enough. And now Santa has something for you," he said, reaching into the basket that sat on a stand at his right. He took out a taffy and handed it to the girl.

Her pupils widened. She slid off his lap and his leg felt cool.

"Say thank you," the mother said, and Melissa did, staring down at her taffy, clutching her mother's hand and walking off.

I did it, Albert said to himself. *I did it. I'll be okay.*

The next kid came forward, a boy about five, and hopped right up on Albert's knee. He instantly started reciting his list, and Albert repeated the items, smiling, his voice at full volume now. *Repeat, but never, ever promise,* Danny had said. "That's plenty for Santa to remember!" Albert said winking and giving the boy his taffy. Next!

And on they came: the bold, the shy, the terrified, the greedy, the polite. The ones who said, "Are you the real Santa? Is that a real beard?" and "Real?" Albert would say, "Go on, give it a tug!" And they would, and leave convinced, the myth preserved.

Hawkins watched from beside a Christmas tree. At last he gave a time-out sign, and Albert said, "Santa has to go talk to his elves a minute, children. Be right back."

"You're hired," Hawkins said outside the men's room.

"Great," Albert said.

"Take a break every hour, stop at ten on the dot. You saw the clock?"

"No."

"It's off to your right, above the exit sign. You can't miss it."

"Okay. Mr. Hawkins?"

"What?"

"Something I forgot to ask you—when do I get paid?"

"When you finish the job. In two weeks."

"Christmas Eve?"

"No, two days later, on Wednesday. That's when our checks are cut."

"After Christmas?"

"Yes. I meant to tell you that before."

"Is there any chance that I could . . . receive an advance?"

"No, that's out of the question."

"I'm in a bad fiscal position right now."

"Sorry, wish I could help." Hawkins looked at his watch. "You're on again."

A few minutes into the session it dawned on Albert: he was a star! For one brief moment, he was the most important person in these children's lives. He resolved to let none of them down—not even the cranky, the surly, the stubborn. All got a pat on the back and a "Ho-ho-ho!" and a taffy and went away pleased.

When his four-hour stint was up, Albert was drained. The last time he'd talked to Laura—how many years ago? Seven? Eight?—she was teaching. Dealing with children day after day, their insecurities, their fears—he had a new appreciation of that now. Maybe he'd try to reach her again. This time he'd call cold sober and maybe she wouldn't hang up.

In the mint-green room he took off his costume, put on his only set of clothes and was just plain Albert again. He didn't much like that feeling—hated it, really. But later, hunched in his freezer box with the river flowing, flowing through the bitter night to the heartless open sea, he realized he didn't want a drink anymore. And he had good dreams.

Each night he enjoyed the work more. He'd go in early, after his lunch at St. Bernard's, and warm himself amidst racks of clothing, stacks of luggage, tiers of sparkling gems. He couldn't wait to don his suit and take his place on the throne. He loved the feel of the kids on his knee, loved watching their awestruck faces. "Let's look at that camera over there and—peanut butter and pickles!" he'd say, and the kid would grin and the shutter would click, and he'd think of Laura so long ago. "And this is for you," he'd say and present the taffy and think: This is why I was put on earth. This is what I was meant to do, what I'm good at, and why did it take me my whole life to learn it? Why did it take an accident, pure chance? All those people who told me I look like Santa, and still, I never caught on. Good grief but I'm thick!

His desire to drink had vanished. His cough had improved, though he still bedded down in a freezer box. Though he still ate his lunch at St. Bernard's, he felt better than he had in years.

After each session as Santa he'd take his sweet time getting changed, chatting sometimes with Freddy, the night security guard, a sour, scrawny, chain-smoking guy of about sixty-five with a holster that looked in grave danger of slipping down his hips. Albert didn't especially like Freddy, but hated to leave the warmth of the store and take the cold walk to Water Street. As he walked he would think of how his stock of days was diminishing. Soon, too soon, this job would end, and he would be plain old Albert again.

Three days before Christmas Eve, as a sad-looking boy expressed his fond wish for a pickup truck, Albert had a disquieting thought: Which of these kids would get what they asked for? Times were not good. How many of those who expressed their desires, cupping their hands to their hopeful mouths, and whispering in his failing ear, would see their desires fulfilled? How many would wake up excited on Christmas morning, their hearts in their throats, and race down the stairs to a shattering disappointment? Maybe the kids who came to this store, to Nelson's, would get what they asked for—but what of the kids who had never set foot in a place like this, who lived in streets where Santa feared to go? Whose parents were out of work in this festive season, or drank up what money there was? What would those children think of Santa on Christmas day? They'd start to learn what all eventually learned: that little was as it seemed in this tattered world.

No, Albert thought as the sad little boy took his taffy and wandered off. They don't have to learn that now, at this age, at this time of the year—the way I did. There'd been no Christmas joy at Albert's house when he was young, with his father constantly drunk and his sick mother slaving to feed nine kids, cleaning toilets twelve hours a day. She would hurry out into the cold after midnight on Christmas Eve to scrounge an abandoned tree, drag it home and trim it alone, and set out the handful of gifts. And once, when Albert had woken from restless sleep and crept downstairs to see the magic, see what Santa had left (for he'd been a good boy), he saw instead his drunken father trip and fall into the tree, bring it down in a shatter of ornaments, a sizzle of lights. *I hate you,* he'd screamed inside his head, and he vowed he would never become like his father. And then he grew up and joined the navy, and years went by and things went bad, and Laura, his precious Laura had shouted the last time they'd spoken, "Your drinking put my mother in her *grave*! You're no father to me. I wish you were dead!"

"Mr. Hawkins?"

"What is it?" A frown, a sharp tilt of the chin.

"I really hate to ask again, but I wonder—"

"An advance on your pay."

"Well—"

"I told you before, it can't be done."

"Yes. Yes, you did."

On Christmas Eve Nelson's closed early, at eight o'clock. Albert's two-hour shift went fast. He felt hollow and sad when the last child left. I can do it again next year, he told himself. I *will* do it again, I'm *good*.

With heavy feet, he walked to the back of the store, toward the changing room. The cleanup crew was already hard at work, trying to finish quickly. They had much to do at home on this special night.

The utility room was next to the changing room. Albert went in and sat down on a wooden box. With his head in his hands, he thought of the past two weeks. He'd loved the work, but had it been right, what he'd done? He hadn't promised anything, but kids that age would *think* he had. He knew they would, and he didn't feel good about that. Still holding his head, he thought of Laura, half a continent away—her husband, Mike, their kids. He hadn't called—had lost his nerve. Instead, he'd sent them a Christmas card. And once he got his check he would send them a present.

He waited till the cleaning crew was gone, then left the utility room. Most of the lights had been turned off and the store looked eerie, dead, the decorations drained of their festivity. And where was Freddy? Off tonight?

Still dressed in his outfit, Albert went to Santa's throne, bent down, and opened the large red sack with the satin bow. As he'd thought all along, it was stuffed with paper. A fake. "But I am not a fake," he said aloud to the empty store. "I'm real. And Christmas is real."

With change from deposit bottles he paid his fare, and saw that he had an excellent choice of seats. Most people had better things to do on Christmas Eve than cruise around town on a bus.

A guy in the back had a wiseguy smile but didn't make any remarks. When Albert got off, the bus driver said, "So this is where Santa lives."

"Used to live," Albert said as he hefted the sack down the steps.

The neighborhood looked worse than ever, and Christmas was when it usually looked its best. The walls of the redbrick houses were scarred by graffiti—none of that when Albert had lived here—and trash had collected against the grooved marble steps. Plastic candles glowed bloodred in the lace-curtained windows, and here and there a cut-out Santa or wreath was tacked to a door.

The first place he went, a fat woman opened the door a crack and said, "We can't give nothin', we ain't got nothin' to give."

"Do you have any children?" Albert asked.

"Get lost," the woman said.

At the next house, a man's voice deep inside said, "Who's out there?"

"Some nut in a Santa suit," the woman said. Her hair was stiff and yellow, her mouth was hard.

"I've brought gifts for your children," Albert said.

"Call the cops!" cried the woman, slamming the door.

At the third house a hollow-eyed woman said, "Who sent you? Where are you from?"

"I'm doing this on my own," Albert said. Behind the woman stood two young children, a boy and a girl. Albert opened his sack and took out two presents, gaily—though far from expertly—wrapped. "Merry Christmas," he said, and handed the gifts to the kids, who looked stunned.

At the next house he stood on the steps for awhile, trying to calm his heart, then pushed the bell.

He heard no ring, so he knocked. After a minute, the door came open. A man with sleepy eyes and a cigarette butt in his mouth said, "Huh?"

"Merry Christmas," said Albert. "I see you have a little girl. Are there any other children?"

"What? What is this?" the man said, squinting.

"Who's that?"—a woman's voice.

"Santa Claus."

"It's not Joe. Is it Joe?"

"I once lived in this house," Albert said. "Can I come inside for a minute?"

The man hesitated; then, taking a drag on his cigarette, said, "Sure," and Albert stepped over the threshold.

So different, and yet—the same. And memories came rushing up: of Laura on that windowseat, reading her picture books; of Eleanor darning a sock in her chair.

"You used to live here?" the little girl said, coming up.

"I did indeed, sweetheart," said Albert, "long ago," and he reached in his sack. "Merry Christmas," he said, and gave her a gift. For a second she looked like Laura.

The man said, "Come on, what's the catch?"

"No catch," Albert said with a shake of his head. "No catch," and he turned to the door. As he went down the steps, he heard the man say, "Gimme that package, don't open it yet."

He managed to give it all away, but it wasn't easy. And when it was gone and he stood on the corner holding his empty sack and shivering, a light snow coating his Santa suit, he knew he was not going to drink anymore.

Then, instead of the bus, a squad car came up, lights flashing, and both of the cops got out and the taller one said, "All done for the night, Santa Claus?"

"All done," Albert said.

"Time to come with us, then, I guess."

"I guess," Albert said.

The cop put his hand on Albert's head as he guided him into the car. "Arresting Santa Claus," he said. "Good thing my kids can't see me." He sat beside Albert and slammed the door. "You got any other clothes?"

"No," Albert said.

"They'll give you some."

The car took off. "Well, anyway, I finished," Albert said. "I thought you wouldn't come for a couple of days."

"The security guard saw you leaving the store with your bag," said the cop.

"Good old Freddy."

"An hour later we started to get these calls. You shook a few people up."

Albert looked at the snow falling out of a street lamp. "I'd have paid for the items," he said, "but the manager just wouldn't give an advance."

"I'm sure the judge will sympathize."

"What will he give me?"

"Two months—maybe three."

"Spring," Albert said.

"Huh?"

"They won't let me out until spring."

"Yeah."

Albert leaned back in his seat, still holding his sack. No drinking till spring. And a warm place to sleep, and food for the winter, and once he got out—no drinking ever. He'd write to Laura and tell her that. And then when his Social Security checks started coming, he'd get a room—an apartment, even—and she would come visit with Mike and the kids, and they'd have a fine time.

He looked at the empty streets, the cold snow, the fake candles in windows. "Well, I'm not a fake," he said.

"Say what?" the cop sitting next to him said.

"I'm real, the real thing," Albert said.

SHOPLIFTER

by Larry Segriff

She walked right by me and I knew she was up to something. She was good, though; I had to admit that. I'd been watching her for two months now and I hadn't figured her out yet. Still, I was sure that every Friday night she stole something from us.

I was in my mannequin act. It wasn't my idea, and I didn't think it was a particularly good one. I would rather have been playing a real Santa Claus, with kids on my lap or a bell in my hand, but Mr. Marvin, the store manager, hadn't wanted me distracted. Or so he said. Personally, I thought he merely relished his ability to make me do things his way.

So there I sat, in a mock-up sleigh with two artificial reindeer arrayed before me. My gloved hands rested comfortably on my wide black belt and, I had to admit, the long white beard and stomach padding did help to hide my breathing. Even so, sitting there, watching over the hundreds of last-minute shoppers, trying to spot potential shoplifters without moving a muscle, I felt pretty damn obvious.

She walked past me and I caught a whiff of her scent: shampoo with a hint of chamomile, body lotion with coconut oil, and the tiniest suggestion of makeup. If my nose had learned anything on this job, she used Lancome. Top of the line stuff, which didn't fit the profile of the typical shoplifter.

I was intrigued, and kept one twinkling eye on her as she approached her usual counter. I couldn't hear what she said to the clerk, but I didn't have to. After two months, I knew her drill by heart.

The salesgirl smiled, turned away for a moment,

and came back with one of the sample bottles we keep out on the counter. My gal sniffed at it, shook her head, and the clerk tried again.

It took nearly ten minutes to go through all the little bottles, from Chanel through Obsession. She sniffed at each one, just like she always did, delicately and daintily, but she didn't try any on. Then the clerk turned away and I tensed. This had to be the moment.

Nothing happened. Her hands were in plain sight, I could see all the bottles on the counter, and nothing moved. Nothing changed. Nothing disappeared.

Damn.

The clerk came back with another sample, one that we do not keep out for just anyone to try, and presented it to the lady I was watching. She smelled it, tried a little on, smelled it again, applied a little more, and shook her head. No sale. She handed it back to the clerk with a smile. Picking up her purse, she turned and strolled past me, the familiar scent of Shalimar trailing in her wake.

I shook my head, too, no longer concerned about maintaining my disguise. She'd stolen something. I knew it, my gut knew it, but I didn't know how. Hell, I didn't even know what.

I considered going over and talking with the clerk, but there was no point. I knew what she'd say. It would be the same story as always. Besides, I'd seen it all for myself. There was nothing more she could add.

God, I hated losing one. I especially hated being taken time after time like this. Christmas Eve or not, I decided then and there that I wasn't going to let her go.

Signaling to one of the closed-circuit security cameras, knowing that on this night Mr. Marvin would be monitoring them closely, I leaped down from the sleigh and started off after her. Let him dock me. Hell, let him fire me. I didn't really think he would, especially if I ended up catching her, but I realized that it didn't matter if he did. I moonlighted more from boredom than from a need for the paycheck.

Besides, any store in town would be glad to get a detective with fifteen years on the force and a willingness to dress up as Santa Claus.

Outside, curses were flying as thick as the snow. I saw one man push a lady down in order to steal her cab, knocking her packages into the dirty slush on the sidewalk. I hurried past, unable to stop without losing sight of my quarry.

Merry Christmas, you bastard, I thought.

She led me through a succession of stores. On any other night, I would have been conspicuous as hell, but this was New York, and tomorrow was Christmas.

In the first, she stopped at the cosmetics counter and went into her now-familiar routine. She was looking at eye shadow, rejecting all the more common stuff and finally trying on a sample the clerk had brought out from beneath the counter. Again, I tensed when the saleslady ducked down, but again nothing happened.

What the hell was going on?

Back out into the wind and the snow, and on to another store. Here, she used a disposable applicator to try on some lipstick, and again it was from the private stock. By the third, where she went straight to the perfume counter and asked for the tiny bottle in its purple velvet box, I was starting to get an idea, but it was so absurd that I didn't know how to handle it.

That third stop seemed to be her last one, and I finally had a chance to act. Stepping back out into the teeth of the wind, she joined the half dozen other last-minute shoppers in trying to hail a cab, and I moved up right behind her.

It took a few minutes, but eventually one pulled up in front of her, and I said, "May I share your cab?"

She turned and regarded me, keeping one eye out for anyone who might try to move in on her claim.

After a moment, she smiled and nodded. "Of course. Who would deny Santa a ride tonight?"

I bowed slightly and followed her into the backseat. The scent of Shalimar was stronger now than it had been, and her makeup was a little more obvious. I grinned to myself, hoping that the beard would hide it.

After she'd given an address and the cab pulled out into traffic, she turned to me once more.

"Sleigh break down?"

My grin widened. "It's in the shop, having the runners rotated. It was supposed to be ready yesterday, but you know how mechanics are."

She lifted her eyebrow and then broke out into sudden laughter. Holding out her hand to me, she said, "I'm Claire Joseph."

I took her hand. "Pleased to meet you, Ms. Joseph. I'm—"

She cut me off. "No introductions necessary, Mr. Claus. Your reputation precedes you."

I nodded. She wanted me to stay in character. All right. "And what would you like for Christmas this year, Claire?"

She gave me a truly wicked grin. "Aren't I supposed to sit on your lap to tell you that, Santa?"

My lips twitched as I fought to keep my own face straight. I didn't think it was a serious offer, but she was an attractive lady. "There are special rules for taxicabs," I said. "No lap sitting necessary."

I realized then that I could get to liking this little flirt. I hadn't enjoyed talking with someone so much in all the long years since my wife passed away. I had to keep reminding myself that I was sharing the backseat with a shoplifter, not a date, and that I was supposed to be gathering evidence against her.

Her eyes were still sparkling as she considered my question. "What would I like for Christmas? Why, I'd—"

I cut her off. "Never mind," I said. "Only good girls get what they ask for. Naughty girls find lumps of coal in their stockings, and you've been a naughty girl, haven't you, Claire?"

For a moment her face froze. In that instant her mask of flirtatious humor fell away and I caught an unexpected glimpse of the loneliness that lay beneath it.

She recovered quickly, so fast that I might have doubted what I'd seen if I wasn't so familiar with it myself. The thing was, I knew that look well. It greeted me every morning when I looked at myself in the mirror.

"Why, Santa," she said as her old self returned, "you sound like you *want* me to be naughty. Just what would you like to put in my stockings?"

I snorted and shook my head. "No, Claire, I'm serious. I know all about your little shoplifting act." Just for emphasis, I slowly named the four stores I'd seen her in.

This time she didn't recover so fast. "What—" she said. "How—"

"Tell me about it," I said gently, but she shook her head. "All right," I went on after a moment, "I'll tell you about it. The way I figure it, Claire, you don't have much going on on Friday nights. You've got money, I can see that, but I can also guess that that's about all you've got. So what do you do? On Fridays, you decide to get yourself all made up, but not with your own stuff. That would be too tame, even pointless. Instead, you go to several different department stores, sampling their best stuff. A dab here, a bit there, and by the end of your rounds you look like you just stepped out of a beauty salon. Am I right?"

She smiled faintly and bowed her head briefly, but that was as close to a confession as she came. "And if you are, Santa, would that really make me such a bad girl?"

And that, of course, was what I was trying to figure out for myself. I mean, sure, she undoubtedly *felt* she was stealing, and there was no doubt that it was a deliberate attempt to defraud the stores, but that was as far as it went. There wasn't a DA in the country who would prosecute, and even Mr. Marvin wouldn't try to press charges. Hell, the stores wouldn't stop her if they could. I'd wager my beard and gloves that she went back to each one on Saturday and bought something she didn't need.

The thing was, I didn't know whether I should tell her that. A part of her probably relished the feeling of wickedness she evoked on Friday nights. Was she seeking absolution from me, or merely confirmation?

I sighed and shrugged and decided to evade the question. "People do some funny things, Claire. I know one guy, a cop, whose life is so empty that he moonlights as a security guard for one of the local department stores. It's not very exciting, but it beats the hell out of his empty apartment. And there was another lady, lived around here a few years ago; like you, she had a lot of money, so much that she didn't have to work, didn't have to do anything she didn't want to, and after a while she found she didn't want to do anything. Her friends, she felt, only liked her for her money, and so she dumped them. Before long, she was in an apartment that, for all its expensive furnishings, was as empty as that cop's. So what did she do? Out of boredom, perhaps, or a sense that her life had no meaning, or maybe even a desire for excitement, she turned to the same kind of petty theft. She'd go down to the local grocery store on the day that they gave out samples of food, and she'd eat her dinner there, one bite at a time. Hardly nutritious, of course, and nowhere near as tasty as the meal she could have afforded at any of the restaurants in town, but those little bites in those little paper cups had the one spice she'd never been able to buy: the spice of risk. The taste of doing something she knew was wrong, even if it was such a little thing."

She listened to my little lecture in silence, and quirked her lips into a wry grin when I'd finished. "A cop, huh?"

I nodded. "No one's immune to loneliness, Claire."

She echoed my nod. "Maybe you're right, Santa." Her gaze went back to the window beside me and we watched the falling snow in silence for a block or two. "This cop," she said as the cabbie started to pull over to the curb, "is he a nice guy?"

"One of New York's finest," I said, hoping once again that the beard was hiding my face.

She nodded. "Maybe he'd like to call me sometime."

"I'm sure he would, Claire. I'm sure he would."

The cabbie pulled to a stop in front of one of Park Avenue's posher addresses. "Here you are, miss," and he named a fare.

"That's all right," I said. "My treat. It *is* Christmas, after all."

"Thank you," she said, and moved to get out. She stopped, though, with her hand still on the handle, and turned back to me. Laying her fingers lightly on my cheek, she added, "For everything."

I smiled. "Merry Christmas, Claire."

She nodded, and smiled, and was gone. Leaning back in the seat, I gave the cabbie the store's address and closed my eyes. I thought of my apartment, with its lack of decorations, and I thought of Claire. I'd call her, I knew, maybe the next day. We could go down to the A&P, if it was open, and eat our Christmas dinner out of paper cups. A bite or two of enchilada; a chicken nugget on a toothpick; maybe even a sample of frozen yogurt in a cone.

Grinning, my eyes still tightly closed, I inhaled deeply of the cab's stale air, seeking a trace of her Shalimar and wondering what in the hell I would tell Mr. Marvin.

A VISIT FROM ST. NICHOLAS

by Ron Goulart

The media, as usual, got it completely wrong. The corpse in the Santa Claus suit hadn't been the victim of a mugging and therefore wasn't an all too obvious symbol of what's wrong with our decaying society.

Actually Harry Wilkie had gotten dressed up as St. Nicholas to commit grand larceny. Things obviously went quite wrong, which is why he ended up, decked out in a scarlet costume and snowy white whiskers, sprawled on that midnight beach in Southport, Connecticut.

It snowed on what was to be Harry's final birthday. That was December 20th last year and the snowfall was fitful and halfhearted, not a traditional New England Christmas-card snow at all. And a foot or so of good snow would have improved the view through the narrow window of the living room of the condo where he'd been living in exile since his last divorce almost two years ago.

Harry was sitting there, phone in his lap, looking out at his carport, his two blue plastic garbage cans, and a bleak patch of dead lawn.

"Didn't I warn you?" his brother Roy was asking from his mansion way out in Oregon someplace. "You take up residence in something named Yankee Woodlands Village, you're obviously going to have problems. There probably aren't any woodlands within miles, are there?"

"Six trees. The point, Roy, is—"

"What kind of trees?"

"Elms. The point, Roy, is that it's been over four

months since I was let go at Forman & McCay. You
may not have heard, but the economy is—"

"You really had talent once. I still remember those
great caricatures you did of Mr. Washburn."

"Who?"

"Our high school math teacher. Washburn, the one
with the nose shaped like—"

"My high school math teachers were Miss Dilling-
ham and Mr. Ribera. The point is, Roy, that I'm running short of cash and—"

"To go from really brilliant caricatures to the worst
kind of commerical art is sad and—"

"Forman & McCay is the second largest ad agency
in Manhattan, Roy. I work on the Kubla Kola account, which annually bills—"

"*Worked.* Past tense."

"And the Cyclops Security System account and—"

"Okay, how much?"

"Do I need, you mean?"

"I can't let you have more than $5000. Abigail
wants to go for her MA degree next sem—"

"You don't have a daughter named Abigail."

"Mistress. Will $5000 help?"

"Sure, yes. I've got a lead on a new art director job
and right after the first of the—"

"Another job in the Apple?"

"No, it's just over in Norwalk. Near Wilton here.
A small, aggressive young agency that specializes in
health food and herbal remedy accounts."

"Have you considered trying one of those career
counselors? It's probably not too late, even at your
age, to start fresh and—"

"*My* age? I'm two years, Roy, younger than you
are."

"Well, I'm nearly fifty."

"You're nearly fifty-one. I'm forty-nine. And I'll
tell you something else—having a damned birthday so
close to Christmas is not that great. This year especially, since I'm not married or seeing anybody seriously, I got hardly any presents or even—"

"You maybe shouldn't become serious about an-

other woman, Harry. Not right yet anyway," advised
his brother. "Four marriages gone flooey is enough
for now."

"*Three* marriages gone flooey."

"Was there one that didn't go flooey?"

"There were only three marriages all told, Roy."

"You sure?"

"Yeah, I've kept track."

"Only three, huh? Let's see . . . there was the fat
one. Was that Alexandra?"

"That was Alice, who was *plump* and not fat."

"Hereabouts we judge a woman who tips the scale
at two-fifty plus as fat."

"At her peak she weighed one seventy-five."

"That's still pretty close to fat, Harry. And then
there was that crazy skinny one. What was her name?
Some kind of flower."

"Pearl."

"That's the one. Loony as a fruitbar."

"Nutty as a fruitcake."

"Exactly.

"No, I wasn't agreeing, I was just correcting your
cliché. Pearl was a mite eccentric, yes, though certainly not crazy."

Out in Oregon his brother made a grunting sound.
"The first one wasn't too terrible. The best of the lot,
in fact. Was her name Amy?"

"Yep."

"She was halfway good looking, too."

Harry asked, "Could you, Roy, FedEx me the
check?"

"Things that bad?"

"The condo payment is a mite past due. And—"
His phone signaled that he had another call. "Hold
on, Roy, I have another call." He pushed a button.
"Hello?"

"Gee, you sound awful. Are you sick?"

"No," he said tentatively.

The woman continued, "You sound absolutely rotten. I bet it's another of those frequent bouts of bronchitis you were always having."

"I've had bronchitis exactly *twice* in my entire life, Amy."

"Most people never have it at all," said his first wife. "Listen, can I talk to you?"

"Hold on a minute. I'm on the other line with Roy."

"Roy?"

"My brother. The best man at our wedding."

"Was his name Roy? That all seems like a hundred years ago and I try not to clutter my memory with all that old junk. Give him my best, though."

He pushed a button and said to his brother, "I've got to take this other call. Send the money and—"

"It's a woman, isn't it? I can tell by the furtive tone of your voice."

"Do I also sound like I have bronchitis?"

"Is this some new lady? You really, Harry, in your present state shouldn't even consider—"

"It's only my ex-wife. It's Amy. She sends you her best wishes, by the way."

"She wasn't half bad, especially compared to what came later. Merry Christmas—and, oh, happy birthday."

"Thanks, Roy. . . . Hello, Amy, what is it?"

And that's when he first heard about what was up in the attic of the Southport mansion she and her latest husband had recently moved into.

The Southport mansion was less than a block from the Sound. A century-old Victorian, it rose up three stories and was encrusted with intricacies of ginger-bread and wrought iron.

Harry arrived there at a quarter past one the day after his former wife's call. Standing on the wide front porch, he noted that they had a new Cyclops alarm system.

"Late as usual," Amy observed as she admitted him to the large hallway. The house was filled with the scents of fresh paint, new carpeting, furniture polish, and cut flowers.

"It took longer to drive over here from Wilton, probably because of the wind and sleet. And then, too, I—"

"You never were very good at planning anything, even a simple visit from one town to another." She helped him out of his overcoat, holding it gingerly and then rushing it into a large closet. "Isn't this the same shabby overcoat?"

"Same as what?"

"It certainly resembles the shabby old overcoat you insisted on wearing back when we were . . . um . . . together."

"Married. We were married." Harry thrust his hands into his trouser pockets and glanced around. There were several small abstract paintings on the walls, bright and in silvery metal frames. He couldn't identify the artist.

"Yes, they're Businos." She smiled thinly and nodded at the nearest painting, which was mostly red.

"Oh, right, Busino." He had no idea who the hell Busino was.

"What happened to your hair."

He reached up and touched his head. "Still there, Amy."

"Not very much of it," she observed. "You used to have a great deal much more hair back when we were . . . um . . . cohabiting."

He asked, "What about the paintings you wanted me to look at?"

"My husband . . . have you ever met Tops?"

"Tops? Your husband's first name is Tops? No, I'd remember if I'd ever encountered somebody who was named Tops. What's it short for?"

"Nothing. It's a nickname. Obviously."

"Is he home?"

"No, he's with his parents over on Long Island. I'll be joining them Christmas Eve day. I find two days with Mommy Nayland is all I can safely tolerate."

"What do they call Tops's father?"

"Jared."

Harry nodded. "About the pictures?"

"I was trying to say that Tops has a full head of wavy hair."

"I once did myself."

She sighed briefly. "Follow me," Amy invited. "We left them up in the attic after we found them last month. You see, as I mentioned to you over the telephone yesterday, many years ago an art director from some New York advertising concern lived in this house. A coincidence, isn't it, since you're an art director, too? His name was . . . um . . . Hoganbanger."

"I doubt it."

"Something like that. Perhaps Bangerhagen." She started up the ornate staircase. "Tops and I think they may be from the 1950s or possibly earlier. Left behind by the art director. It's old artwork by various artists, stuff he must have brought home. This Hagenfarmer seems to—"

"Do you mean Faberhagen? Eric Faberhagen?"

"That sounds about right. Have you ever heard of him?"

"Sure, he was a famous art director in the 1930s and 1940s. He still gets written up in advertising graphics magazines now and then," Harry answered. "He worked for the agency that, back then, had the Kubla Kola account."

"Yes, some of these awful paintings have cola bottles in them."

Harry felt a sudden tightening across his chest. He let out an inadvertent gasp, took hold of the bannister. "Really?" he managed to say.

"Have you had a physical exam lately? Climbing a few flights of stairs shouldn't—"

"It's the bronchitis, that's all."

"With all the weight you seem to have put on, you have to think seriously about your heart."

"I weigh exactly what I did while we were . . . um . . . married."

"C'mon, Harry." She laughed. "You used to be quite slim."

"I was never slim, no."

"Well, certainly slimmer than you are now," she insisted. "Two more flights to go. Can you make it?"

"Yes, ma'am."

"I understand you're not married just now."

"I'm not."

"I've been meaning to call you before this. Ever since Tops and I bought this place five months ago and I quit working with Thigpen Reality," his former wife told him as they began another flight. "The thing is, Tops isn't that keen on my seeing old beaus . . . or old husbands. But when we came across these old advertising paintings, it occurred to me you were the perfect person to tell us what they're worth. I got Tops to see it my way. And, really, there's no reason why you and I can't be friends again—in a distant way at least."

"When you moved out you implied you never wanted to see me again. Let's see . . . the exact words were 'I never want to look at that awful pudgy face of yours as long as we both shall live.'"

"Well, then I guess you were overweight back then, too," she said, nodding slowly. "As I told you, I weed out my memories fairly often. I have no recollection what I might have said to you eleven years ago. Did my remarks hurt you?"

"Not as much as the bricks."

"Oh, my. Did I throw a brick at you, Harry?"

"Bricks, plural. Three."

"I have no recollection. Wherever did I get bricks?"

"The bookcase in my den was constructed from boards and bricks."

"Oh, that ugly thing. Yes, I remember that," she said. "Tops and I got to talking, after we discovered this small cache of old advertising art that had been mouldering in the attic for untold years, and I suggested that it might be worth something. Tops simply wants to donate it to St. Norby."

"Another nickname?"

"St. Norbert's Holy Denominational Church. You must've driven past it on your way here."

"Big building with a cross on top?"

"That's dear old St. Norby, yes." She started up another flight. "But before we donate this stuff to their fair next month, I thought I ought to get an expert opinion. And, after some debate, Tops gave in and allowed me to ask you over. Maybe this crap is worth something after all."

When they reached the large, chill attic and he saw the seven canvases, it took Harry almost a minute to get himself to where he could speak. He had to sit down on a highly polished humpback trunk and cough a few times.

Six of the unframed canvases were, indeed, crap. But the seventh, as he'd hoped ever since he'd heard the old art director's name, was a large oil painting of Santa Claus in his shirtsleeves sitting in front of a roaring fireplace after a long night of delivering toys. He was relaxing by drinking Kubla Kola straight from the bottle. It was, beyond doubt, an authentic Maxwell Van Gelder.

Although most people knew nothing about the long-dead commercial artist, who'd been a favorite of the equally long dead Faberhagen, his Kubla Kola Santa paintings were highly prized by certain collectors. He'd done fifteen during his lifetime, but only five had surfaced thus far. The last one that had been sold, over three years ago, had been purchased by a Kubla executive for nearly $400,000. This one, which was much handsomer, ought to bring at least $500,000.

Harry was finally able, after another cough, to inform his ex-wife, "They're not worth anything, Amy."

"Nothing, not anything?"

"Not exactly nothing, no. There are people who collect old advertising art. I'd say you could get probably a hundred dollars or so for each of these," he said. "That Santa, since it has a Christmas theme, might bring as much as two or three hundred."

Amy looked disappointed for a few seconds, then smiled. "Tops was right this time," she said, starting for the attic door.

"Wait a minute." He rose off the trunk. "I collect this sort of stuff myself."

"I didn't realize that. Although you did tend to clutter up the house with all sorts of silly—"

"How about a thousand dollars for the lot? I'd like

to hang that Santa in my den, to remind me of my days with Kubla."

"That seems a fair price, and this stuff is only gathering dust up here."

His brother's check ought to get here tomorrow. He could write Amy a check for a thousand and still cover his condo payment and some of the other bills. And if he could sell the Van Gelder, very quietly, for even $450,000—hell, he could live on that for years. Sure, if you invested that wisely, you could even live well here in Fairfield County.

"I'll take them with me, Amy, and send you a check first thing—"

"Oh, I'll have to talk it over with Tops first."

"Sure, of course. Can you phone him over in Long Island? Now, I mean."

"Well, he's off at lunch somewhere, I'm not exactly sure where, with Mommy Nayland and Dr. Boopsy and—"

"Dr. Boopsy?"

"His real name is Bublitzky. When Tops was little, he couldn't pronounce that and his cute way of—"

"You can get in touch with him tonight, though?"

"Or tomorrow morning, yes."

"I could take them along now, save me another trip and you more bother. He's likely to say okay and—"

"I'd better not, Harry. I don't want to annoy Tops by making a household decision without consulting him first. Unlike the days when you and I were . . . um . . . living in the same house, Tops and I have a very democratic marriage."

"So did we, Amy, until you declared yourself fuhrer and . . . But that's, as you say, all lost in the dim past." He forced himself to smile. "Do call me as soon as you talk it over with your husband. And be sure to wish Tops a joyous Noel."

Harry waited until noon the next day before phoning Amy. He didn't want to convey undue eagerness, which might make his erstwhile wife suspicious.

He let the phone ring eleven times.

After pacing his living room for what seemed a half hour but was actually only thirteen minutes, he tried the Southport mansion again. This time he got their answering tape.

While Chopin music played softly in the background, a thin, nasal male voice said, "Well, hi, this is, as you no doubt expected, the Nayland residence. But, as you may not have expected, neither Tops nor Amy can come to the phone just now. You know the drill, so wait for the beep, won't you?"

Not waiting for the beep, Harry hung up, muttering, "What an asshole."

A chill, heavy rain was falling outside and it made his narrow view even bleaker. Harry sat there, phone waiting in his lap, watching the view for another twenty-six minutes.

Then he punched out Amy's number again.

She answered, sounding impatient and out of breath, on the sixth ring. "Yes, what?"

"This is Harry and—"

"Oh, you picked a rotten time to call, dear heart. I've got Mr. Sanhammel in the parlor in his shorts and—"

"Beg pardon?"

"It's because of the Santa Claus Choraleers," she explained. "I'll be right back, Mr. Sanhammel. He's going on eighty, poor dear man."

"But why is he in your parlor in his underwear?"

"That should be obvious. As people grow older, they tend to put on weight, as you well know. His Santa Claus suit doesn't fit him anymore and has to be let out, quite a bit in fact, especially around the middle. But poor old Mrs. Sanhammel happens to be in intensive care at the Norwalk Hospital because of her—"

"What are the Santa Claus Choraleers?"

"A Southport tradition."

"Oh, so?"

"Every Christmas Eve they roam the streets and byways of our town, every man jack of them dressed as St. Nicholas, stopping at various spots to sing carols and unoffensive hymns."

"That's fascinating, Amy. Now about—"

"You don't think it's fascinating at all. I can tell by that familiar patronizing tone in—"

"Actually I was wondering if you'd talked to your husband about those second-rate old ad paintings. I'm going to be over your way this—"

"Yes, I did. Tops feels that if they're really only worth one thousand dollars, why we'll donate them to St. Norby."

"I'll go up to twelve hundred. I'll donate the money to St. Norby and save them the trouble of—"

"Let me be absolutely candid with you, Harry," she cut in. "Tops says he'd rather toss the paintings on the landfill than sell them to an odious toad such as yourself."

"What gave him the notion I was an odious toad?"

After a few silent seconds she answered, "Well, I may have exaggerated my accounts of some of the low points of our wretched marriage, Harry."

He said, "Fifteen hundred dollars."

"It's no use. He won't sell them to you. But, hey, you can go to the fair at the church next month. I'll have Father Boody send you an invitation."

That was too risky. If the Van Gelder got out in public, somebody else might recognize it. "Wouldn't it be much easier if—"

"Poor Mr. Sanhammel is getting all covered with gooseflesh. I really have to go. Merry Christmas and maybe I'll see you at the church fair next month."

"Yeah, Merry Christmas."

The most difficult part was finding a Santa Claus suit. Harry didn't come up with his plan until the afternoon of Christmas Eve and by then the few costume shops in his part of Connecticut had long since sold or rented what they'd had in stock.

He persisted, however, and finally located a used-clothing outlet over in Westchester County that had one threadbare Santa costume for sale. They wanted two hundred dollars for the damn thing, but since the check from his brother had come in, he was able to rush over into New York State with the cash to buy it. The beard was in bad shape, stringy and a dirty yellow color. When he got it home, Harry used some ivory spray paint on the whiskers and livened them up considerably.

The rest of that gray afternoon and into the evening he sat at his drawing board, studying all the material he'd saved about the Cyclops Security System from the days when he worked on the account. It seemed to him definitely possible, just by using the tools he had on hand, to outfox the type of alarm setup they were using at Amy's mansion.

His plan was a simple one. There'd be a dozen costumed Santas—he'd found out how many choraleers there were from the back files of the Southport weekly at the library—roaming the streets of the town from nine until midnight. Nobody was likely to pay much attention to a thirteenth. Especially not on Christmas Eve. Amy and Tops were now over in Long Island and their house sat empty.

The Van Gelder Santa painting was resting quietly up in the attic. All Harry had to do was disarm the alarm system, enter the house and gather up the picture. To throw suspicion off himself, he'd also swipe whatever silver and jewelry he could find. And he'd take all those awful Busino paintings that decorated the hall. The police would assume that the thief had stolen the advertising art under the assumption that it, too, was valuable.

Then, after a safe interval, he'd sell the painting and live on the $500,000. There wouldn't be any more job interviews with art directors who were ten or twenty years younger. No more loans or lectures from Roy.

To explain his income, he'd pretend he was doing gallery painting. As a matter of fact, he'd been a damn good painter once and he might really give that a try again.

His plan wasn't a bad one. But what Harry hadn't anticipated was the fourteenth Santa Claus.

A strong wind came up at nightfall and the rain grew heavier. When Harry went running out to his carport, shortly after ten P.M., the rain hit at him hard.

He was carrying the Santa costume in a large, cloth laundry bag. Later, after he'd changed into the outfit, he was going to use the sack to carry off the Van Gelder and the rest of the loot. No one would pay much attention to a Santa Claus with what looked like a bulging sack of toys.

The Southport library sat less than a block from Amy's mansion. The building was dark and there were only two other cars in the unlit parking lot. Harry parked there and opened the sack. He took out the jacket to the Santa suit.

After glancing around at the rainswept lot, he started getting into the jacket. The sleeves had several moth holes in them. Next he struggled into the pants, which were tough to tug on over his jeans. He heard a ripping sound, but when he felt at the trousers he couldn't locate a rip.

The rain was drumming on the car roof, the wind rattled the tree branches overhead.

"Oh, shit," he said aloud. "Where's the beard? Where's the damn beard?"

He thrust his hand deep into the sack again.

"Ow! Damn it."

He'd stuck his forefinger with one of the screwdrivers he'd brought along for working on the alarm system.

"Ah, here it is." He yanked out what felt like the false whiskers. It turned out, however, to be his Santa hat.

"I had the beard. I know I put it in the sack."

Then he noticed something white on the floor of the car, over on the passenger side. He grabbed up the beard and attached it with the wire ear loops. Stretching up, he attempted to get a look at himself in the rearview mirror. The thing was all steamed and there wasn't enough light anyway.

Harry started to open the door. "Half-wit," he reminded himself. "Gloves! You almost forgot the damn gloves."

They were in the laundry bag someplace, too. "Ow!" He found them and slipped them on.

Nodding to himself, Harry gathered up the big laundry bag and left the car.

Wind and rain struck at him, shoving him off in the wrong direction. He fought, gasping, and managed to get himself aimed right. The wind caught at the beard, and unhooked it from one ear.

Harry rescued it, got the whiskers back in place. As he stood on the sidewalk watching Amy's dark mansion across the way, a Mercedes drove by on the wet street.

The driver honked and someone yelled, "Merry Christmas, Mr. Sanhammel!" out a briefly lowered window.

Harry waved. Maybe he *was* putting on weight.

After the car had been swallowed up by darkness, he ran across the street. He sloshed swiftly across the lawn, circled around to the backside of the Victorian house.

He intended to enter by the back door, which couldn't be seen from the street and was sheltered by a stand of maples. Down across the back acre of lawn was a narrow stretch of beach. The water on the Sound was dark and foamy.

"This is typical of Amy," he muttered when he reached the rear door. "She was always going off and leaving things wide open."

The door stood an inch open. Gingerly Harry reached out with his gloved right hand and pushed at the door. Creaking faintly, it swung open inward.

After listening for a half minute, he crossed the threshold and started along the back hall. The house smelled exactly as it had the other day.

In the front hall, he stopped and frowned. Even in

this dim light he noticed that the Busino paintings weren't hanging on the walls anymore.

Then he spotted them, stacked and leaning against the bottom steps of the staircase.

That was just ten seconds before he became aware that somebody was coming down the stairs.

"Well, sir, hi there," said Harry, affecting what he hoped was an older man's voice. "I'm Mr. Sanhammel from—"

"You walked in at the wrong time, friend." The man approaching him had a suitcase in his right hand and a .38 revolver in his left. Tucked under his arm was a lighted flash.

He was also wearing a Santa Claus suit and a handsome beard.

"Damn! Somebody else with the same idea." Harry pivoted and made ready to run.

The other Santa came diving down the stairs. He dropped the suitcase and it hit the floor with a metallic rattle. He grabbed Harry by the arm, swung him around and hit him hard across the temple with the butt of his gun.

That wasn't what killed Harry, though. It was falling to the floor and cracking his head against the frame of the topmost Busino.

What the burglar did next was to gather up the loot he'd left downstairs, add it to the loot he'd gathered upstairs, and stash it all in his suitcase along with Harry's laundry bag. Leaving it behind for a few moments, he carried the obviously dead Harry out of the house and down across the back acre. He left him lying at the edge of the water.

Returning to the house, he collected his things, took his leave and reset the alarm system. When they found Harry's body down on the beach, it probably wouldn't occur to them that a burglary had been committed. Not immediately anyway.

None of the advertising art in the attic was stolen. In January, Amy and Tops did donate the paintings to the St. Norbert fair.

A young commercial artist from Westport picked up

the Van Gelder for $225. Harry, by the way, overestimated the value of the Santa painting. It brought only $260,000 when it was auctioned at a Manhattan gallery last month.

THE LAST HAPPY TIME

by Morris Hershman

"My dear, I thought that after all these long years of living in New York City, I had finally lost my mind. I opened up this morning's *Times* and saw your ad in the first section."

"It's not really mine. I didn't pay for it."

"Belinda, you're not going to deny that today's *Times* has a full-page ad for Gaynor's, 'the Crown Jewel of Department Stores,' and everybody's favorite in the city. An ad in *today's* paper, when the store closed down over a year ago."

"If you had done just a little more reading, you would know that the store is going to be reopened only to raise money for charity."

"I saw enough of the ad to know that there's going to be a sale of the same sort of first-quality merchandise that Gaynor's always sold."

"For one night only."

"Better than nothing if it's Gaynor's. I'll bet you feel good knowing that your store will be open again even for a few hours."

"It was never mine. My great-grandfather's and grandfather's, yes; my father's definitely, but never mine."

"The last chief executive officer at Gaynor's was your husband."

"He's not my husband anymore."

"I'll let you off in just one tiny sec, Belinda. I heard a rumor that your ex will be at the re-opening."

"He won't want to go near the business he managed so carelessly it went bankrupt. He'll probably make it his job to be in Paris or the Riviera or Yucatan."

"I do hope you're right. A recently divorced couple under the same roof can make for one ugly evening."

"Then I'm sure *you'll* be there to see any fireworks, dear."

And now, on the evening itself, with world premiere lights flogging the cold sky and women with their men crowding the Fifth Avenue building on this rain-touched icy December night, Belinda Gaynor Stoddard left her car and gestured for Powers, the chauffeur, to drive off until needed.

Her paternal grandmother, who had raised Belinda after both her parents died, took in the sight and said ruefully, "It looks like you've got a success on your hands, Bel."

Not only had Belinda suggested the type of fund-raiser, but taken an active role in gaining permissions and determining the character of this night's activities. Gam was probably edgy, in part because Belinda had won the battle to make the whole affair a benefit to help the Animal Protection League, of all little-known causes, but more importantly because she must have resented such efficiency from a younger woman who was a blood relative. Women of Edna Gaynor's generation and social position attended theater parties and dinners for charity, but never worked very actively behind the scenes. They didn't really participate, period. Even as far as sex was concerned, the grandmotherly advice to Belinda had been almost in so many words to close her eyes and think of Tortola. Gam and her peers weren't so much professional courtesans, any of them, as they were full-time consumers.

"Everybody who can afford it will be upstairs, Bel, and everybody else on the lower floors." Reluctant approval, there, issuing from a dry throat.

Belinda looked startled. "Do you think that Hub will be here, too? I had a phone call from Bitsy Cannon the other day, and she put the idea into my head."

Required to be soothing, Gam performed like the

veteran she was. "Hub Stoddard won't come near this place tonight or ever again."

"I wouldn't think he'd miss a chance to try making me uncomfortable inside the store."

"There's no sense in his going near the store he ruined because of his laziness. He knows that he cost the original workers their pension money, and if you yourself hadn't set up a contingency fund for emergencies, some of the older ones would be on the street. Not even Hub Stoddard can distort the truth about his own guilty fecklessness if he comes here. The past is a dangerous country, Belinda, numbing the innocent and stinging the guilty."

An older woman's ruminations were beside the point. "Suppose he does come."

"Avoid him."

"And if he comes over to me and tries to be his sweet self, how do I get rid of him, Gam, *how*?"

Edna Gaynor turned to one side, too busy gathering up the folds of her coat to offer advice on tilting against a windmill, stemming a flood.

"Well, dear, let's go in now and look at your very special Christmas toy."

The line in front of the main entrance stretched raggedly for a half block, with elaborately courteous women and many husbands waiting patiently to get out of the cold. Belinda would have liked to take her place on the line and see how smoothly it moved, but Gam might not be able to keep standing much longer. She touched the older woman on a papery shoulder, urging her to follow to a side entrance. For once, a silent Edna Gaynor did exactly what her granddaughter wanted.

Belinda smiled at the deferential nod of recognition from a uniformed private guard opening the side door swiftly. At her instructions, given this afternoon, a long table had been set up twenty feet from the main entrance for people to pay admission fees by credit cards. Women who hadn't said a word before payment

was made were now congratulating each other at being
on the scene.

"It's a miracle, like it was never closed," one
woman said huskily to a new friend. "Do you have
any idea how much time I spent in Gaynor's?"

The other woman, cheerful rather than awed,
asked, "Do you suppose they've re-opened the dining
room, too?"

Belinda felt self-satisfied as the strangers hurried off
happily. She had taken care to make sure that Gaynor's looked the same, with that familiar indirect lighting, those dark display cases, the somber mannequins,
the twenty-foot columns spaced decorously across two
acres of selling area and freshly painted in the familiar
pitch-black.

Gaynor's, the crown jewel of department stores,
had been put up to last. True enough, the five subur-
ban branches could be shut and turned into parking
lots or mini-office buildings, whatever, but bad eco-
nomic times in New York City had made it impossible
to destroy this Taj Mahal and put up another plastic
office building in its place—to reset this crown jewel.

Edna Gaynor whispered, "It really does look just
the same."

Indeed, it was possible to shut both eyes and hear
muffled sounds while *seeing* Daddy walk through the
store, *seeing* Gamp striding along the aisles while dic-
tating notes to his secretary, notes describing exactly
what was being done wrong and by whom.

With the same magic, it was easy to make out a
blank space to represent the time when her ex had
been chief executive officer of Gaynor's, had let his
work go and provoked the smashing of this once-solid
business. Taking time off for vacation, delaying his
return, neglecting to keep in touch during a spree.
Recollections of Hub slipping out of harness were so
many lessons in the art of watching some over-aged
child, testimonials to energy in pursuit of laziness.

The past is a dangerous country.

But it wasn't the authoritative Daddy, the dictato-
rial Gamp or the founding great-grandfather she had

never known that she looked out for so warily as she and Gam walked farther into this family domain. It was the absent Hub Stoddard.

One of the perfume salesclerks nodded at them, a woman rehired for this night. Gray-haired and with eyes to match, she was pausing between sales.

"Is everything all right so far, Doe?"

"Oh yes, Mrs. Stoddard. Everything is in the same place it always was."

"I'm glad you won't have any trouble finding what you need."

Instead of spurring the saleswoman to praise arrangements that Belinda had conscientiously supervised, a grim look crossed her face. "I can find everything except the store pension that I paid into and should be getting by now."

Which was far from Belinda's fault, but she said no word to defend herself.

The women went on, "I know there's a special fund set up in your name for longtime employees, but I'd be ashamed to draw on it till I got absolutely desperate. If not for the Social Security money, I don't know what I'd do."

Gam said softly, "I think we'd better go upstairs, dear."

Belinda wanted to hear more, stoking her anger against the man who had forced the company union to invest its pension fund in the store's future, then let the corporation slide into bankruptcy and dissolution.

But she was turning away obediently, in the main to make sure that Gam got upstairs and could sit among friends. Just as she started to say farewell and add good wishes, the saleswoman suddenly looked over Belinda's right shoulder, attracted by some sound, and now she seemed a little less careworn, even elated.

There was a happy commotion nearby, holiday greetings offered and returned in a voice that she had dreaded ever hearing again, although it was a cheery voice with a movie hero's pseudo-carefree tones.

She turned even while telling herself not to look, and was in time to see Hub Stoddard revealing pearly

white teeth as he smiled and answered a question put
by some older woman.

"No, sweetheart, I'm pretty sure you can't use the
Gaynor silver credit card tonight, though I'm not surprised you've never been able to destroy the thing."

Gam, at Belinda's side, ordered quietly, "Take me
to the elevator."

"No, I won't do that." She was surprising herself,
in light of the success she had helped make of this
special evening. She was disagreeing, giving expression to feelings to which she had earned a right.

Hub's royal progress, bringing him closer, had
stopped at a male clothing salesman who offered a
respectful smile of greetings and a tired observation.

"I decided to come by again," Hub responded
cheerfully and loudly. "After the work I'd done here
I can treat myself to one last happy time at Gaynor's
before it closes forever."

As if he had lifted a finger to bring this occasion to
life, as if he had ever cared a damn about the corporation itself. His lazy inattention to business sometimes
made her wonder what Daddy would have said after
his promise, "If I think you can run Gaynor's when
you're old enough, then no matter who you marry,
you'll be the person who runs it officially." And
Gamp, speaking tyrannically a while after that killer
plane crash in Dallas when the reins had returned to
him, "How could a female ever be in charge of Gaynor's? Impossible that she could do all the hard work.
Impossible!"

What was the sense in waiting like royalty for Hub
to come closer whenever he wanted to? Purposely not
hearing Gam's expelled breath of vexation, which demanded immediate attention, Belinda walked easily
toward him.

She had sometimes wondered what first words she
would say if she ever saw him again, one-on-one, but
the choice had always been obvious.

"Hub, you're looking very well, as usual."

Indeed he did, the face and neck and hands sun-
burned, eyes clear, teeth shiny, the perfectly fashioned

clothes over a sturdy body without an ounce of excess weight. His appearance still spoke of exercise as well as travel and more than one willing woman in a charmed life. Most likely he never put a foot indoors until the sun had set.

"You look fine yourself." He had been reading her lips because of the crest of surrounding noise, and returned the courtesy as quickly as if following some serve at tennis.

The surging crowd made it easy for Belinda to excuse herself and go back, however slowly, to Gam.

"I'll take you to the elevator, if you like."

"And you, Bel?"

"I'm in the mood for a floor-by-floor view of the crown jewel back in operation."

"You've earned it." Without assistance, Gam walked stiffly at Belinda's side over to the silver-painted escalator, but reached right away for the moving black rail. "I don't suppose that you and Hub had much of a conversation at the most crowded part of the floor."

"He didn't needle me," Belinda mused while the escalator rose smoothly. "I could see it was on his mind, though. Do you remember that malicious stare of his, like a child who's done something wrong on purpose? That look has been on his face a thousand times, especially just before he used to call me 'princess.' Why he kept from doing it this time, Gam, I don't know."

"I'd be surprised if a stampeding elephant could make itself clear among that first-floor crowd."

"Then I guess he'll have his chance later on."

Gam offered a sovereign remedy for social awkwardness. "I'll stay close, dear. He'll have to contend with me if he tries to give you the least difficulty."

"Really, I don't know what I'd do without you, Gam."

Belinda spoke as sincerely as she could, trying to make the older woman feel she was still competent and needed as ever. But she knew she could turn to no one but herself to take charge of Hub Stoddard.

The stronger, more self-assured Belinda Gaynor was certain that she'd manage him. Somehow.

"If only the Landmarks' Preservation Commission had been able to keep from dawdling over permission to add extra floors for office space, I could certainly have saved the store."

Hub had followed behind them to the escalator, speaking to every worker who answered his greeting, responding to any question aimed at him, oozing calm and sunny take-it-for-granted confidence. Didn't those smiling workers know he was a living and breathing lie?

Belinda walked across the second floor, having left Gam briefly with her consent. When Daddy had inspected and she was with him, Belinda was always assigned to check the ladies' room on each floor for neatness. She did it this time, too, and approved what she saw, but decided against doing it once more.

On the third floor she saw a woman of Gam's age telling Hub happily, "I always said I would buy my great granddaughter's first dress at Gaynor's, and thanks to you I'm going to do it."

The cheap politician in Hub responded happily, "God bless you, ma'am."

Children's goods dominated the fifth floor, clothes in two corners while the center was taken by electronic toys. A Santa Claus dummy looked benignly down at a small chair in front of small desk with a thumb-sized computer. Enough to beguile any child for at least ten minutes, Belinda thought.

She stayed longer than expected in the sixth floor dining room, where longtime patrons freshly admired the discreet Christmas decorations and the wrap-around mural of a summer garden scene while nibbling at finger sandwiches and drinking tea or coffee out of cups that looked as if they were on the wrong end of binoculars. Belinda sternly told a kitchen helper to make fresh coffee and serve nothing else, ignoring his what-difference-does-it-make look.

And Hub, just off the escalator, was telling yet another well-wishing former employee, "Don't you think I tried hard to have the pension fund restored to the union? You know for a fact that the idea was voted down."

And wasn't the former employee fawning on him? Of course.

The executive elevator, carpeted and noiseless, opened its doors soon after Belinda and her grandmother rang for it. The loudly defensive Hub Stoddard had planted himself at the center of the well-dressed men and women on their way up to the executive quarters.

"Hello Belinda, and Gam," he greeted them as they stepped in. He was clearly interrupting his flow of speech, but didn't resume until the women had turned to face the closing elevator door. "Belinda could tell you how I twisted her arm and her lawyer's to get her to institute a contingency fund for the corporation's older employees. If I'd had the money in my own hands, I'd have done more."

Gam closed two fingers on Belinda's arm, urging her, imploring her to keep silent for the sake of strangers' comfort. For Gam's sake alone, she did.

The door opened on a party scene. Men in tuxedoes mingled like penguins in a summerhouse among colorfully dressed women. Musical notes chittered along the PA system, largely unheard by the generous people who had paid a thousand dollars apiece for the opportunity to dance and dine above the city, seeing friends, starting or cementing relationships, and positioning themselves to cut business deals. The location was fresh, the cause worthy, but the matter in hand for most participants was the pursuit of pleasure as usual.

Belinda couldn't help hearing Hub's over-friendly greeting to the waiter providing a drink on request. A too loud greeting was reserved for Mr. Juro Yoshitomi, the small, poised man who had bought Gaynor's to convert all the stores into office buildings and had been prevented by hard times from doing it only in

New York City. Mr. Yoshitomi was polite, but hardly interested.

Hub, a salesman with some product in which he felt perfect confidence, allowed the waiter to offer him one more drink rather than approach new arrivals. The waiter, a longtime staff member, had been selling personal computers when Hub's fecklessness shot down the Gaynor's stores. How could the man possibly be favoring Hub as if Hub had been a thoughtful boss, a well-wisher, even a friend?

Belinda, turning away in silent anger from the demeaning sight, decided to make one last inspection of the dining area and be sure that everything was up to the mark. She had been premature. Hub's voice was raised even higher in a regretful farewell to the totally indifferent Mr. Yoshitomi, and then Hub materialized in front of her.

"Dance with me." That was an order, although he must have known, too, that divorced couples were supposed to be almost painfully polite to each other in public. "Hey, where are you—?"

She had turned to Fred Gartner, her arms outstretched as if he had asked her to dance and she had already agreed.

"A shame you decided to call it quits with him," Gartner said, moving around the floor with the agility of a circus elephant. "He's a lot of fun, Hub is." Somehow, Gartner avoided the shiny Christmas tree.

The fun producer remained nearby, watching, brows drawn down. The set was only long enough to include "Night and Day," "Just One of Those Things," "Don't Fence Me In," and "Anything Goes." Old songs to make listeners like herself feel nostalgic for a sunny-seeming time they never knew. It had become possible to recognize a charity dance by the number of Cole Porter songs that an orchestra ground out.

Gam was starting over to join her as soon as Gartner waddled back to his long-suffering wife, but Hub got there first. He'd been favored with more drinks since she'd seen him last. His swaying balance proved it.

"You won't dance with me 'cause you don't want me to talk to you." Dutch courage was putting a sharp edge on most words. "Right, isn't it?"

Which meant that Hub was now going to become louder and abusive in painting himself as an honorable man accused unjustly. Listening to him would be hell.

"Let's go into the hallway." She was taking it on herself to risk discomfort in the cause of letting time pass more pleasantly for others on this evening she had planned with such painstaking care.

She was aware of the waiter who had served Hub keeping what seemed like a wary eye on him as she moved slowly so Hub could follow with the least possible difficulty. She picked her way carefully around the younger dancers moving to the floor now that the orchestra had switched to more modern music. Older dancers, leaving the floor, reached for wine from passing waiters.

She accepted the nods and smiling congratulations of friends, exchanging quick vacant pleasantries with a few other guests. Keeping the hall door open for him would anger Hub even further, so she shut it and waited. There was a half-empty drink in his hand when he weaved his way into the hall and scowled at the sight of Belinda turning from him to find a quieter area.

He raised his voice. "Made my life miserable, you did . . . Only married me so you could tell me how to run the stores and instead of happy times I'd be jumping when the princess said to jump."

What he had done was to stay lazy after he married money instead of being man enough to do a hard job in any way that would prove himself.

"And after all's done, you set up a pool of money for stupid useless salesclerks, for no reason!" Whiskey breath sailed uncertainly between twin rows of gleaming teeth. "Little mother wants to kiss the place and make it well. We can all depend on little mother."

Almost like a deep breath, the door of the party

room opened and the saturnine waiter hurried into the hall, his tray left behind.

"You should be working," Belinda snapped.

He paid no attention, dark eyes on Hub in what seemed his typically concerned manner, a prisoner worrying about the welfare of the judge who had sentenced him.

"This way, Mr. Stoddard." In front of a closed door down the hall, he carefully opened it into an area with egg-white walls setting off egg-yolk-colored fire stairs. "You need a little air, sir."

As soon as Hub zigzagged his way to the other side, Belinda went to close the door completely so that no one's evening would be spoiled by any unpleasant action by her queasy ex-husband. Unable to get it shut entirely, she heard a shout deepening to a yell before halting abruptly after the sound of a weight landing. Making the best of a difficult situation, she opened the door and walked in, prepared to offer help. She was in a chilly area, with no one in sight.

Looking anxiously down the stairs, she saw the waiter staring at the heap that had fallen to the floor below. The waiter kicked Hub Stoddard in the head as she was hurrying down to join them.

"A man has to settle scores with somebody who did so much harm." That intent look toward Hub, which had seemed so much like concern for him, was now revealed as naked hatred. "Some staff people still can't bring themselves to believe he ruined us all, but that can't delay a reckoning, particularly when the destroyer comes to smile over who and what he destroyed."

The past is a dangerous country. Hadn't Gam said so, and wasn't she often right?

To her own surprise later on, Belinda cared nothing about the fate of one lazy and negligent man who had left a trail of smashed lives behind him. What Hub deserved he had received. With interest, as the rich little girls of her generation used to say, gloatingly.

No wonder she responded practically. "If the police are sent for, they'll question our guests eventually, and the night"—She didn't say *my night*—"will be ruined." *Not even as a dead man will he ruin my night.*

"We can behave as if nothing happened," the waiter said.

"The body will be found when the store is inspected afterward, and it'll certainly be a scandal. Besides, you're likely to be questioned, too, and you might give yourself away."

"He can't be taken out of the store because too many people are hanging around outside."

She had been coping with emergencies for weeks and the recent inspection alone had refreshed her memory of the store's layout. From those experiences she drew courage and craft.

"If you can get cooperation from others on the staff who feel like you do," she said, with confidence that couldn't be questioned, "I can tell you how to get rid of it."

Hub Stoddard had never been inside the store after closing time when he was active in the firm. Now, in the children's department, his sun-touched body was clothed in a Santa Claus suit—a destroyer dressed as the icon of generosity. On Monday morning, in the course of cleaning up, his mortal remains in costume would be set aside with the dummies, a sales tool currently considered outmoded by most of New York City's remaining department stores, and burned.

To announce the closing of the selling areas for every night over a period of forty-nine years, a recording made in the 1940s had been played. Once again the voice of a tenor rang out, *". . . That's why without you I'm nothing . . ."*

Gaynor's, the Crown Jewel of Department Stores, was closing to the public for the last time.

THE NIGHT BEFORE CHRISTMAS

by Bill Crider

For as long as the little delegation of high-powered Pecan City residents was in his office, Chief of Police R. M. (Boss) Napier was the very picture of the Christmas spirit—His eyes, how they twinkled! His dimples, how merry!—but as soon as the last of the influential citizens had departed and closed the door behind him, Napier's expression changed. His eyes narrowed, his mouth drew itself into a thin, tight line, and his dimples, such as they were, disappeared.

What did those people want from him, anyway? Hadn't he already done enough to make the Christmas season a success in Pecan City? Hadn't he played the part of Tiny Tim in the college's readers' theater production of *A Christmas Carol*? Hadn't he solved the mysterious case of shoplifting that had been going on at Cameron's Department Store?

OK, sure, Carl Burns had helped him out on that last one. He had to admit that. But it had been his idea to dress Burns up in the Santa suit and—Napier's eyes suddenly began to twinkle again. That was the answer! All he had to do was to get Burns into that Santa suit again. He was humming the theme from *Hawaii Five-O* as he picked up the telephone.

Carl Burns, who taught English at Hartley Gorman College, was determined to enjoy what was left of his Christmas vacation. He hadn't really minded helping Napier out with the shoplifting case, but he was determined not to get involved with the police chief again. Whenever he did, he always wound up getting hurt.

"That woman didn't hurt you much," Napier told him. "Besides, you assaulted her kid."

"I didn't assault anybody," Burns countered.

There had been a time when he'd been a little afraid to speak up to Napier, who was bigger and stronger than he was and who had the reputation of being a man who liked to go out into the woods and crack a bullwhip and shoot his .45. But the two had gotten to know one another in the course of two murder investigations in which Burns had played a major role in bringing to a conclusion, and now they were almost friends.

"You tackled the kid in the parking lot," Napier said.

"I didn't assault anybody, and I didn't tackle anybody," Burns said. "Besides, I thought he was the shoplifter."

"You shouldn't jump to conclusions," Napier said.

The two men were sitting in Burns's den, Burns in a recliner and Napier on an old couch that Burns didn't have the heart to get rid of. Christmas music was playing on Burns's cassette stereo, the kind of Christmas music that both men approved of: "White Christmas" by the Drifters, "Blue Christmas" by Elvis Presley, "Rockin' Around the Christmas Tree" by Brenda Lee. They had just finished off the bag of tacos and burritos that Napier had brought over for lunch.

"You can't buy me with a cheap lunch, either," Burns said. "Besides, I might have other plans."

"But you don't," Napier said. "I talked to Elaine."

Burns had sort of figured that Napier might have done that. Both men were dating Elaine Tanner, Hartley Gorman's librarian, but so far the rivalry had remained more or less friendly.

"What did she say?" Burns asked.

Napier stretched out his legs to the side of the coffee table. He was wearing cowboy boots and baggy Levi's. "She said that she was leaving this afternoon and that she'd be out of town for a week and a half. That she was going to visit her folks in Houston. So unless you've got another woman stashed away some-where, you won't be busy tomorrow night."

"Maybe I'm going to a party," Burns said. "I'm a popular guy. There are a lot of parties at this time of year."

"Not on Christmas Eve, there aren't," Napier said. "Not in Pecan City."

The police chief was right. Burns couldn't deny it. Everyone in Pecan City did the same thing on Christmas Eve. They drove to River Bend and looked at the Christmas decorations.

Pecan City wasn't an especially prosperous town, but it did have one residential section that had what the developer referred to in his advertising as "real plush" homes. "Real plush" meant that no two houses were built on the same floor plan, at least not in the same block. The name of the area was River Bend, despite the fact that there was no river anywhere nearby, and most of the town's prominent citizens lived there. The mayor lived there, for example, and several doctors, a few lawyers, and a banker or two. And the president of Hartley Gorman College.

"Franklin Miller was in my office along with the rest of them," Napier said. "I know he'd appreciate it if you'd help me out on this."

Burns sat up as straight as he could in the recliner. "You didn't mention my name to him, did you?"

"Sure I did," Napier lied. "He knows we've worked together when the college was involved. It was only natural for your name to come up."

"I'll bet it was," Burns said. "You rat."

"Watch it," Napier said. "You're presuming on my good nature."

Burns wasn't even sure that Napier had a good nature, but he said, "OK. Tell me again about the problem. Maybe I'll help you after all."

Napier smiled. "I thought you'd see it my way," he said.

The problem had to do with River Bend and the Christmas lights, but there was more to it than just the lights themselves.

Every year the people who lived in River Bend made Christmas Eve a real production. All the sidewalks, curbs, and driveways were lined with lighted candles set inside weighted paper bags. The electric lights were another part of it, and every homeowner tried to outdo the others with spectacular displays that brought joy to the hearts of the power company's stockholders, if not to the world. People from all over the county, their car lights turned off, drove through the area after nightfall to see the elaborate spectacle.

But the lighting effects were only part of it. The spirit of competition was so great that people in River Bend had begun to do other kinds of presentations.

One yard might feature a dazzling array of cut-out figures representing characters from every animated feature the Walt Disney studios had ever turned out, all in Christmas dress. The next lawn would have a living Santa's workshop, with busy little elves slaving over a long workbench filled with toys. And on the next would be a scene right out of Dickens, with someone playing carols on the violin while the little Dickensian beggar children capered in their colorful costumes. Burns remembered that one year there had even been Christmas dinosaurs.

"It's a real mess, all right," he said. "Maybe you could just persuade them to cancel the whole thing."

Napier was horrified. "You've gotta be kidding me! People from all over come to see that stuff. And your boss, Miller, seemed really anxious for it to go on this year."

Miller was anxious, all right, and Burns knew why. Every year the HGC president, whoever it might be at the time, drove Eula Deen Nipperson through River Bend to show off the lights. Ms. Nipperson was ninety-eight years old and didn't do much driving herself, but she liked to look at the lights. And as HGC was hoping to cut itself in for a generous portion of her considerable fortune at her demise, the president was more than glad to cater to her in any way he could.

"I know about that," Burns said, "but if someone is breaking into the houses—"

"No one's breaking into anything," Napier said. "But every year a few houses are burglarized. Dammit, somebody's taking presents right from under the trees. There are so many people around, driving and walking from house to house to see the decorations, that nobody can keep up with all of them. There's certainly nothing unusual about somebody walking around with a present under his arm. And a lot of the homeowners don't lock up the way they should."

"Maybe you could talk to them about that."

"I did. Last year. But it didn't do any good. The little elves have to go to the bathroom all the time, and the Mrs. Clauses have to go to the kitchen for a fresh batch of cookies, and the carolers need to wet their whistles from time to time, and—"

"I get the picture," Burns said. "But why don't you put some officers out there?"

"Napier gave him a look. "I put all I could spare. You citizens just don't understand about Christmas. It's the worst time of year for crime. People who don't have money want to get it any way they can. You've got your burglars, your convenience store robbers, your shoplifters—"

Burns thought about Cameron's Department Store and about Mrs. Branton hitting him with her purse. "Never mind about the shoplifters. What you're telling me is that you need your officers elsewhere."

"That's right, but try telling that to most of the biggest taxpayers in town. That's why you can help me on this, Burns."

Burns leaned back in the recliner. "I don't see what I can do."

"You can look," Napier said. "You can listen. You're good at that stuff." He paused. "And you can wear the Santa suit."

Burns hated the Santa suit, and he absolutely refused to wear the padding that went underneath it, carry the bag of presents, or wear the wire-rimmed glasses. The padding made him waddle like a duck, the bag was too heavy, and the glasses made it hard for him to see.

"You'll be the skinniest Santa in the world," Napier said, eyeing him critically. "People are gonna wonder about you. And you should carry the bag, at least."

"It's too heavy," Burns said. "And I don't care if people wonder about me."

"It's gonna be bad if some little kid starts asking his mother and daddy why Santa is anorexic," Napier said. "And we could just put some empty boxes in the bag."

"I suppose you'd wrap them," Burns said.

"Maybe you don't have to carry the bag. But you could at least wear the padding."

"Why don't you wear the outfit, then?" Burns asked, stroking his fake whiskers to make sure they were affixed firmly to his chin.

Napier frowned. "Is that a crack?"

"No," Burns said. "What costume *will* you be wearing, then?"

"Costume? Me?" Napier was amazed. "I'm not going to wear a costume."

"If you're not, why should I?"

Napier tried to sound patient. It wasn't easy for him. "Look, I'm just there for backup; I'll be part of the sight-seeing crowd. You're the one who has to blend in with the homeowners. The Santa suit'll give you a chance to look like you belong there."

Burns still wasn't convinced that he wanted any part of this operation. "What if I do spot the robber? What am I supposed to do then?"

"Burglar," Napier corrected him. "You're looking for a burglar. And if you spot him, don't do anything. Lots of people get out of their cars and walk through the neighborhood, and I'll be one of 'em. If you see a burglar, I'll be right there. Just let me know."

"It's going to be really cold tonight," Burns said.

Napier nodded. That was one of the things he didn't like about Christmas. He thought wistfully about Steve McGarrett, policing the blue waters and white sands beneath the warm skies of Hawaii.

"Sure it's going to be cold," he said. "That's another reason why you should wear the padding."

"Never mind," Burns said. "When will you pick me up?"

"Ten till eight," Napier said. "The festivities run from eight until ten. I don't have a sleigh, and it wouldn't do for the kiddies to see Santa getting out of a police car, so I'll have to let you out at the end of River Bend Drive. You can walk from there."

"Great," Burns said. "Just great."

It was cold, all right. The temperature was already right around thirty and dropping fast, but at least there was no wind, for which Burns was grateful. The sky was perfectly clear, and if it hadn't been for all the lights in River Bend, the full moon would no doubt have been spectacular.

The cold didn't seem to be bothering anyone except Burns, however. There was already a slow-moving line of cars wending its way through the housing addition when Burns started trudging along the empty half block that began River Bend Drive. Someone had bought the lot years ago but had never built on it.

Burns looked down the street. The lighting displays clustered atop the houses and scattered through the trees gave a lustre of midday to objects below.

He could see mechanical reindeer prancing, wise men (without camels) looking for inns, Little Mermaids dancing in what were supposed to be undersea Christmas scenes, Cratchits hunched over high desks while admonishing Scrooges stood by.

What Burns wished he could see was someone dressed as one of the Beagle Boys. Maybe that would be a clue.

But of course there was no one like that, no one who resembled a robber—make that a burglar—in any way at all. There were carolers who looked as if they'd stepped right out of the pages of *The Pickwick Papers,* and in one yard there was even a group of rap carolers: "Yo! *We* three *kings* of *O*-rient *are!*" Burns wouldn't have believed it if he hadn't heard it. He saw another Santa, who was wearing his padding and carrying a bag, and a Mrs. Claus with a cookie tray in her hands. Well, at least there were no dinosaurs this year, not on this block at any rate.

Burns's feet were freezing in the cheap plastic Santa boots, and his ears were like little cubes of ice. He tried to pull the Santa hat down over them, but it didn't work out. He saw Napier looking at a display of giant gumdrops, and he hoped the police chief was as cold as he was.

Burns thought about the burglaries. Why would anyone want to come out and steal at a time like this?

Well, for one thing, it would be pretty easy to pass unnoticed. The streets were full of cars and pedestrians, and the yards were full of people. No one questioned Burns at all as he walked from one house to the next. He was just a skinny Santa, looking not that much different from any of the other people in costume.

But what if someone were carrying presents out of the houses? Surely someone would say something to him. And how could a stranger just walk into someone's house and walk back out uncontested? It didn't seem possible. Sooner or later, someone would see whoever it was and say something.

Burns looked back at the street and saw a long, dark blue car pulling over to the curb. The driver's door opened, and Franklin Miller plunged out. With a distraught look on his face, he raced around the back of the car and to the other side.

Burns sprang across a flower bed and ran to see what was the matter. He arrived at the car just in time to see Miller fling open the passenger door.

"Are you all right, Ms. Nipperson?" Miller asked, a note of panic in his voice.

"Mummmmph," Ms. Nipperson said, and then she threw up on Miller's shoes.

Burns looked around for some way to help, but there was nothing much he could do except get something for Miller to use in cleaning his shoes. He walked up to the nearest house and knocked on the

door. There was no answer, everyone being involved
in recreating the Dance of the Wooden Soldiers in the
yard, so Burns simply opened the door and walked
in. He saw the Christmas tree glowing in the den,
surrounded by stacks of presents, and by the tree
lights he could see the kitchen, where he found a roll
of paper towels on a rack.

Tearing off a generous handful of towels and wet-
ting them at the sink, he had started back outside
when he heard a little voice say, "Hi, Santa!"

Standing near the doorway was a little girl about
seven or eight years old in pink tights and a ballet
costume, over which she was wearing a fake fur coat.
"I had to go to the bathroom," she explained. "Did
you come to bring our presents?"

"No," Burns said, holding up the towels. "I had to
get these to help a sick person."

The girl nodded as if she understood. "Will you be
back later with the presents?"

"Sure," Burns said. "You can count on it."

"And you're bringing me the new Nintendo cartridge I asked for?"

"Absolutely," Burns said, hoping he wasn't lying.

"Thanks! You'd better go help that sick person
now."

Burns agreed. He carried the towels outside. The
girl stood by and watched him leave, smiling at the
thought of her new Nintendo cartridge.

Miller had gotten Ms. Nipperson out of the car and
was holding her with one hand cupped under her
elbow. He was asking her again if she was all right.

"I'm fine," she said in a quavery voice. "You were
just driving too fast. All the lights and the motion
made me sick."

Burns tore off a couple of wet towels and handed
Miller the rest. The college president looked at him
closely. "Oh, it's you, Burns. What are you doing in
that get-up?"

"Getting in the Christmas spirit," Burns said. He
handed Ms. Nipperson the rest of the towels, and she
began rubbing her face with them.

"Are you enjoying the lights, Ms. Nipperson?" Burns asked.

"He was driving too fast," Ms. Nipperson complained, her voice muffled by the towels. "I told him not to drive too fast."

Miller looked at Burns and shrugged. He hadn't been driving fast at all, since the line of cars couldn't have been moving at much more than five or six miles an hour.

"I'll tell him to slow down," Burns said. "Everybody does what Santa says."

"Ha," Ms. Nipperson said, handing him the towels, now wadded up.

"Thanks, Burns," Miller said, also handing him a soiled wad of towels. "And merry Christmas."

Burns looked down at the towels, which didn't smell too good and which he could almost feel turning to ice in his gloved hands.

"Merry Christmas," he said.

Miller grinned, got Ms. Nipperson back into the car, promised her he'd slow down, and drove away.

Burns wondered what to do with the towels, and then decided that he'd just go back in the house and toss them in the trash, which is what he did. When he came back out he started looking for Napier. He had an idea.

Boss Napier was looking over a scene where all the creatures were stirring, even the mice. They were in fact stirring a big electric cooking pot in which Napier was pretty sure fudge was bubbling. It *smelled* like fudge, anyhow, and fudge was one of the few things Napier liked about Christmas. There was a large veined slab of imitation marble on a heavy wooden table near the pot, and Napier was just waiting for the creatures, including a dog and couple of cats, plus the mice, to pour the fudge out on the marble to cool. He was certain they'd cut it and offer a piece to everyone who was watching, and he was determined to be there to get his share.

His mouth was practically watering in anticipation,

and he'd even forgotten how cold he was, when Burns walked up and touched him on the elbow.

"What is it?" Napier asked. One of the dogs was carrying the pot over to the marble. "Don't tell me you've caught the guy."

"Not yet," Burns said. "But I think I know—"

"Tell me in a minute," Napier said, his eyes fastened on the creamy candy that flowed out of the pot and onto the cold stone.

Burns wouldn't wait. "I have to tell you now."

Napier groaned. He just knew that he wasn't going to get any of the fudge. Not now.

"All right," he said. "What is it?"

"Think about this," Burns told him. "Who do you think can go pretty much anywhere he wants here, no questions asked?"

"I give up," Napier said, looking at the fudge. He wondered how soon it would be ready to cut. Maybe there was still a chance.

"And who can get by even if there *are* questions asked," Burns went on, "especially if a kid asks them? And maybe even if an adult does?"

"You got me," Napier said without looking at him. "Do you like fudge?"

Burns waved a gloved hand in front of Napier's eyes. "Why do I get the feeling you aren't listening to me?"

Napier turned. "All right. I give up. Who?"

"Santa Claus," Burns said. "And I saw some guy dressed just like me. Except that he was carrying a bag."

Napier caught on quickly. "He could grab a present, stick it in the bag, and leave. Who'd know?"

"Nobody," Burns said. "He could have a couple of cheap things in there already, and say he was delivering them if someone caught him in the act."

Napier forgot about the fudge. "Where is this guy?"

Burns looked down the block. He was sure the Santa wouldn't have strayed too far. "About three houses that way," he said, pointing.

Napier looked in the direction that Burns indicated and nodded. "Let's go," he said.

The Santa that they strode up to was a right jolly old elf, full of ho-ho-hos and carrying a large canvas bag over his shoulder.

"Hello, Santa," Napier said. "Mind if I have a look in your bag?"

"Ho, ho, ho!" Santa said, though he didn't sound quite as jolly as he had only a moment before. "Why would you want to do that?"

"Just to check the tags on your gifts," Burns said.

"Here," Santa grunted, heaving the bag over his shoulder and thrusting it toward a surprised Napier, who opened his arms to take it.

The bag was much heavier than he'd expected, and the police chief staggered backward for a few steps under its weight, then fell on his rear. Santa, meanwhile, dashed away with alacrity and surprising nimbleness.

Burns looked at Napier, who seemed to be all right except that he was struggling to get out from under the bag, and then took off after Santa.

Thinking about it later, Burns knew they must have made quite a sight—a skinny Santa chasing a fat Santa through a chaotic Christmas landscape of lights and noise. People were watching, most of them yelling and pointing, but no one seemed to know quite what was going on, so there was no help forthcoming for Burns. He had to stop the fleeing Santa himself.

Because he wasn't wearing any padding, he had a slight advantage in the race, and he was catching up quickly when he got tangled in an extension cord that ran across a yard to a gaily lighted hedge bush. He pitched forward, tearing the cord from its socket. He saw the lights go out in the bush as he hit the ground and rolled over.

He got back to his feet, but the fat Santa had gained on him, leaving carolers, elves, dancers, and musicians scattered in his wake. He might even have gotten away if he hadn't made one serious strategic mistake.

Two yards down there was a house whose yard was surrounded by a low stone wall. Instead of running into the street, the fat Santa decided to leap to the top of the wall.

He looked decidedly ungraceful to Burns, but he made it. However, he landed heavily, and his ankle twisted beneath him. He fell over the wall and into the neighboring yard.

When Burns reached the wall, he was more careful. He slowed to a stop and put his left leg over first. Balancing with his hands, he lowered that leg and followed with his right.

The fat Santa was staggering along, listing heavily to the left. He was shoving his way through a gang of elves that surrounded a model sleigh pulled by nine tiny reindeer. The ninth was Rudolph, of course, and he had a shiny red electrified nose.

"Stop that Santa!" Burns yelled, and to his surprise one of the elves gave the man a solid push, causing him to topple into the sleigh.

"Don't let him out!" Burns yelled, and the elves piled in on top of Santa.

That'll teach the old guy to go shoving his elves around, Burns thought.

When Burns reached the sleigh, the Santa was struggling to get up, but the elves were sitting all over him. Burns looked over his shoulder and saw Napier clumsily negotiating the wall.

"Take your time," he called. "The elves and I have everything under control."

Napier didn't laugh.

It took a while for things to return to normal, but finally all the elves were back in their places outside the sleigh, the neighbors were calmed, and the viewing of the Christmas scenes proceeded pretty much as if nothing had happened.

Napier led the fat Santa away in handcuffs, leaving Burns alone at his own request. It didn't seem so cold to him any longer, and there was something he liked about sitting in the sleigh in his Santa suit. Besides, there was something that he'd always wanted to do.

So he sat there and smiled and saluted all the passing cars, and when the last one was finally pulling out of River Bend, he stood up in the sleigh, took off his Santa hat, waved it in the air, and called out, "Merry Christmas to all, and to all a good night!"

THE MAN
WHO KILLED SANTA

by Douglas Borton

Christmas Eve, and the phone rings.

"Great," Margie says. After eight years of marriage she's heard the shrilling of the telephone at odd hours often enough to know that it generally means trouble.

"Maybe it's just one of your relatives calling to wish us a merry yuletide," I tell her as I pad into the kitchen, not believing it any more than she does. Then the phone is in my hand. "Taylor residence, Jim speaking."

The voice I hear belongs to Lieutenant Tom Gavin, night-watch commander at the station. He says what he always says: "Jim, there's been a homicide."

Hell. The kids are upstairs getting ready for dinner, Margie and I have bought cookies and chocolate milk to leave out for Santa at bedtime, and now I'm called away on a case. Why do people have to get themselves killed on holidays?

Gavin gives me the details. A Pine Valley man named Robert Welder was murdered in his home on Crest Road an hour ago, apparently by an intruder. Welder was a professor at the local college; the name strikes me as familiar, though I can't quite place it. And here's the interesting part: his wife was present and claims to have witnessed the whole thing. In fact, she's the one who called the station to report the crime.

"Beat cops say she's somewhat incoherent," Gavin says. "Some kind of crazy story."

"All right, I'm on my way. Have you called Cartwright?"

"He's next on my list. Might as well spoil his Christmas too."

As I hang up, I hear the tromping of eager feet on the stairs. The kids are coming down for dinner. Two boys and a girl, ages four, six, and eight. All still young enough to believe in Santa Claus. That's why there are no presents under our big artificial tree; everyone knows Santa delivers them personally while children sleep.

Margie has overheard my end of the conversation. She's not looking too happy as I enter the living room.

"Case," I say. I never use the words "homicide" or "murder" in the children's presence. "Sorry, but I've got to go."

"Will you be back at a reasonable hour?"

I know she's thinking of the gifts hidden in the back of the hall closet. We'd planned to wrap them later tonight once the kids are in bed. "I hope so," I say, feeling guilty for no good reason.

"Is Santa coming soon, Daddy?" our youngest asks.

"Real soon, Mike. In no time at all." I point at the fireplace. "Down the chimney."

His eyes are very big as he studies the dancing flames.

Crest Road, true to its name, runs along the summit of a thousand-foot range in northwestern Connecticut, near the New York and Massachusetts borders. Snow has been falling since midafternoon; the road is slippery under my tires as I guide my Mercury Sable to the address Gavin gave me.

Squad cars are slant-parked out front. Pulsing domelights throw the ice-silvered branches of leafless trees into stark relief against the black sky.

The house is a well-kept split-level that reminds me of our own place. A lot of gray granite was quarried to lay down the front walk and put up the facade. Snow bleaches the roof; icicles drip down like candelabras.

Cartwright meets me at the door. He lives nearer to Crest Road and got here first.

"Hey, Pete," I say with a nod. "Merry Christmas."

He exhales a plume of breath. "Ho, ho, ho."

The body lies sprawled on the white pile carpet in the living room, near a Christmas tree larger than ours, and real. A lake of blood outlines the victim's head. The walls are dappled with teardrop-shaped splashes of red, evidence of wildly looping arterial spray.

Cartwright and I circle the body without touching it. Neither the coroner nor the evidence team has arrived; the man's hands have not been bagged, and no incision has been made for a livor mortis reading. Other than the beat cops and Mrs. Welder, we are the first to see the man like this, his eyes blank and bulging, his hands fisted in cadaveric spasm, the side of his face mottled with the initial signs of postmortem lividity.

He is neatly dressed: white button-down shirt, jeans, leather boots. Even in death he has a rugged look for an academic, a look of square-shouldered durability enhanced by his Hemingway beard and broken nose. I guess his age at late thirties, forty at the most. My age, roughly.

Two wounds were opened in his abdomen, one at belt level near his navel, the other slightly higher, in the rib cage. But what killed him was a swipe of something sharp—a knife or a straight razor, probably—that opened his left carotid artery just below his ear. Spurting blood, he spun and stumbled; I can see patches of bloody footprints on the carpet like a lunatic dance pattern. Finally he collapsed on his side, leaking life away.

"He struggled with his assailant," Pete says, summing up what we both can see, "was stabbed twice in the torso and once in the neck. He expired and the assailant fled."

"Look there." I'm pointing at a pinkish stain a few yards from the body, then another a yard farther away. "Blood trail."

The killer got spattered or wounded. Either way, he was dripping when he left. We follow the spots into the dining room, then the kitchen. The linoleum is an unpleasant mauve that makes the stains harder to see. We track them anyway, all the way to the back door.

Outside, the yard slopes down to a rickety wooden fence at the edge of a brush-choked ravine. A scatter of lights, Pine Valley's skyline, lies on the horizon winking at the indifferent stars.

The yard is drifted with snow, but no footprints are visible in it, and no further blood spots; the continuing snowfall, light and powdery but relentless, has covered everything in a spread of arctic white.

Arctic. The word teases the nerve endings of my memory, though I can't say why. Then a voice is calling from the kitchen doorway: "Detective Cartwright? Detective Taylor?"

We return to the house, where a patrol officer named Lacy is waiting.

"I think Mrs. Welder is capable of being interviewed now," he says.

"Where is she?" Pete asks.

"Upstairs in the bedroom. We found her there when we responded to the call. She was lying in bed and shivering all over like . . . like a wet dog."

"You the first officer on the scene?" I ask him.

"Yes, sir."

"We'll need to take your statement. But first I want you and Collins to see if you can get down into that ravine behind the yard." I explain about the blood trail. "It's possible the killer escaped out this door and through the ravine. There's even a chance he's still in there, hiding or wounded."

Lacy licks his lips. He stares past us at the blowing cold. "The little man."

"What?"

"That's who did it, Mrs. Welder says."

"A dwarf, you mean?"

"I asked her that, but she just kept saying 'the little man' over and over."

"You call an RA for her?" Pete asks, meaning a rescue ambulance.

"Yeah, but there was a bad accident on Highway Forty-four, and right now all the paramedic units are tied up over there. Coroner too."

"Hell of a Christmas," Pete says.

I'm thinking the same thing. "Okay," I say, trying to sound brisk. "Check out that ravine. And exercise caution. If there is a little man—or anybody else—hiding in there, I want you to see him before he sees you."

"Right, Detective."

We find Mrs. Welder in the bedroom, just as Lacy said. Like her husband she has a young, vigorous look, augmented in her case by a salon tan. I should say, ordinarily she would look vigorous. Not now. Now she lies supine, blank-faced, staring at the ceiling, listening perhaps to the creak and groan of wind-lashed trees.

"Mrs. Welder, I'm Detective Taylor. This is my partner, Detective Cartwright." I show my badge but she doesn't bother to look. "I'm sorry about what happened."

Her mouth quivers. She makes a whimpering sound.

I glance at Pete and we read each other's thoughts. She's flipped out. Question is, did she crack as a result of seeing her husband killed—or did she commit the murder herself?

I glance at her clothes, her shoes. I see no blood, no melting snow, nothing that would tie her to the killing or the blood trail that led out back. But she might have wiped herself clean.

"From what I understand," I say quietly, "you reported the crime. Is that correct?"

Her voice is a whisper: "Yes."

"You witnessed the killing personally?"

"Yes."

"You saw who did it?"

She nods, not with her head but with her eyelids, briefly shutting her eyes in a way that signifies assent.

"Who was it, Mrs. Welder?"

"The little man."

"Tell us about this man."

"He was very small. Like a child. That's why Robert let him in, I guess. He looked through the window and saw what he thought was a child at the door. Perhaps a lost child."

She is distraught but coherent. Her facial muscles twitch and flutter.

"Where were you when he let the man in?"

"Upstairs. In the bathroom next door to this room. I heard the doorbell, and then I heard Robert speaking with someone. So I started walking down the hall to the stairs."

"Could you hear what they were saying?"

"As I got nearer, yes. The little man had such a funny, squeaky, high-pitched sort of voice. He was saying things that made no sense, and Robert was arguing with him."

"What were they saying?"

She doesn't seem to hear me, just keeps talking. "I started down the stairs just as they began to fight. Then I froze up. I had never seen Robert fight anybody before. And I saw that the little man had something in his hand that flashed when it caught the light. They struggled, I heard the little man scream, and then Robert was doubled over and the man was slashing at him and there was blood. . . ."

She drifts away. I touch her wrist and pull her gently back. "Where did the little man go?"

"Into the kitchen, I think. He ran away. No, not ran—scampered, scurried. Like a mouse. Squealing and squeaking and chittering in that horrible way mice have. And Robert was . . . flopping on the carpet. Then he was still."

"Do you know of anyone who might want to kill your husband?"

"Of course not, he was a teacher, a scientist, he had no enemies. . . ."

"What subject did he teach?"

"Geology."

"His name seems familiar to me. Is there some reason I should know it?"

"Well, there was the expedition last summer. He . . ."

She sits up suddenly, her body snapping upright, eyes darting with a thought.

"Oh, God, do you think that's it? Do you think that's what the man meant? Do you think it had something to do with *that*?"

"With what, Mrs. Welder?"

"With the trip! No, it can't be. It's too . . . too *crazy*."

"What trip, ma'am? Where did your husband go last summer?"

She looks at me, fear and bafflement competing in her eyes. "To the Arctic. He was part of a five-person team that went dogsledding to the North Pole."

Now I remember the name, the local news coverage, the proud headline in the Pine Valley *Citizen*: LOCAL TEACHER CONQUERS POLE.

Below the headline, a photo in bleary color. Five snowsuited figures huddled around a small American flag planted at the northern end of the earth's axis.

"What would that have to do with what the little man said?" I ask.

She doesn't hear me, doesn't react.

"Mrs. Welder? What did the little man say?"

Her answer is breathless and faraway. "He said Robert murdered Santa Claus."

An ambulance arrives shortly afterward and takes the woman away. Lacy and Collins are still struggling through the snowy ravine. Pete and I talk in the kitchen.

"Think she did it?" he asks me.

"Entirely possible. Her story is bizarre enough. On the other hand . . ."

"What?"

"Suppose some nut read about that expedition and got it in his head that Welder did kill Saint Nick at the North Pole. So he waits till Christmas Eve and comes here to take revenge."

"Why Welder? Why not one of the other people on the trip?"

"I seem to recall that something went wrong at the pole, something that was Welder's fault. His homecoming was a little bit tarnished once that part of the story came out."

Pete shrugs. "I didn't follow it."

"Neither did I, not too closely, anyway. But you can bet the Welders did. Let's see if we can find a scrapbook or a file folder full of clippings."

The Welders' den is a burrow of richly varnished wood and bookshelves bowed under the burden of a thousand books. In a metal file cabinet I find a manila folder labeled POLAR EXPEDITION. The file is thick and dog-eared. In it are newspaper accounts clipped from the *Citizen* and the *New York Times*.

"Here it is." I read from the *Times* story. " 'The team's triumphant arrival at the pole was marred by a potentially serious accident when Dr. Robert Welder, a Drake College professor of geology and earth sciences, attempted an experiment to determine the depth of the ocean below the ice pack.

" 'Drilling a hole in the ice, Dr. Welder inserted an explosive charge. Near it he placed a microphone wired to a tape recorder one hundred yards away. He and the other members of the team then retreated behind a wall of ice that had been upthrust over time by the gradual buckling of the ice pack. Dr. Welder detonated the charge remotely.

" 'The purpose of the experiment was to record both the sound of the blast itself and its echoes off the sea floor. Analysis of the recording would yield an accurate measurement of the ocean's depth.

" 'The explosive charge, however, was apparently formulated incorrectly, and the detonation set off a terrifying blast of tremendous magnitude. If not for the protection afforded by the ice barrier, the five scientists might well have been killed.

" 'The explosion ripped a hole ten feet in diameter in the surface ice and threw a fifty-foot fountain of ice and snow into the air. Team members heard distant groans and creaks attributed to the collapse of underground ice caves, a consequence of shock waves generated by the blast.' "

I lower the paper. Cartwright is staring at me.

"You think Santa could have been offed in that explosion?" I ask, straight-faced.

Pete plays along. "Doesn't seem likely. They'd have seen him if he was right in the area. That red suit would stand out against the snow."

"White beard would blend in, though."

"I still think they'd see him. And they'd hear him laughing and singing Christmas carols and stuff."

"Right." I nod soberly. "Unlikely Santa was there, then. But suppose our hypothetical nut believed otherwise."

"That's possible. But I don't believe it."

"No?"

"No. I don't think there is any nut other than the one upstairs. I think Mrs. Welder cooled her husband, and now she's hallucinating or fantasizing, whatever you want to call it."

"So there's no little man?"

"None."

I'm inclined to agree with him, and I'm about to say so when I hear Lacy's voice from the backyard: "Detective Taylor! We found him! *We found him!*"

He's a little man, all right, no more than three feet tall. I stare at him as the paramedics haul him out of the ravine on a collapsible gurney. He's thin and white-haired, with a pinched, wizened face and gnarled roots of hands. Snow has bleached his fur-collar coat and black corduroys. I wonder if he bought them in the children's department of a clothing store.

Frost sparkles in the air above his mouth in time with his shallow, irregular breathing. His skin is fish-pale. Blood pastes one leg of his trousers to his thigh.

Apparently Welder did manage to wound him in the struggle. But the little man fought back and got that knife into the professor—twice in the abdomen to force Welder to double over, then once in the neck to end it all.

"How is he?" I ask one of the paramedics as he and his partner lower the gurney's wheels.

"Unconscious. Pulse is weak. Severe blood loss."

"He's in shock," the partner says.

"Will he live?"

"No way to tell."

They wheel him through the house and down the driveway, then retract the wheels and slide the gurney into the ambulance.

"You follow them," Cartwright says. "I'll meet you there."

I tail the RA unit to the hospital. The ambulance is moving fast, going lights-and-siren on the slick ice-polished roads, and I have to sweat to keep up.

At the hospital there's a lot of waiting. The desk nurse keeps saying, "He's still in surgery," in answer to my irritating persistence. I keep expecting a doctor to come out and tell me that he lost the patient in the bitter, fatigued voice they always use.

Cartwright arrives at three A.M., while I'm on the phone with Margie, apologizing for having missed Christmas Eve. "Did you get the wrapping done?"

"Wrapping?" She sounds sleepy and vague.

"The presents. Are they under the tree?"

"Oh. Oh, yes. I . . . I think so."

"Go back to sleep, hon. Sorry I woke you. I'll be home when I can."

It pains me to think of missing Christmas morning too, the priceless moment when the kids descend the stairs and stare goggle-eyed at the heap of loot beneath the tree's garlanded, ornament-laden branches. Well, maybe I can make it home by then.

"Talk to Margie?" Pete asks.

"Yeah. She sounded funny. Sort of confused."

"It's three in the morning."

"That'll do it." But the conversation leaves me feeling uncertain, my world knocked off center in some way hard to define.

At four-fifteen the doctor enters the waiting room.

I've seen him before, but I don't recall his name till I scan his I.D. tag: Patrick Rupert.

"He's still critical," Rupert says. "There was internal hemorrhaging and enough blood loss to make brain damage a strong possibility. Even if he survives, he may never recover fully."

"Is he conscious?" Cartwright asks.

"Touch and go."

"Can we talk to him?"

The doctor hesitates. "All right," he says finally. "But for no longer than five minutes."

As he leads us down the hall to the critical ward, we pass a trio of nurses clustered around a portable radio, listening intently to a news broadcast, their faces a strange blend of slackness and tension. The announcer's voice has the same quality, a strained balance between joviality and concern. I've heard enough bad news tonight; I tune out his words.

"What is he, anyway?" Cartwright asks the doctor as we approach the ward. "A dwarf or a midget or what?"

Rupert pauses to look first at Pete, then at me. "I don't know. He doesn't seem to fit the physical characteristics of either type precisely. Can't judge his age either. One staff member thought he might even be a child."

"A child with a wrinkled face like that?"

"There is a condition that causes premature aging in children. They acquire a, well, a gnomelike appearance. It's extremely tragic, obviously. Tragic and grotesque. This might be a case of that kind. But I don't think so. Although," he adds thoughtfully, "he does have a rather childlike quality, somehow."

Rupert guides us into the patient's cubicle and leaves us there with a warning that he'll return in five minutes to escort us out. I bend over the bed and touch the little man's arm. His eyes flutter open and swim into focus.

"I'm a police detective," I tell him, keeping my voice low so as not to disturb patients in adjacent cubicles. "Do you want to tell me what happened tonight?"

There is a long silence, his eyes unblinking, unmoving. I begin to wonder if he has fallen asleep with his eyes open, or if the neurological damage Rupert mentioned has robbed him of speech.

Then his lips part and he whispers, "I'll tell you."

His voice is high and strange, a Munchkin falsetto.

I think about Mirandizing him. Oh, hell. We've only got five minutes and he's dying anyway. Forget about it.

"Who are you?" I ask. "What's your name?"

"It would mean nothing to you."

An odd accent clings to his speech, one I can't identify. "Where are you from?"

"North."

"Canada?"

He almost smiles. "Much farther north than that. The pole."

"I see." I keep my tone even. "Did you meet Dr. Welder there?"

"Meet him? No. But that is where I *encountered* him."

"Tell me."

He shuts his eyes, and for a moment I think he is dead. Then I hear the reassuring beep of the heart monitor, see the rise of his chest with an intake of air, and he says:

"I lived there with many others like me, at the top of the world, beneath the ageless snow. It was a good life. We were happy and we made others happy, the children most of all. It was for the sake of the children that our hammers clanged all day long in our workshops, and our forges glowed, and our sewing machines rattled and hummed."

"Jesus Christ," Cartwright mutters. "I think he's saying he was one of Santa's elves."

He says it softly, but the little man hears. "Yes. That is how you would know us, though 'elf' is not a term we use. We are the *malinoi*, the unchanging ones. Or at least"—he sighs—"we believed our manner of existence would never change. But it did. One day the roof of our world was split by thunder. Ice showered down like a rain of glass. Our escape tunnels were blocked by debris. Walls crumbled. Light was extinguished, and in the darkness there were screams.

"They all died that day. All the *malinoi*—and the magical deer in their carved-ice stalls, and the master and his wife. All are dead now, all but me. By chance I survived. Then, by desperate digging over many days, I freed myself from the deathtrap that had been our home. And I began my trek south, to join this world of men and learn who had done this thing.

"It was necessary to have justice. To take revenge against the one who cheated the children of their happiness.

"Now I have done so. Now I may die."

Our five minutes are nearly up. I don't know whether or not to pursue the conversation further. But I have to ask the obvious question. "You really believe all this?"

"I believe. The one you knew as Santa Claus was the being I served. He was very real, more real than any mortal adult knew."

"You built the toys that children get on Christmas?"

"Yes."

"All of them?"

"Yes."

"Look." I hate to argue with the man, but his calm certainly is infuriating somehow, and after all, he did kill Welder. "I'm a parent. Every Christmas I buy toys. Nobody has to deliver them in a sleigh drawn by reindeer. I buy them. So does my wife. We wrap them and we put them under the tree."

That strange smile is poking at the corners of his mouth again. "You only think you do. It is a shared delusion, a collective fiction, which you maintain to protect yourself against a truth you cannot permit yourselves to see. To believe in the magical would kill you, and so you do not believe. But tell me, sir . . . are you sure you bought these toys?"

"Of course."

"Then which toys, exactly, did you buy this year?"

I look at him. My mouth works, but there is no sound.

A light knock on the cubicle door. Rupert is there. "It's been more than five minutes."

I move away from the bed, trying not to show my relief.

The three of us are at the door when the little man says suddenly, "There will be no toys this Christmas." His voice is stronger than before, his eyes gleaming with anger and grief. "And no toys from Santa ever again. That part of childhood is over now, over forever."

Rupert hurries to the bed, tries to calm the patient, but the little man goes on speaking.

"Can't you hear them, doctor? Can't you hear them? Even now they rise at dawn, they stalk the tree, they find no gifts. And the milk and cookies left for Santa remain on the table, untouched."

A nurse brushes past me into the cubicle and Rupert orders a shot of Valium.

"Hear them, hear them: their wails of sorrow, the sound of magic dying, of childhood betrayed and banished!" He is shrieking now, his voice high and keening like a bird's wild cry. "They weep, weep for their lost Santa, weep for a world grown gray without the luster of fantasy! They weep, and I weep with them, I weep, I weep . . ."

The syringe is poised over his arm when abruptly his slight body sags, his head lolls, his eyes roll.

The heart monitor drones a monotone and displays a horizontal line.

"We can run a print search through the FBI," Pete is saying as we leave the hospital an hour later. "If he has a record, they'll I.D. him."

"Uh-huh." I'm barely listening. I'm still trying to remember what Margie and I bought this year. We went shopping together, I'm sure we did.

"Maybe check the local mental institutions too. His

description is pretty damn distinctive. One of them may have tried to mainstream him or something."

Margie didn't seem all that groggy with sleep when I called her. Just confused about wrapping the packages. As if she honestly couldn't remember doing it. Just like I can't remember what the hell we bought.

"Hey, Jim? You awake?"

"Huh? Oh, sure. I'm fine."

"Go home, get some rest." Pete stops by his car. "And by the way . . . Merry Christmas."

The sun is rising as I steer the Sable along the salted roads. I can't shake the memory of the little man's eyes or the sound of his comical cartoon voice saying, "The roof of our world was split by thunder."

The *Times* said that ice caves at the pole were collapsed by the explosion's shock waves.

Oh, come on. You're losing it. Anyway, if all the children of the world were crying out, you'd know about it by now. Hell, it's been Christmas Day in Europe for hours already. . . .

Then I remember the huddle of nurses in the hallway. The glazed panic on their faces. The announcer's voice, giddy with tension.

Something big has happened. Something frightening and unreal and incomprehensible.

As first light crept across the countries of Europe and now grazes the eastern seaboard of North America, as a billion children wake, are they finding no presents this Christmas? Are they learning Santa Claus is dead?

No. Impossible. Insane.

I pull the car onto the shoulder of the road. For a long moment I sit at the wheel, breathing in and out, in and out, watching my breath frost the windshield, listening to the hammer blows of my heart in my ears.

Then slowly I reach for a knob on the dashboard.

My hand is trembling only a little as I turn on the radio to hear whatever the news may be.

SLAY BELLE

by John Lutz

Krista Lefarge said, "You gotta be kidding."

But she knew by the basset-hound sadness in Lieutenant Smyth's somber brown eyes that he was serious. He shifted position behind his cluttered desk. The sounds of the precinct house filtered in from outside his office: the indecipherable metallic chatter of a police radio, a losing argument at the booking desk, two detectives in the squad room discussing last night's televised football game. The lieutenant said, "You know you shouldn't even be here, Krista."

Well, she knew that. She couldn't help glancing down at her swollen stomach. Policewomen in their third trimester of pregnancy usually were sitting at home on leave, waiting. She was still working because she wanted it that way, and Smyth had bent the rules for her. But he could bend them only so far, and sometime during the week there would be a surprise inspection by Headquarters, and Krista, with her drastically altered shape and uniform, couldn't be seen doing the desk work Smyth had assigned her to a week after the funeral.

Her husband, patrolman Jerry Lefarge, had died in a motorcycle accident, his skull crushed because he hadn't been wearing his helmet as proscribed by law. After the agony of the funeral and memorial service, Krista had begun going insane sitting around the apartment watching herself become more swollen with child, observing the happiness of everyone else in the world as Christmas approached, and missing Jerry. Missing Jerry in a way she never thought she'd miss anyone or anything, even though there'd been times when he hadn't treated her so well. The doctor had said her pregnancy might be intensifying her grief; a hormonal reaction. So she'd asked to come back to work, and old friend Smyth had obliged against his better judgment; a human reaction.

Now Smyth said, "He's a cop killer, Krista."

She nodded. He was talking about notorious drug dealer Nick Denham, whose prints were found on the gun that had killed Patrolman Sam Schneider in his bed two nights ago. Schneider had been scheduled to testify against Denham, who'd been out on bond at the time of the murder. Denham, always too cute for his own good, had seen to it that he stood a chance of being acquitted on the pending drug charge now that Schneider was dead, but he'd messed up and dropped the murder weapon and now he was wanted on a homicide charge that would stick and send him to prison or worse. Never one to learn from experience, Denham was now evading the police dragnet by being cute again. An informant had tipped the police that Denham was masquerading as a Santa Claus instead of trying to slip out of the city.

"He would actually do this?" Krista asked. "Dress up as Santa Claus instead of fleeing?"

"It's not a bad idea when you come to think of it," Smyth said. "It's the week before Christmas and there are hundreds of Santas wandering around the city. How will we know which one is Denham? We can't watch the airport, bus and train station forever. Or keep up a statewide alert in case he tries to get out by car. So he lays low by playing Santa, then after Christmas, when things loosen up, he slips away on us. Not so dumb."

"What's dumb," Krista said, "is having a pregnant policewoman dress up in a Santa suit and try to find him."

"It's sort of a version of setting a thief to catch a thief," Smyth said, flashing his sad, novocaine smile to show he was joking.

Krista, who didn't smile much these days, didn't smile this time, either.

"It's a way to get you out of the precinct house and keep you on the job, Krista." Smyth couldn't help smiling again. "And you gotta admit, you're kind of a natural for this one."

Krista stared out the window at the light snow that had begun to fall.

"So how about it, Krista?"

She said, "I'm trying to decide if this is sexual harrassment."

Serious as ever now, Smyth said, "It isn't. And you don't have to do it if you're dead set against it. Maybe we can hide you down in the file room when the inspection team shows up, which could be any day now. Any hour."

Krista didn't tell him that actually she yearned to be back out on the street, that the precinct house was beginning to close in on her the way the apartment had. Jerry, why did you have to be doing sixty on an icy road? Why did you have to die? On top of everything else you did, why did you have to do this to me?

Immediately the guilt lay heavy on her. Selfish, thinking about herself and not about Jerry. He hadn't been perfect, but she'd loved him. Still did. And he hadn't deserted her, hadn't died on purpose.

She said, "Give me the details."

Smyth nodded, looking relieved, and said, "Our informant tells us Denham is one of the Santas hanging around downtown, in or near Craigle's Department Store. You'll take a crash course in being a Santa this afternoon at Craigle's, then get outfitted. Tomorrow you play Santa in the vicinity of the store." He frowned to show her how serious he was now, making him look even more like a morose basset hound. "Here's the big thing, Krista. I don't want you in any danger or doing any physical stuff. You observe, and that's all. Denham might let his guard down in front of another Santa, not figuring you for the police. If he does, or if for any reason you suspect which Santa is Denham, you report to one of the patrolmen in the area, or you phone or radio in the information. Is that understood?"

She nodded. "Sure. I'm not exactly in any condition to give chase."

"Go easy on yourself, Krista. If you get tired, go inside Craigle's and sit down. I mean that. You'll have your service weapon for self-defense, but for nothing more. I don't want you or the baby in harm's way. Jerry wouldn't want it."

He had her there. In fact, she wondered what Jerry would think of this whole idea.

A gaunt woman named Verna who was in charge of training Santas as well as elves, took Krista to a room on the top floor of Craigle's and explained how to comport herself as Santa, how to give out peppermint canes with a broad holiday smile, and emit a credible "Ho, ho, ho!"

The next morning, bolstered by even more than her natural padding, her sex disguised behind white beard and reddened nose, Krista was roaming the square block taken up by Craigle's, ho-hoing and handing out candy canes to surprised and grateful children. She found herself enjoying it, gaining some measure of hope from the shining faces gleaming up at Santa. This was how saints were stared at, she decided. There were fringe benefits in this Santa job.

She counted a half dozen uniformed patrolmen in the vicinity, and two plainclothes detectives. She made herself known to all of them. They were surprised to learn there was a woman behind the red suit and white beard. They would have been even more surprised if they'd known she was pregnant and not merely padded. What they all expressed was a powerful desire to nail Sam Schneider's murderer. For a cop to be killed in the line of duty was one thing. Even worse was when one was killed by someone sneaking into his apartment and shooting him in the back while he was asleep in his bed. Krista was glad she wasn't Denham. She was also glad that Denham was Denham.

Like every cop in the city, she'd studied Denham's

photograph. He was an average sort of guy, average size with dark hair and blue eyes. His face was hardly memorable, and the Santa beard would probably conceal most of it. And there were more Santa Clauses walking around downtown than Krista had imagined. She had to admit the lieutenant was right; Denham wasn't so dumb.

Krista found the shelter of a doorway and gazed again at the photograph she carried in her baggy red pocket, concentrating on the eyes. Maybe she'd be able to recognize Denham by his eyes despite the beard and paste-on bushy white eyebrows. And if his *Ho, ho, ho!* wasn't up to par, or if he snarled at one of the children, she'd know for sure.

On the second day, she settled on one of the countless Santas roaming the downtown area as a possible suspect. He seemed disinterested, standing by a donation kettle and ringing his bell. Near the kettle was a sign lettered AID FOR AIKERMAN'S DISEASE. It was a charity Krista had never heard of. And there was a special wariness in the Santa's constantly moving blue eyes.

After he'd failed to acknowledge several donations, then apparently said something upsetting to a boy about twelve years old, Krista approached a uniformed patrolman standing in the doorway of a florist shop.

"That one," she said, nodding toward the Santa standing with his kettle and monotonously ringing his bell near the Pine Street entrance to Craigle's. "He doesn't ring true to me."

The patrolman smiled slightly at her unintentional pun. He was a handsome, dark-haired guy wearing the shiny black boots of a motorcycle patrolman and a billed cap with POLICE DEPT. on it in large letters. Krista had introduced herself to him yesterday. Don, she thought was his name.

He knew her name. "I've been watching him myself, Krista."

"I figured that's why you were standing here. He could be Denham."

"Or he could be some con man running his own

fake charity racket. You know how many of them are roaming the streets this time of year."

It was something Krista hadn't considered, that there might be more than one fake Santa in the area. "We better move on him one way or the other," she said. "Get him off the street."

Watching the Santa, Don said, "You call in for backup while I keep an eye on this jolly character. Then stay clear." He smiled again. A warmer smile this time. "That Santa suit doesn't cover up as much as you think. I don't want you or the baby in danger."

She couldn't help smiling back. "Okay, we'll do it that way." She felt a sudden thrust of anguish. Jerry. Something about Don made her think of Jerry. Maybe it was his dark, droopy mustache trimmed to regulation length.

"We can talk about it afterward," he said, looking directly into her eyes.

"No," she said, "I don't think so." Her emotions were whirling: guilt, anger, grief. All in a turmoil. Hormonal, she told herself, remembering what the doctor had told her about pregnancy and mourning. All hormonal.

"Maybe some other time?"

"Maybe," she heard herself say. She walked to the corner and used her walkie-talkie to call in the troops.

Santa didn't know what hit him. Within less than a minute his red suit was surrounded by blue suits. He tried to run but he tripped over the tripod supporting his donation kettle and fell. Coins from the kettle scattered on the sidewalk. He scrambled to his feet and was immediately tackled by one of the cops. Three more were there when he got to his knees. They yanked him to a standing position and handcuffed him. The cop who'd made the tackle began reading Santa his rights. Checking them twice, doing it right. Nobody wanted this case to be tossed out of court on a legal technicality.

Krista walked across the street to the scene, listening to the shrill, warbling sirens of converging patrol cars.

Santa's beard was dangling askew from one side of his chin. He was an elderly man with smooth, pale skin. He kept saying over and over that his name wasn't Denham, it was Aikerman, and he was sick so he hadn't violated any law. Krista stared at the AID FOR AIKERMAN'S DISEASE sign by the overturned kettle. A judge would hardly interpret the law as leniently as Aikerman, but she knew Aikerman had no reason to fear a murder charge.

She looked around, feeling a sudden pain deep in her bowels, and went inside Craigle's and used one of the public phones to call Smyth. At that moment she felt burdened by her pregnancy, and very vulnerable.

"Lieutenant," she said, "can you check on something for me while I hold?"

"Could be," he said, his voice wary.

"Find out if one of Schneider's uniforms was stolen."

Smyth said, "I don't have to check. One of his uniforms was missing."

"Was he with Traffic?"

"That's right. Rode a cycle. His gun was stolen, too. The only thing left in his closet was his helmet and his civilian clothes."

Krista hung up the phone and went outside. She used her walkie-talkie again. Across the street, Don, still in the doorway of the florist shop, was watching her.

Suddenly he left the doorway and began walking fast along the sidewalk, away from her, elbowing holiday shoppers aside. A man shook a fist at him. A woman dropped all her packages and fell to the sidewalk.

Krista hurried across the street. Tried to hurry, anyway. The bulk of her pregnancy seemed to grow larger and heavier with each step, causing her to waddle, and her rapid breath steamed in the cold air. Cars honked at her. Someone cursed her.

Think of the baby! she cautioned herself, trying to run as smoothly as possible. Think of Jerry's baby!

When she reached the other side of the street she

could barely make out Don a half block away, still forging a violent path through the sea of Christmas shoppers.

Krista drew her gun.

"Down! Everyone!" she screamed, and fired straight up into the brittle winter sky.

The shot echoed like cannon fire in the canyon of the downtown street.

Everyone stopped and stared at her. "Everybody down!" On the second command, the second reverberating shot, they dropped to the sidewalk, some of them screaming and covering their heads with their arms.

The only one standing between Krista and the intersection was Don.

He stopped.

Turned.

He drew Schneider's nine-millimeter handgun and aimed it at her. Death from a distance. She knew how quickly it would arrive.

Standing with her legs spread wide, her hands steady, she didn't want to squeeze the trigger. Until she thought again of the baby.

As her gun roared and bucked in her hand, the sound of the shot was joined by a half dozen other shots. Blue uniforms closed in on the blue figure lying on the sidewalk near the gutter.

Krista walked slowly toward the scene, her gun holstered again beneath her Santa suit.

She'd suddenly understood why Don had made her think of Jerry, and why she'd known that Denham wasn't masquerading as Santa but as an anonymous and indistinguishable member of society, that he was pretending to be a cop. It was his cap. A motorcycle patrolman would be wearing or carrying a helmet, not one of the department's soft, billed caps.

It was the law.

When the baby was born in late February, Krista found herself the mother of a healthy and noisy boy. She considered named him Jerry, Jr., then decided to name him Noel.

By summer the pain was gone and only the memories remained.